SECRETS & RIVALRY

Book Three

Salvaggio's Light

An Epic Contemporary Romance Serial

By C. L. Cattano

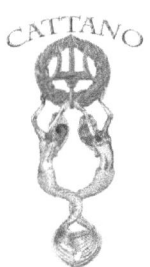

VAGARY PUBLISHING

Secrets & Rivalry
Book Three
Salvaggio's Light
A Vagary Publishing Book
Copyright © 2017 by C. L. Cattano

Cover Art, Title Page Art and Typesetting Copyright © 2017 by Chynsia Hinesley

Published by:

VAGARY PUBLISHING

www.vagarypublishing.com
inquiry@vagarypublishing.com

Rogena Mitchell-Jones, Independent Literary Editor
RMJ Manuscript Services LLC *www.rogenamitchell.com*

ISBN 978-0-9980906-7-2

First Edition

WARNING

It is suggested readers of this story be adults over the age of eighteen.

This dramatic romance series has many scenes describing sex as well as intense emotional scenes and acts of violence.

This is a serial story with themes that flow from one book into another with lots of twists and turns. Reading this series from the beginning is highly suggested, or the reader may not be able to follow all of the story lines.

Go to the Salvaggio's Light Facebook page to join other readers who are talking about the series.
www.facebook.com/SalvaggiosLight/

Join the C L Cattano mailing list and check out my website at
www.clcattano.com

Acknowledgments

THANK YOU TO everyone who made it to book three with me! I know the work doesn't get easier, so I appreciate you all hanging in there. Thank you to my great editor, Rogena, for all her hard work and to my significant other, Marie, for her time and patience—and for folding all the laundry. Many thanks to those who have read this book along with the many rewrites until I was happy. Thank you to everyone who has been patiently waiting as I get each book ready for publication.

Dedication

For Marie — who grew and found me.

Salvaggio's Light

An Epic Contemporary Romance Serial

Shattered Paradise
Blue Inferno
Secrets & Rivalry
Wildling's Claim*
Sowers of Discord*

Coming Soon

"I did not die, and yet I lost life's breath."
—Dante Alighieri, *The Divine Comedy*

1

Two days later...

ON MONDAY MORNING, Rafe Salvaggio only felt like she was on the *edge* of hell—but it was still hell. She was up, but it didn't mean there was anything good about the morning. Rafe was still not feeling well after finding out Eden Kingsley was playing games with her, and Jake Thompson had been helping. She called in to let the school know she was sick and wouldn't be there today. After going through the motions of being alive, she showered and dressed, then made her way out of the house.

Living at the moment was a surreal sensation. The mind and the body were living separately, but somehow, the body knew what to do while the mind was occupied elsewhere. Rafe knew she had to drive to Katheryn's office, and she made it there in her car, but she had no memory of making the drive. She only remembered the painful thoughts demanding she make the drive to see her lawyer. Apparently, her body just took over and went on autopilot.

She walked into Katheryn Hardam's law office unannounced, pale with dark circles around her eyes. The secretary saw her walk in and didn't stop her as she went straight into Katheryn's office without a glance or a word to anyone.

The secretary was familiar with the routine and had buzzed Katheryn. Hanging up the phone, Katheryn watched as Rafe entered and went straight to the built-in hidden bar, pressed the latch, and opened the cabinet panel. Rafe made herself a drink and then sat limply in one of the leather chairs.

"What can I do for you, Rafe?" Katheryn asked, surprised and shocked at the dark-haired woman's pale, sickly appearance.

"I want to talk to you about the injunction," Rafe informed her softly before taking a sip of her drink.

"Everything is going as expected," Katheryn told her. "Do you have a specific question?"

Rafe sat her drink on the arm of the chair and then leaned forward, rubbing her temples. "No," she said calmly. "I'm thinking maybe I shouldn't be fighting it."

Katheryn looked at Rafe surprised. She got up and walked around her desk to sit next to Rafe. "Why are you thinking you shouldn't fight it?"

"I don't know," Rafe said still looking down at her now shaking hands. "Maybe it isn't the right thing for Bronte... or Eden." She picked up the drink and took another sip, holding the heavy crystal tumbler tight to stop her hands from shaking.

Katheryn looked at Rafe with concern. "Eden said she wanted it, and she thinks it's the right thing for Bronte," she reminded her.

Rafe was silent for a while working to force words out. "Maybe you should talk to her about it again and make sure. I'm thinking maybe I should just," she paused, "not do this thing."

"You mean the adoption," asked Katheryn trying to understand where Rafe was going with her thoughts, and wondering if Rafe might fire her from the adoption case after all the work she had been done to get it on a docket.

"Yes," Rafe answered shakily holding back the sorrow wanting to overwhelm her.

Katheryn took a breath and looked intently at Rafe. "Rafe, are you sure you know what you're doing?"

Rafe shook her head despondently. "No, but I think Eden does." She looked up at Katheryn with watery eyes. "You should talk to her and do whatever you think is best."

Troubled by Rafe's demeanor, Katheryn was determined to get to the bottom of what was happening. "I think I will."

"Good. That's all," said Rafe as she got up and sat her glass on the cabinet. She left the office before Katheryn could ask more questions.

As Rafe left, Katheryn went directly to her desk and dialed the phone. "Eden Kingsley, please. Yes, I'll hold."

2

AN HOUR LATER, Katheryn Hardam had Eden Kingsley sitting before her in the same chair Rafe Salvaggio had been in earlier. The tenacious lawyer wasted no time when it came to protecting her clients' interests and making it her business to find out answers to questions even they didn't know to ask.

Eden had rushed to the office as soon as Katheryn called. She worried something bad was happening with the injunction because Katheryn had insisted they speak in person. "Why did you need to see me, Katheryn? You said it was an emergency."

"I think it is," said Katheryn firmly becoming acrasial. "Do you know who was just in here an hour ago?"

"No," Eden answered confused and worried.

"Rafe was in here looking like shit warmed over," Katheryn informed the nervous blonde. "Is there something going on between you two?"

"Rafe was here?" Eden asked surprised. "We've been getting along well lately. Why?"

"She asked me to make sure you still wanted the adoption," she stated plainly. "Why would she ask again if you two are getting along so well?" She paused hoping for a reply, but instead of speaking, Eden looked nonplussed. "Do you still want the adoption to go through?" she asked staunchly, following her client's instructions

Eden looked at Katheryn flustered. "I don't know why she wanted you to ask me again. She's been sick. She's been under a lot of stress because of the abuse accusations. Maybe that's why."

"It seems to me she thinks you've changed your mind," said Katheryn pointedly. "She told me to do whatever I thought best after talking with you. You haven't answered my question. Have you changed your mind?"

"No, Katheryn, I haven't changed my mind, and I'm not going to," Eden snapped angrily. "I want you to keep fighting the injunction and make sure the adoption happens."

"Okay, fine." Katheryn took a breath regaining control of her temper wanting to flair on Rafe's behalf. "Eden, I think you should go talk to Rafe about this immediately. She went just a step below firing me. If she fires me, I can't help her."

"If she fires you, then I'll hire you to keep working on it," Eden insisted. "She's just sick, Katheryn," she said, flustered Rafe would come in and fire Katheryn, thinking she wanted to stop the adoption when she knew the opposite was true. "I'll talk to her tonight."

3

THE REST OF the day at work, Eden Kingsley was useless and unproductive. She couldn't get Rafe Salvaggio on the phone, and she was getting worried. By the time Eden was able to leave the office, her anxiety was bad enough she had to use her inhaler. She thought after leaving Jake she wouldn't need to use it again, another thing she had gotten wrong. Pulling up to Rafe's house, she saw all the lights were on inside and outside. When she opened the back gate, she could see almost everyone they knew was on the patio or in the house. Before going through the gate, she took in the scene, finally spotting Rafe sitting by the pool on a lounger next to Julia.

Rafe was still showing signs of being sick—pale with dark circles around her eyes, and she was drinking. Both she and Julia were drinking from bottles as they talked. Eden shook her head at the sight. Jude and Flynn were swimming, and Stacey was sitting on the edge of the pool with a glass of wine and talking with Erica. Inside, Letty and Ephraim were in the kitchen making food.

Abby walked out of the house carrying a tray of snacks Ephraim had made and took them over to Rafe and Julia. "These should be good," said Abby popping one in her mouth.

Clearly drunk and smiling, Rafe looked up at Abby. "Abby, I know what good is. Do you want me to show you?"

"Abby, you should take," Julia hiccupped, also inebriated, "take advantage of her while she's drunk."

"Ha, ha. I don't think so," said Abby with a smirk. "Do you want one of these?" She held out the gourmet snacks.

Eden was bewildered at the scene and walked angrily up to them. "What the hell is going on?"

Abby turned to Eden and smiled. "Oh, hi! Rafe invited everyone over for a little dinner party." She held out the tray of snacks as an offering.

Eden ignored the tray of food and looked past Abby. "Rafe, I need to talk to you."

"Not now," Rafe waved her away not wanting to look directly at the golden heart crusher. "I need to finish my drink." She then took a drink from her bottle.

"Rafe, I'm so glad you called for an emergency financial meeting with me today. Mondays are the worst," Julia slurred and hiccupped again before taking another drink from her bottle of wine. "I love meetings involving a good wine!"

Eden looked at Abby crossly. "How could you let her get drunk? She's sick." She looked at the bottle Rafe was drinking from. "She's drinking scotch?"

Abby unceremoniously dropped the tray of food on one of the tables and held out her hands in surrender not wanting to take the blame for anything. "They were both drunk before I got back here. I think they've been drinking all day. There's not much left in the liquor cabinet." She looked at Rafe and cocked her head to the side. "She does seem like she's feeling better, and she did sleep all day yesterday."

Rafe smiled up at Abby. "I am feeling better, Abby. And it's all because you are a very... funny... girl!"

"I wish you would stop saying that," said Abby in annoyance.

Julia laughed and slapped Rafe on the leg. "Why are you saying she's funny?"

Holding her bottle up in a toast to Abby, Rafe grinned. "Because she makes me laugh." She took another drink of scotch from the bottle.

Eden walked up and snatched the bottle from her angrily. "Rafe, I'm serious. I need to talk to you!"

Rafe frowned at Eden and the loss of her drink. Shaking her head, she spoke in Italian. "*Beh, lo sono non grave affatto più lungamente,*"[1] Rafe mumbled. She called back over her shoulder into the house. "More drinks out here! Letty, I think there's still some limoncello left! Bring the bottle to me, bella!" she said in a heavily Italian-accented slur.

Julia reached over and grabbed Abby's shirt pulling her down close to her. "Watch this." She giggled and released her. "Hey, Rafe, you need to be nice now. You didn't even say hello to Eden."

Rafe looked at Julia with a frown. "She wasn't nice to me," she mumbled and looked around for a drink. "I need a drink."

---

[1] Well, I am not serious any longer,

"But you're the host," Julia slurred and handed Rafe her bottle of wine. "So welcome her to your home. Go on," she waved toward Eden.

"Welcome to the party, Eden," Rafe said politely but with reluctance, because she would prefer she went away. She then took a drink of Julia's wine.

"Thank you," said Eden not sure what Julia was doing.

Rafe looked at Julia. "Happy now?" she asked sarcastically.

Julia laughed loudly. "Yes, welcome, *Adan*," she said making fun of Rafe's slurring accent. "Show your love for this poor sick soul, *Adan*," she said patting Rafe on the shoulder. "Drink some wine, *Adan*!" Julia laughed hysterically and winked at Abby, who rolled her eyes.

Rafe drank more wine, unhappy Julia was playing games with her. She looked up at Eden and thought about how many people were trying to play games with her lately. Rafe took another drink of wine to push away her thoughts of Eden and the things Jake told her. She looked at Julia and smiled darkly. If Julia liked games, she would play too.

"Julia," Rafe said softly with a drunken smile. "Come here, bella." Julia moved closer still giggling at making fun of Rafe's accent. Rafe leaned close to her ear and made several clumsy attempts to move Julia's silver hair. "It's not funny. You know," she moved more hair. "You know what is funny?" she asked in her accented English.

Julia leaned back and grinned. "What?"

Rafe pulled Julia close and whispered in her ear again, "Tess." She laughed softly. "She thinks I..." she wheezed, "I fucked her much better than you did." Rafe bent over laughing as Julia looked at her in shock. Rafe sat back up and grabbed at Julia pulling her back to whisper in her ear again. "Can't you," she stopped, having to control her urge to laugh before she could speak again. "Can't you make a girl come more than once?" She grinned and pushed Julia away as she fell back in her chair laughing.

Julia pushed through her shock and got her voice back. "Fuck you, Rafe," she hissed angrily.

Rafe sat up and grinned at her. "Oh, I said yes when she asked for that too!" She laughed hard and tried to drink more wine but missed her mouth spilling some on herself. "Fuck," she mumbled as she tried to wipe the wine off her chin.

Abby and Eden looked at the two of them wondering what had just happened because they hadn't heard the exchange, but they could see Julia was suddenly in a fury.

Julia jumped up out of her lounger and stood over Rafe threateningly. "You're a fucking piece of shit! I thought you were my friend!" Julia pushed Rafe back in the lounger, but Rafe just looked at her and laughed. "What? That night, in your car? Were you mad because I was late? So, after then? When?" She grabbed Rafe by her shirt and pushed her back hovering over her menacingly, but Rafe just kept laughing. "When did you do it?"

"What happened?" asked Abby frantically as Eden watched unsure what to think as the dark woman laughed, and the lighter one was yelling with anger and making threats.

"Well?" Julia fumed, but Rafe just continued to laugh. "You're fucking with me, aren't you?" she said nodding her head, but Rafe was wiping tears of laughter from her eyes and drinking from the wine bottle. "You better be," she said threateningly, showing her a fist. "You better be lying."

"Lying about what?" asked Abby in frustration. "What the hell is going on?"

Rafe looked at Abby as she forced herself to stop laughing. "You're still the only funny girl here, Abby," she said with a lopsided smile. She looked at Julia and pulled her close again. "Don't fuck with me if you don't want me to fuck with you," she said cheerfully. She pushed Julia away, lifted the wine bottle in salute, and took another drink.

Julia sat back down unsure if it meant Rafe was lying or not. "I'm sorry," she slurred with regret. "I just wanted Abby to hear you saying Eden's name when you slipped into your accent more." She grabbed the wine bottle back from Rafe and took a drink. "I can make a girl come more than once," she said with a whimper as she looked at Rafe with a pout. "I can."

"Good for you," said Rafe as she laughed and patted Julia on her silver head as if she were a little girl.

"What the fuck," screeched Abby. She was looking at Eden, who threw up her hands at the whole exchange.

Letty walked out of the house with a glass of wine and handed it to Rafe. "Maybe you should take it down to a glass full of something instead of a bottle."

Taking the glass, Rafe smiled at Letty. "*Grazie, cugina.*[2] Is the food ready?"

"Yes. Ephraim is bringing it out now," she said and went to help him.

---

[2] Thank you, cousin.

Rafe stood up unsteadily, the game with Julia forgotten and replaced by thoughts of food. "Okay, everyone," she shouted out, "the food," she stumbled forward and caught herself, "is coming!" She staggered her way to the patio table, where Letty was setting out food, and sat down again.

Eden followed her dismayed. "Letty, I need to talk to Rafe," she said anxiously. "Please, help me take her inside."

"Okay, sure," said Letty, "but I'm not sure how coherent she'll be in her current state." She lifted Rafe up from her chair and started walking her to the door.

Rafe leaned heavily on Letty. "Where are we going?"

Letty stopped to adjust Rafe and stand her up more. "Eden wants to talk to you inside."

"Eden?" asked Rafe with an accented slur Julia would have made fun of if she had heard.

"Yes, Eden," confirmed Letty.

"But the food is coming. We can talk later," said Rafe. With that decision, she broke away from Letty and stumbled back to the patio table where she sat down in her chair again. Ephraim was putting more food out, and Rafe's mouth watered. "Ephraim, it smells so good." She smiled at him then drank the rest of the wine in her glass. When she looked up, she saw Eden, who was suddenly standing over her, and Rafe smiled up at her drunkenly.

"You are so freaking drunk!" she accused angrily.

Rafe just continued to smile up at her. "Yes, I am," she agreed, "and I'm going to be this way all night! Come on, everyone. Let's eat!"

"What's wrong with you, Rafe?" pleaded Eden not understanding why she was being so difficult.

Rafe gave her a baffled look. "Wrong? You already know what's wrong." She looked at Eden and held her gaze for a moment. Rafe visibly paled as she looked into her eyes and struggled with the rising bile from her stomach burning her throat. "You know what? I'm not feeling very good anymore. I think I'm going to bed now. You all stay," she told everyone. "Stay."

She got up and staggered into the house as Eden followed on her heels. Making it to her bedroom, Rafe opened the door and noticed Eden had followed her. "What?" she asked, sickly.

"I told you I need to talk to you," Eden said in frustration.

Rafe put her hands on Eden's shoulders and looked into her eyes sadly before looking away. "No," she said, "you don't. Goodnight." She went into her room and shut the door, locking it behind her.

Eden banged on Rafe's door with her fist. "What is wrong with you, Rafe? Open the door! I really need to talk to you!"

Abby saw Eden banging on Rafe's door and went to investigate. "Eden, what's up? What's with the banging?"

Eden turned to her, the frustration showing on her face. "Were you with Rafe all day?"

"Some of it this morning," Abby confirmed. "So... sort of. Why?"

"She went to see Katheryn today and told her she didn't know if she wanted to fight the injunction or go through with the adoption," Eden said despondently. "I need to find out why."

"Oh, man," she said as she shook her head. "Let me see if I can find out what's going on." She knocked on Rafe's door. "Rafe, it's me, Abby. Can I come in?"

A few seconds passed, and Rafe opened the door. When Abby went inside, Rafe had sat down on the floor next to the door. Once Abby had closed the door, Rafe got up on her knees and locked it again before sitting back down on the floor. She looked curiously at Abby. "Did you come to hold my hair?"

"Are you going to throw up?" Abby asked warily, not wanting to have to deal with puke breath again.

Rafe thought about her question. "No."

Abby sighed relieved. "Rafe, let's sit on the bed." She pulled Rafe up, led her to the bed, and sat her down. "Did you go see Katheryn today?"

"Katheryn." Rafe gave Abby a crooked smile. "She is a fucking hard-ass lawyer."

"I know," said Abby. "Did you go see her?"

Rafe nodded her head once. "Yes, I did."

"Did you tell her you didn't want to fight the injunction?"

"Yes, I did." Rafe nodded her head again.

"Why?"

Tilting her head to one side, Rafe frowned as she looked at Abby. "Because, Abby, I can't win. You see, even if I win, I lose."

"I don't understand," said Abby.

"I know. It's hard to understand things sometimes." Rafe closed her eyes and laid her head on Abby's shoulder. When she opened her eyes, she found herself looking at Abby's hair and the many shades of blond blended together. She reached up and stroked her head. "Why do you have so many colors in your hair?" she slurred.

"It's highlights," Abby explained with a frown. Rafe had never cared about her hair before, so she was sure it was the liquor talking.

Rafe wrapped a strand of hair in her fingers and pulled.

"What the fuck!" Abby screamed. "You fuckin pulled my hair out!" She rubbed her head to ease the pain of having hair ripped from her head.

Rafe held out the blond strand of hair. "Here," she said softly. "I was helping you. You don't want this color."

"I want all my fucking hair!" she shouted and pulled the hair from Rafe's fingers. "Why the hell are you pulling out my hair?"

Rafe leaned into her again. "Abby, I'm tired. Will you stay here with me for a while?" She crawled to the middle of the bed, curled up, and closed her eyes. "I still hurt."

Abby just looked at her unsure if she should stay pissed or feel sorry for her. "You're so fucking drunk," she said and sighed. "Okay, just for a little while." She climbed in next to her spooning her as she put her arm around her. "What did you say to Julia to piss her off?" she asked softly.

"I was fucking with her," Rafe mumbled. "She thinks she can fuck with everyone, but I'm not gonna let her fuck with me," she slurred.

"I thought she was going to take you out," Abby admitted then laughed softly.

"Her daddy is too far away for her to take me out," rasped Rafe churlishly. The bed shook slightly as they both tried not to laugh out loud.

About twenty minutes later, Abby came out of Rafe's room, leaving Rafe as bed ready as she could and asleep. She managed to get Rafe's shoes and jeans off her. Then Rafe told her to fuck off, so she left her alone. She looked around and saw everyone was eating and talking out on the patio except Eden, who was sitting on the couch.

"Did you talk to her?" Eden asked anxiously.

"She was just too drunk to talk much," she said and rubbed her head. "After practically snatching me bald, she fell asleep."

"Did she say anything at all?" Eden pressed not sure what to think about the hair pulling.

Abby scratched her head absently. "She just said she couldn't win." She looked over at all the delicious smelling food she was missing.

Eden leaned forward and put her face in her hands. "I think she's talking about those abuse accusations. I think the stress and worry are wearing her down." She looked up at Abby. "She must be terrified another complaint will be filed, and she won't be able to dispute it."

"Do you think she believes it'll cause her to lose the injunction hearing?" Abby asked with a frown.

Eden looked at Rafe's bedroom door then up at Abby sadly. "I think so," she said softly. "She came so close to firing Katheryn. I think she's giving up." Tears filled her eyes. "I don't know why she did it. I don't know how to help her anymore."

Abby sat next to Eden and hugged her. "Don't worry. We'll all try to help her through this."

4

SATURDAY EVENING WAS filled with the sounds of shrill screams from Bronte and peals of laughter from Abby Van Falkov as Rafe Salvaggio worked at her computer.

After the art lesson, the three of them had spent the day swimming and playing together so Rafe wouldn't be alone with the baby. She had made sure not to be alone with Bronte since receiving her warning from Jake. Rafe didn't want to give Eden, or anyone else, any reason to file another complaint against her.

Now Abby was playing with Bronte in the living room waiting until Eden arrived to pick up the baby. She was also trying to get the petite dark-haired devil child to put her clothes back on. Rafe was working on a PowerPoint for a class she was substituting for on Wednesday as well as her presentation for a lecture she was giving Friday. Surrounded by research materials, she was engrossed in work on her laptop.

Eden knocked on the door and entered trying to be positive and upbeat. She had left after the art lesson to run errands. At least, it was her excuse. She could just feel Rafe didn't want her there, so she left to give her time alone with Bronte. "I'm back," said Eden as she walked over to Bronte and Abby. "Hi, baby. Are you having fun playing with Mama and Abby? What are you wearing?" she asked as she picked her up and noticed the baby was just in underwear.

"She's been great!" said Abby with a smile. "Rafe said she likes being in big girl panties. Rafe said she could wear them when she's here. You know she wants to wear them when she starts stripping off all her clothes!"

"You're such a big girl!" Eden smiled as she hugged Bronte and was caught off guard again at the positive things Rafe was exposing Bronte too. "Mommy will get some for our house."

"She's worn them almost all day," said Abby impressed with Bronte. "She knows the sign for 'potty' now, and she shows it to Rafe when she has to go! She's a really smart kid."

Eden looked over at Rafe with surprise then back at Bronte. "Mommy will have to learn to sign," she said to the baby and kissed her. "You're such a smart girl!" She looked at Abby. "I didn't think we'd start on underpants until after she was two," she said as Bronte hugged her.

Abby looked over at Rafe. "Rafe, Eden is here," she called out.

"Yes, I can see her," Rafe said coolly but did not look up from her work.

Eden looked anxiously over at Rafe. "How are you feeling tonight, Rafe?"

Rafe stopped working and looked at Eden, forcing a smile before she spoke calmly. "I'm doing fine, thank you. When will you be bringing Bronte back?"

"Well, I was hoping you could pick her up from my place on Wednesday," Eden said as she shifted Bronte on her hip.

She hoped Rafe would come to her apartment, and she could have dinner ready for them as a family again.

Rafe looked thoughtfully at her. "No, you'll have to bring her here, or I can meet you at the Kiki."

"Rafe," said Eden frustrated, "it would be so much easier if you could just come over to my apartment and get her."

"I'm sorry," said Rafe solemnly, "but I can't. I'm meeting a colleague on Wednesday."

"I can pick her up for you," Abby said, trying to be helpful.

"Great! Thanks, Abby." Rafe smiled at her in appreciation.

"No! Rafe," Eden said, trying not to show her anger, "lately, you seem to be too busy to pick her up, or you make some excuse to send someone to get her, or you want to meet somewhere to get her. On top of that, I feel like you're avoiding me and not wanting me around. For the thousandth time, what's going on?"

"I'm never too busy for her," Rafe said calmly ignoring her question. "I'm sorry my schedule doesn't align with yours. It would be better if you brought her here, or I can meet you at The Kiki Bistro. It's on the way to my meeting."

Eden looked at her in disbelief. "You're taking her to your meeting?" It was not lost on her how Rafe had ignored her question and what she had said about avoiding her.

"No, I was going to see if Letty could watch her until I got back," Rafe said as she made sure she gave her a full disclosure, so neither she nor Jake had anything on her.

"Why don't I just keep her at home if you're going to leave her with someone?" she asked in frustration.

"Fine," said Rafe very calmly. "If you think it's best."

"If I think it's best?" Eden asked in exasperation. "Rafe, I've been putting up with your crap all week. I'm not leaving until you answer my questions." She put Bronte in Abby's lap. Clenching her jaw in irritation, she took a moment to calm herself. She then went over and sat at the table where Rafe was working. "We were doing so well before you got sick. What's going on?" she asked softly.

"Hey, guys, I'm just gonna take off now," said Abby as she sat Bronte on the floor with her toys. "Yeah, it sounds like you two need some privacy. Call me if you need me to pick up Bronte."

"No," said Rafe abruptly. "I'd like you to stay Abby." Rafe looked at Abby and raised her eyebrows. She then nodded for her to sit back down. Abby sighed and sat down near Bronte again.

Eden shook her head not believing the two of them. She looked back into Rafe's eyes and tried to stare her down. "Well? What's going on?"

Rafe leaned back in her chair and crossed her arms, not phased in the least by Eden's stare. "I think maybe we were just going too fast. I need to go slower."

"Slower?" said Eden not understanding. "Rafe, you were the one who wanted to jump into bed almost immediately!"

"I know," said Rafe as she nodded her head in agreement. "It's a good thing it didn't happen. I can see now it wouldn't have been fair to you, to either of us."

"Fair?" Eden repeated as she reached out and touched Rafe's arm. "I don't understand."

Rafe closed her eyes for a moment at her touch. She could hear Jake's words in her ears and see the image of him walking out of her apartment behind her eyes. She snapped open her eyes and looked at Eden's hand on her arm.

"Yes, fair." She shrugged Eden's hand off her arm. "I just don't think I've been very fair to you. I feel like maybe I was pushing you into feeling something for me when you still aren't sure what you want."

Eden looked down, caught off guard at Rafe's words because it sounded too close to the truth. "So, you're sure of what you want?"

"I thought I was," said Rafe sadly.

Eden threw her hands up. "What does that mean?"

Rafe looked hard into Eden's eyes. "I don't know. I don't have a plan for us. Do you have a plan for us?" *Like your plan to get me out of your life for good and take Bronte away,* she thought bitterly.

"Rafe," Eden said then pulled away from Rafe's gaze. "I just want us to get along," she said softly.

"We are getting along," Rafe said coolly. She wished Eden would just leave her alone now.

"No," Eden said upset. "I don't think we are. You just... You give me these short answers and never come to my apartment anymore. You still won't be alone with Bronte, and you do your best not to be alone with me. You don't want to kiss me or hold me anymore, and there are hosts of other little things you're doing. I'm not surprised you made Abby stay." She looked into Rafe's unyielding steel gray-blue eyes. "And then there's the look you're giving me right now. I don't know what that look means." She looked down trying to compose herself. "I feel like you're cutting me off again."

"Cutting you off from what?" asked Rafe with a small laugh.

"I don't know," answered Eden in misery. She just wished Rafe would tell her what was wrong.

"Why does anything I do or say make you feel cut off, Eden? What is it I have you want?" she asked then looked at her expectantly. *Just tell me the truth, you want me out of your life forever*, she thought as she waited for an answer.

Eden closed her eyes. "I don't know."

"Eden," Rafe paused to reign in her pain. "The only thing I have to offer you—is me. But you're still not sure if I'm who you want." She looked at Eden who had looked down at her hands. She fought the sick feeling inside her because she knew it was Jake who Eden really wanted. "Look at me." Eden lifted her head slowly, and when she met her eyes, Rafe continued. "I've always been open and honest with you. I've never lied to you about how I felt about you, or us."

"I know," Eden said and swallowed the knot in her throat.

"Be sure to take Bronte to the restroom and have her try to go before putting a diaper on her," Rafe said as she got up. She went over and gave Bronte a kiss and a hug. "This is the sign if she needs to go potty," she said and made the sign for Eden by making the ASL letter P and tilting her hand side to side. "Right now, I need to be away from you for a while," Rafe informed her as she went back to her desk and closed her computer. Then she walked toward the hallway.

"Why?" Eden asked as she followed her. "Why do you need to be away from me?" Eden's head spun. She was thrown off guard at this revelation and the sudden subject change.

Rafe turned and looked at Eden intently. "Because, Eden, I just don't think you've been honest with me. I feel like you're hiding something from me," Rafe said firmly. "So I need to go slower."

Eden avoided those intense gray-blue eyes. "See, this is what I mean. I just don't ever know exactly what you're talking about. Why are you making this so hard for me?"

"Believe me," Rafe said with a sigh because Eden knew exactly what she was talking about, "this is much, much harder for me than it is for you. You have nothing to lose, no matter what decisions you make," Rafe said evenly. "I don't have the luxury." She turned and walked to her room, taking her work with her and leaving a stunned Eden behind.

5

WHILE BRONTE FELL asleep in her car seat, Eden Kingsley cried almost the entire car ride. She had managed to hold it together just long enough to call Flynn Ogden and leave him a message to meet her, but then she couldn't stop crying.

She didn't know what she did to make Rafe treat her so differently, and she didn't know what to do about it. She couldn't talk to her because Rafe refused. She couldn't do anything for her because she had no idea what to do. Rafe would barely spend five minutes in the same room with her, and when they did spend any time together, they were never alone.

Eden had just laid Bronte down in her bed when there was a knock at the door. A wave of relief came over her knowing there was at least one person she could confide in who would listen.

Flynn had been worried when he got Eden's call. He could hear she was upset and came as fast as he could. When she answered the door, he could see she was still upset.

"I got your message," said Flynn. "What's wrong?"

"Come inside. It's Rafe." Eden led Flynn to the kitchen.

"Did something happen?" Flynn asked with worry as he sat down across from her at the kitchen table.

Eden burst into tears again but forced herself to stop and stay calm. "Something must have happened, but I just don't know what. Tonight, she was telling me she feels like I'm hiding something from her, and she has been impossible to talk with about anything lately."

"Then maybe we should tell her what's going on," suggested Flynn.

"I can't," sniffled Eden wiping the tears from her face with her hand. "I'm not sure what she's talking about," she explained as she pushed her blond hair from her face. "Is she talking about the Stewards and Bronte's adoption and all of the things going on with it and Jake? Or is it about my feelings for men and the thing with Michael, or my feelings about her? She just said she feels like I'm hiding *something*. So which something does she mean?"

"You're hiding a lot from her," agreed Flynn as he nodded. "I sort of understand the injunction stuff, but why would you want to hide your feelings from her?"

"I don't know," she groaned miserably. "I'm not sure what my feelings are." She gave a desperate laugh. "I lay in bed at night and my body aches, but I'm not sure if it's for Rafe or Jake or Michael or for any man."

"You can't want Jake!" Flynn cried out with alarm.

"No, no, I don't," Eden reassured him miserably. "I just mean what Jake gave me, not him specifically. Flynn, I've only dated two men since Rafe, and they both turned out to be huge mistakes. But what if the next one isn't? I can't go back to Rafe, and then one day, tell her I'm leaving her for some man again."

"Eden, Rafe is a real person who loves you," Flynn said not understanding Eden's thinking. "This man in your mind may not even exist. How can you compare them to each other?"

"I don't know," admitted Eden with a sob. There was a tremendous amount of turmoil going on inside her, and she didn't know if she could explain it all to him. She hadn't even figured it all out for herself. This was just one of a thousand things it seemed like she was trying to figure out. "I just feel like, since Jake and Michael were such disasters, maybe I need to try dating another man, any man, to see if my feelings are the same. I just need to be sure. It's why I wanted to go slow with Rafe. I really don't want to hurt her again."

Flynn was very uncomfortable with what Eden was saying. He saw his mother go from man to man and, it seemed to him, without a thought or reason. It got her nowhere but in a hospital. He always wished she would just stop and really look at them to see what kind of a person they were before letting them move in.

"Why do you keep saying any man?" he asked tentatively. "Why don't you say the right person?" He decided to take a risk and tell her his own thoughts on love. "If you want someone to love you and give you the things you need in a real relationship, it can't be just anyone. It has to be the right person, a person who loves you and wants to give you the things you need, and has your best interests in mind all of the time. Defining people by whether or not they're a man or a woman shouldn't happen. It can take a long time to find the right person. Rafe wants to be that person for you. Why can't you let her?"

"I don't know if she wants that anymore," she said in misery. "She said she wants to go slower. I don't know what I did wrong. Maybe she can just feel I'm hiding all these things."

"Why don't you think she can give you what you thought Jake gave you?" asked Flynn trying to understand her. "Was it just the sex?"

Eden leaned on the table with her head in her hands. "Oh, Flynn, I don't know. I guess, at first, it was about sex when it was online," she admitted. "It was different and exciting, something that was just a memory from my past. I convinced myself it was okay and that I wanted—needed to relive it. After what happened online, I knew it was wrong, and I didn't do it again. But the memory was still there, and it stayed."

She looked up at him needing him to understand why she couldn't go to Rafe yet. She felt like she couldn't go anywhere until she could get through the chaos constantly tearing through her emotions, and then pull herself out.

"I've been dealing with all these doubts and feelings for a long time," she said softly, "and I thought they went away, but I was wrong." She hesitated but then decided to try to explain a few of the things she was going through so he would understand and keep helping her.

Eden wiped her tears and looked at Flynn. "After the baby was born, I was home on my own because Rafe had to go on another work trip, and I couldn't reach her. You would have thought I'd have cared or even wondered where she was, but I didn't. That night, when I thought about why I didn't care, I knew it was because deep down, I wasn't sure if we should be together anymore. I cried because we had been through so much. Everything is my fault because the feelings I started having about being with a man just wouldn't go away," she said as tears ran down her face again.

"When Rafe came home and wanted to make love, I felt so guilty. Guilty because everything she did to me felt right. My body wanted her, but my mind and heart weren't in the same place. So I avoided being close to her until I finally just had to tell her what was happening."

She looked at Flynn and rubbed her hands over her face. "You know what happened after I told her," she said softly. It was the beginning of the end when Eden had moved out of their bedroom and into the guest room. "When Rafe made me move into the guest room, I felt like I was in a void and didn't really belong anywhere," she continued. "Then I met Jake. The next thing I knew, it was happening, sex with a man in real life."

She looked down at her hands, again wishing she had never met Jake. "A few weeks ago, Rafe asked me if it was better." Eden released a sad laugh. "But it wasn't about better. At the time, when I first knew him, I felt comfortable and safe. It was like, suddenly, everything was right again. I knew where I belonged and felt like I found stability for myself and for Bronte."

Flynn shook his head in confusion. To him, it sounded like Eden was running away, just as his mother always had. Then one day, she would wake up and find out she had to run away again from the man who was supposed to save her, all because she wouldn't look where she was running.

"So you think it was all because you were with a man? It didn't have to be Jake or even Michael? Could it have been any man? Is that love?" He knew he could never be with just any man, even for all the things she listed.

"I don't know what it is," Eden said distraught.

"Did you feel the same way when you were with Rafe?" asked Flynn hesitantly. "Could she have been just any woman?"

Eden snuffed out a sad laugh and shook her head. She remembered how unhappy and unsatisfied she felt when she had her affair with Regan. She remembered, at one time, it seemed as if whenever Rafe walked into the same room, the world suddenly made sense and nothing else mattered. Now she just felt confused about everything.

Even now, it seemed Rafe didn't have to do anything but be close enough so Eden could smell her scent to make her body react and her head spin. Sometimes she thought she could actually feel Rafe's touch and hear her voice, even when she wasn't around. Every time she saw Rafe and looked into her eyes or heard her voice, or even felt her presence, her heart beat hard in her chest, and she felt like she had to touch her. She dreamed and thought about her all the time, even when she had not wanted to have those feelings for her.

"I don't think there's anyone else out there like Rafe," she said and dropped her face into her hands.

"Well, did you ever think it's not you picking the wrong man," asked Flynn hesitantly, "but it's that you're picking the wrong person? You know she loves you and wants what's best for you and Bronte. So, pick the person who loves you. Pick Rafe."

6

Wednesday: 6:45 a.m.

THE BREAKFAST CROWD at The Kiki Bistro was buzzing. Abby Van Falkov and Julia Hawthorn were getting coffee and a quick bite at the counter before they had to start work. They were enjoying the food they had chosen from the new breakfast menu Chef Ephraim had created. The food was a big hit with everyone who was fortunate enough to have ordered from the special menu.

"So, were you at Rafe's again last night?" asked Abby as she looked at her watch excited for her protégé Erica to show up so they could go shoot a bunch of new promo videos around town.

"Yes," said Julia and sipped her coffee, "she was going on and on about some class she has to teach today and her big presentation she'll be giving Friday. She was pulling out books and putting last minute things together for the presentation on her laptop."

"What did you do?" Abby asked as she tucked into her breakfast. "Did you mess with her again," she teased with a grin remembering Rafe's joke about Julia needing her daddy to finish her fights.

"No," said Julia with a smirk. "We played with Bronte most of the time and had dinner," she said with a shrug. "Then I just watched Bronte play and read some information about some new compliance rules until Eden got there while Rafe worked." She sipped her coffee and sighed heavily as she sat it down. "Eden came in and tried to talk to Rafe again, and she just looked at her, said hello, hugged Bronte, then picked up her laptop and went into her room. Basically, the same thing she does when you're there. Those two are driving me crazy."

"I'm just glad Rafe's looking healthy again," said Abby. "I was really worried. Whatever she had was hard on her. She's lost a lot of weight."

"I noticed too," said Julia thoughtfully. "I don't think she's been eating much unless Bronte is there. Her cupboards are bare again because of the party. I may pick some things up to take over for her tonight."

"Has she talked to you about why she's being so polite but aloof to Eden?" Abby asked curiously.

"Not a word," Julia said and took another sip of her coffee. "I've asked her, and all she says is, '*sempre guardare con attenzione prima di saltare*,'[3] whatever that means."

"Uh, what does it mean?" asked Abby. "I don't speak Italy."

"Italian," Julia rolled her eyes. She knew Abby said things wrong on purpose because she thought it was funny to annoy her. "I think it translates to 'always look carefully before you jump,' but I don't know what she means by it translated either." She took a bite of her food wondering if this meant she should set aside her vow of just being a friend.

"It's like one day they're kissing and all smiles, and the next, nothing," said Abby exasperated. "She said she wasn't, but," she hesitated, "do you think she was just messing with Eden."

"I'm not sure. It doesn't seem like something Rafe would do to Eden," Julia said hoping she was right. She knew, though, Rafe had been very skillful at cutting people off in the past. "She still won't be alone with Bronte even though they got a letter Monday saying no further action was going to be taken on the complaint filed with child services."

"It's the stupid injunction," complained Abby and took another angry bite of her food. "She's been out taking pictures a lot. I think she's spending too much time alone. She's driving Eden crazy too, with her weird, short answers to all of her questions."

"She's been spending a lot of time with Jude," said Julia and laughed at the thought.

---

[3] Always look carefully before jumping

Abby rolled her eyes. "Yeah, have you seen how they spend their time together? They just sit on the porch or by the pool and drink beers saying absolutely nothing for hours. It's maddening."

"They have a lot in common," Julia postulated.

"Like what?" scoffed Abby.

Julia and sipped her coffee. "They both have messed up relationships with the people they love."

Abby laughed. "Well, then, we all have a lot in common with her."

"True." Julia sighed as she thought about the pain of her break up with her last girlfriend, Andrea. "But I think those two handle things differently than us. They just keep everything inside."

Abby couldn't deny what Julia had pointed out. She knew she had never been one for keeping things inside. She left her baggage out all over the place, and sometimes, she opened it up in places where she shouldn't have. People told her more than once she needed to declutter and lighten her load, but she was a sentimental girl. "What I don't get is why Eden can't just make up her mind about what she wants," said Abby frustrated.

"I know," said Julia wryly. "I don't know if she's even interested in going to the clubs anymore. Maybe I'll ask her if she wants to go this weekend."

"Speaking of Eden, there she is," said Abby as she waved to her. "Eden, over here."

Eden made her way over and sat next to Abby. "Good morning." She looked at the waiter who appeared at the table. "Just coffee to go, thanks."

"Hey, do you need me to pick up Bronte tonight?" asked Abby.

"No." Eden sighed. "I'm keeping her home because Rafe has a meeting with a colleague or something tonight. I wish I knew what was going on in her mind."

"Did you get anything out of her Monday?" Abby asked even though she probably knew the answer.

"Just more confusion," said Eden as the waiter handed the take-out coffee to her. "I've got to go. I'll see you guys later."

Abby watched her leave. "She ran out of here fast," she said with a frown and spotted Erica outside on the sidewalk. "Finally," she muttered and started gathering her things. "Let me know if you talk to her about going out," Abby called back and gave a wave. "See ya!"

"Laters," Julia said as she swallowed and waved. "I think I may go see her and..." she started, but Abby was already gone.

7

Wednesday: 9:00 a.m.

SHIFTING THROUGH ALL of the paperwork on her desk Eden Kingsley was unable to concentrate on her tasks at work this morning. There was a brief knock on her office door and Gail, a production assistant, walked in frantic. "Eden, I can't find the preproduction schedule for the crane shots they supposedly sent up for *Zombies under the Midnight Moon.* Do you have a copy in your files?"

Eden threw the paperwork down in frustration. "I don't know where anything is right now."

"What's wrong?" asked Gail concerned because, through the office rumor mill, she knew Eden had been going through some personal troubles.

"I don't know. I just can't concentrate this morning," said Eden as the phone on her desk buzzed. "Eden Kingsley," she answered. "Oh, send her in," she said and hung up. "Gail, I'll look to see if I have a copy of the schedule and get it to you as soon as I can. I have a visitor."

"Sure," said Gale. "Please, don't forget. I really need it if you have it."

"I won't," promised Eden. As Gail walked out, Julia walked into the office. Eden looked up at Julia hopefully. "Have you found out what's going on with Rafe? Did she say anything to you last night?"

Julia breezed in, sat in the chair in front of Eden's desk, and gave her a peevish look. "I wish because you two are driving everyone crazy. Abby thinks she's still upset about the abuse charges and the injunction. I think she's getting tired of waiting for you to make up your mind about her," said Julia and looked at Eden pointedly. "Do you love her or not?"

Eden lowered her head. "It's not so simple," she said softly feeling guilty because she couldn't answer the question for Julia—but she couldn't answer it for herself yet either. "We were doing so well. Then she suddenly says she wants to go slower, and her slower seems almost like a complete stop," she said wearily. "I don't understand the sudden change. Has she mentioned anything to you?"

"No, she's just been very cryptic and strange. She's working late a lot lately too," Julia said in her lilting British boarding school accent, and then she paused for a moment. "This is why I came to see you. It seems like every time I'm over, she either gets a call or has to make one at about seven at night and takes it to her room. Not to mention she gets all these text messages. Her phone going off all the time is really getting annoying."

"Does she say what she's working on or who it is?" Eden asked.

"No. She just said it was a colleague," Julia said as she sat back in the chair.

"A colleague?"

"Eden, you really should figure out your feelings for Rafe soon. I hope you don't think she's going to wait for you forever." She hesitated for a moment. "There may be a reason she wants to go slower," said Julia wondering if Eden was really taking reconciling with Rafe seriously. It seemed like she couldn't see some pretty obvious things.

Eden looked at her confused. "What do you mean?"

"What I mean is her colleague may be another woman. Think about it," Julia said and waited a moment for Eden to process her words. "The calls are at night, and sometimes on the weekends, and last from thirty minutes to a couple of hours. No business call I've been on lasts that long at night, and I usually don't take business calls into my bedroom, and who texts someone so much? It has to be another woman. If there's any chance you love her, you really should figure out how you feel soon. You may not ever get the chance to make up your mind about her before she makes up her mind to love someone else."

8

Wednesday: 10:00 a.m.

IN THE SEMI-DARKNESS of the classroom, Dean Rafe Salvaggio stood behind her smart-desk giving her students time to make notes about what she had just presented to them. Today was the day she was lecturing to a special topics art class as a substitute. She was happy for the opportunity to be in the classroom. It was a place she had not been since she had to teach for her master's in college. Preparing for the lecture distracted her from the turmoil in her life, and the painful thoughts in her mind put there by Jake. To be engaged and challenged by the students was good medicine for her too.

Rafe continued her lecture to the class. Behind her, a screen displayed the presentation from her laptop. "Caravaggio was a womanizer who went after married women as well as the daughters of some of his patrons. He was a drunkard, a street brawler and," she paused for effect, "he was a murderer." She changed the photo on the screen. "So why is it the church and other patrons ignored the trouble he was constantly in and continued giving him commissions? Anyone?" She pointed to acknowledge a student. "Yes?"

"Well, the church needed artists to help promote their agenda," answered Mark confidently.

Rafe nodded. "Possibly. But the reason they wanted *him* specifically was because he was one of the very best, and he had something new, and everyone wanted what only he could give them at the time. They all appreciated him for his discovery of *tenebrism* and the power it added to his work. Remember the word *tenebrism*. What you'll see in your book is that tenebrism is a style of painting with distinct chiaroscuro, creating violent contrasts of light and dark. You'll note how the darkness becomes the dominating feature in his work. Today you may see this exact type of style in photography and in filmmaking. We owe this to Caravaggio." She paused again to give the students a chance to look at the painting in the book and take notes. "But not everyone had a positive reaction to his paintings. Some said they were unsuitable since they didn't respect the subject. Who can give me an example of his work showing this so called unsuitability?" Rafe acknowledged a student, "You."

"His *John the Baptist*," answered Laura timidly.

"Yes, *John the Baptist*," confirmed Rafe and rewarded the student with a smile. "As you can see in your books, this particular *John the Baptist* is now hanging in the Nelson-Atkins Museum of Art in Kansas City, Missouri. Caravaggio painted John the Baptist in such a way that when a worshiper approached the painting, at their eye level, the first thing they would see was his dirty feet. Who can tell me what else—"

A jolting crash cut off Rafe without warning as the door to the classroom was opened and slammed against the wall.

Everyone looked up in shock and surprise at a desperate gunman holding a glinting black semi-automatic handgun as two deafening gunshots rang out over their heads. Panicking students fell to the floor and frantically covered their heads and ears, falling and crawling chaotically away from the danger.

"Everyone, stay where you are!" shouted the gunman as he pointed the gun at the students. "Don't move or I'll blow your fucking heads off!"

Rafe stood frozen behind her desk as her vision shaded with the color of thick red blood. Her mind struggled to keep up the walls around the echo of painful memories from her childhood as the familiar sound of the gunshots threatened to bring back. As more shots rang out, screams of terror joined them as a metallic smell filled the air.

9

Wednesday: 11:00 a.m.

AT HER MASSAGE company, Sweet Sensations, Jude Atwood had finished with a client and was taking a break in the lounge. She got herself a drink from the refrigerator, crashed on the couch, and turned on the television with the remote.

On screen, a news reporter stood in front of one of the buildings at the California Conservatory of Art and Design talking into the camera. "...again, hostages are being held in the CCAD building behind us," the reporter appraised the viewers. "We have just been informed it is a lone gunman and the police are awaiting his demands. The Conservatory has not released the names of the hostages, but we do know all of the male students were sent out of the building just twenty minutes ago. We also know there are eight students being held along with one instructor. We're staying live at the scene. Back to you, Bill."

"Stay tuned," the news anchor instructed the audience. "We will be bringing you more on this hostage situation in a moment. But now we need to take a station identification break."

"Oh, shit!" breathed Jude as she recognized the Conservatory in the background. It sank in this place was where her friend and neighbor Rafe worked. She pulled out her phone and connected a call. "Abby, have you been watching the news? You should turn it on. Something's going on now at the Conservatory where Rafe works. Someone's holding some students hostage in one of the art buildings." She listened to Abby's questions. "They haven't announced any names yet. No, I haven't tried to call her. I just found out and called you. Okay, call me back." She hung up and turned her attention back to the television and the surreal feeling it gave her to know a friend was close to the situation on the news. She was sure since it wasn't the administration building, Rafe would be okay.

10

Wednesday: 11:30 a.m.

JUMPING OUT OF Erica's car, Abby Van Falkov rushed into The Kiki Bistro and was frenzied as she looked for anyone she knew who she could tell her news. She was hoping Rafe would pick up her phone so she could get some inside information, but there was no answer when she called. She found Letty, Ephraim, and several customers already listening to the news. Letty motioned her over, and they listened to the announcer together.

"...still have no word from the police for a reason behind the hostage situation here at the California Conservatory of Art and Design," reported the dark haired anchor. "The Conservatory, also known as CCAD, has not yet released the names of the students or the instructor being held inside the arts building pending notification of the families..."

The phone on the countertop rang, and Letty answered it and stepped away from the counter. "Hello, the Kiki Bistro." She listened to the caller. "Yes, this is Letty Carver. What? Oh, no, no. Oh, my god no. Not Rafe!" she cried. "What, what should I do?" She tapped Ephraim on the shoulder and motioned to him frantically. "I understand." She hung up the phone with a worried face. "It's Rafe. She's the instructor being held hostage." She looked at Ephraim with distress then burst into tears as her legs gave out, and she slumped almost to the floor before he caught her.

"Oh, my god! Letty!" Ephraim cried out as he caught her and lifted her back up looking to Abby for help. "Letty. Letty, what did they say to do?"

"We have to," Letty sobbed, "we have to go there! They said to stay by the phone, but I have to go!"

"Oh, shit no!" Abby said in a daze as she realized what had happened. "You guys go. I'll call everyone." She started dialing.

"I'll forward the phone to the cell," said Ephraim as he led Letty out back to their car.

Erica rushed in from parking the car and saw Ephraim leading Letty out the door. "What happened?"

Abby gripped Erica's arm and looked at her with worry as she spoke into the phone. "Eden Kingsley, please. It's an emergency!" cried Abby. "Eden. Eden, it's Abby. Have you been watching the news? You have?" she swallowed hard so she could continue. "Rafe is the instructor being held..." she choked and looked at Erica whose eyes got round, "...being held hostage. Letty and Ephraim just got the call and are on their way now. No, I'll call everyone. See you there." Abby started out the door pulling Erica with her. "Let's get over there!"

11

Wednesday: 12:00 P.M.

INSIDE THE DIMLY lit classroom, Rafe Salvaggio waited in silence, along with the eight female students lined up against the outside wall sitting under the large metal-framed windows.

A few of the girls cried silently and held each other in fear while others stared blankly at the floor.

Rafe remained in place behind the smart desk, the presentation behind her still projected and glowing on the screen. She had recovered herself from her initial shock at the situation, but the sound of the gunshots and the smell they left behind had left her head aching. It was a black ache tinged with the red edge of memories she would rather not revisit. With each breath she took, the sharp sweet scent of gunpowder filled her nose. It brought wakefulness to the memories she had worked to put to rest long ago and created a bad taste in her mouth. She was sitting in her chair, lying across the desk and resting her head on her arms, listening to their captor with loathing.

They had been in the room for two hours.

Their captor, Wade, had his semi-automatic rifle slung across his back, and he had one hand gripped tightly around his pistol. In his other hand, he held his cell phone, the only way left to communicate with the outside world. He was talking with the police negotiator and pacing in front of the desk where Rafe was sitting.

"What else do I want?" asked Wade manically into the phone. "I don't know." He listened for a moment "Lunch? Sure, I'm hungry. Pizza? Sure, I guess it's okay. Just have them set it inside the building door. I'll have a hostage," he reminded them unnecessarily, "so I better not see anyone anywhere near the door," he warned the caller. He hung up the phone then went and sat at the desk he had placed next to the doorway, out of view of anyone looking in the windows.

Unable to stand his stupidity anymore, Rafe sat up and looked at Wade with scorn. "Wade, *you—*" she said with disgust, "you are a fucking idiot." She sneered, wishing she had something for her headache.

Wade pointed his gun at Rafe. "Fuck you, teacher!" he spat.

"No," said Rafe calmly. "Fuck you. You have nine hostages and a gun. They ask you what you want to eat—" she waved her hand and motioned toward the window where police waited below, "—what may just be your last fucking meal on this earth, and you order fucking pizza. Idiot! Why do people like you always order pizza?"

"You don't fucking like pizza?" Wade asked not understanding why she even cared when no one else seemed to care about anything.

"I like pizza, Wade," Rafe said with false sweetness. "But this may be my last fucking meal too, and I don't want it to be pizza."

"Well, then, what the fuck do you want?" Wade asked sarcastically.

"I don't know," answered Rafe as she looked at the girls sitting on the floor under the windows. "What do you think, people? Steak and lobster?" The girls just looked at her with disbelief. "Yeah, steak and lobster is what I want. That would be a fucking great last meal." She looked over at the girls. "Anyone allergic to shellfish? No? Good." She looked back at Wade. "I think we should have some wine too."

Irritated with her, but unable to see a flaw in her logic, Wade got up and walked over to Rafe and handed her the phone. "Here, you order it," he demanded as he pointed the gun at her head and pressed it into her temple. "Just don't try anything that'll make me use this."

Rafe just smiled up at him then hit redial on the phone. "Hi, this is Dean Rafe Salvaggio." She paused, waiting for all the questioning on the other end to stop. "No, no, I'm fine. I just have a god damn gun to my head," she said irritably. "Listen, Wade here has changed his mind about lunch. No, he still wants lunch. He just wants something different. He wants steak and lobster for everyone. Right, nine of us plus him," Rafe confirmed. "Well, you better get it. Oh, and he wants six bottles of wine and not the half bottles, he wants the regular size. Red and make it a nice one." She paused listening. "I know this is a zero tolerance school, but I think an exception can be made in this particular case, don't you? Oh, one more thing," she said and smiled mockingly up at Wade, "he says not to forget the silverware, lobster bibs, and wet naps. Sure, salad and rolls would be good too. Just send the works. Bye." She hung up the phone, leaned forward, and sneered at Wade. "Just let me know if you need any more help being smart. Like you said, I am the teacher here."

Wade snatched the phone from her and shoved her head back with the gun. "Fuck you!"

12

Wednesday: 12:30 P.M.

AFTER FIGHTING TRAFFIC, and finding a place to park as close as they could to the building where Rafe was being held, Letty Carver and Ephraim Holden made it to the California Conservatory of Art and Design grounds. Frantically, they made their way through the crowds to the police line. They finally found the police captain who was talking with the president of the school, Clarice Biggalow.

"I'm Letty! I'm Letty Carver, Rafe Salvaggio's cousin," she said adamantly so they would let her through. "Where is she? What's happening?" Letty questioned them. She was desperate for information.

"Ms. Carver," the captain began in an annoyingly calm voice, "we're doing everything we can at the moment. The negotiator talked with your cousin on the phone about a half an hour ago, and she indicated she was fine." He didn't bother to ask her why she was there even though they had told relatives to stay home at this time. He knew it was a waste of breath. Some people followed directions, and some did not. It was clear this woman was in the latter category.

"Of course, she did," Letty said, agitated because she heard what they were saying on the news about the hostages being held at gunpoint. "What else could she have said with a gun to her head?"

"He made her order steak and lobster for lunch," Clarice, the CCAD president interjected, and then looked at the captain. "Is he going to get it?"

The captain sighed and tugged his hand down his face in frustration. "Yes, he's going to get it," he said gruffly. "Who the hell orders steak and lobster during a hostage situation?" he asked in frustration. "This guy is a real piece of work! Can you believe he asked for wine too? They're going to be in there having a god damn dinner party!"

13

Wednesday: 1:30 P.M.

TAKING IN THE crowd on the Conservatory grounds, and based on the news reports they had been watching, Julia Hawthorn and Eden Kingsley could see the crowd had grown as more students and onlookers migrated to the scene. The arts building was surrounded by an inner ring of police vehicles, which was, in turn, circled by a ring of television news crews, and then again, with a ring of spectators.

Eden and Julia made their way through the crowd to the edge of the ring of television crews, but they were denied access to go further by the police. Abby, Jude, Stacey, Erica, and Flynn arrived not long afterward. They were all trying to locate Letty and Ephraim as a nearby reporter began broadcasting another update.

"We're back live at the California Conservatory of Art and Design where nine people have been taken hostage in the building behind me," said the reporter as the camera zoomed in on the building. "We have just been informed the instructor being held is Dean of the Department for the Advancement of the Arts, Rafaella Salvaggio. Dean Salvaggio was formerly CEO and owner of *Eroina Conservazione e Design* a company with offices in Milan, Italy as well as in the US in New York and California. The company is responsible for the restoration and conservation of some of the most precious historic buildings and homes in the world. This footage was taken just about a half an hour ago as lunch was delivered to the captor and his hostages."

The video playback was displayed on a large screen mounted on the side of the news van. On the screen, a SWAT officer, all in black with a bulletproof vest, helmet, and faceguard, wheeled in boxed meals on a hand truck as several similarly clad officers covered him with assault rifles. One officer had taken a knee and was aiming his rifle at the doorway. The meals were pushed carefully just inside the door and left on the hand truck. Then the officer went back for the other hand truck holding the box of bottled wine. He wheeled it to the door and took it inside, placing it next to the meals. As the officer walked out, he moved away from the building slowly making sure his hands were in full view until he made it back to his base site.

The camera zoomed in on the building and the window next to the door. It revealed a hostage inside who was pushed violently forward against the glass to the side of the door and forced to her knees. The camera zoomed in further on the hostage and revealed the face of Rafe Salvaggio to the world. Behind her, all they could see was the black barrel of the gun placed against her head. Rafe, unknowingly, looked straight into the camera and then closed her eyes.

Panning right, the camera caught two student hostages wheeling the food away from the door and further into the building away from the sight of the camera. The camera was again on Rafe and showed she now had her forehead against the glass. With the gun still against her head, she was jerked away from the window and disappeared from view.

On the screen, a still picture was displayed to the world of Rafe kneeling with her eyes closed and the malicious black gun against her head. The text below her image said only the word HOSTAGE in an angry red and brutally ragged font.

Eden, Abby, and all of Rafe's friends were staring at the screen and the image of Rafe in horror. The blood drained from Eden's face as she began to shake, losing the strength in her legs. She grabbed Erica's arm, pulling her down with her as she fell. "No!" she choked out.

"Abby, help me," cried Erica holding onto Eden as her legs folded under her.

Abby reached out for Eden and helped guide her gently to the ground. "Eden! Are you okay?"

"No!" screamed Eden in anguish. "He's going to kill her!" The image of Rafe swam before her eyes, and it felt as though her heart would beat out of her chest and her lungs had stopped working. "He's going to kill her!" She gasped for air.

Julia rubbed Eden's back, trying to calm her, and could see she was having an anxiety attack. "He's not, Eden. The video was from a half hour ago. Rafe's okay. She's okay," she reassured her.

Eden fought to regain her breath and control. "No," she croaked out. "No, her eyes," she wheezed in a breath as her anxiety tightened her throat. "There was no hope, she knows. She knows." She sobbed. "He's going to kill her. It's why she closed them! My god," she moaned. "My god, no." Her body shook as she gripped Erica's arm.

"Eden, everything is okay. It's just the camera," Erica said as she grimaced in pain from Eden's grip.

"Stacey, help us! We should get her away from this screen," said Abby as she looked around for a place to go.

Stacey grabbed Eden's elbow to try to help her stand. "Hold it together, woman!"

Jude and Flynn ran over to them when they saw Eden on the ground. "What happened?" asked Jude.

"Eden is just shaken," said Julia, trying to keep things calm. "Let's move her back under those trees."

"Okay, maybe we should all go," suggested Jude. "I'll meet you there. I'm going to find Letty and tell her where we're gathered." Jude took off across the grounds.

Flynn took over for Stacey and grabbed Eden's arm to help lift her and lead her away from the television screen with the disturbing image of Rafe still displayed. "Eden, it'll be okay."

They helped Eden to a spot under some trees and away from the news van. Everyone sat on the ground under one of the trees, and Abby knelt in front of Eden holding her hand to try to help calm her. "Come on, Eden. It'll be okay. Jude will find out what's going on and tell us. Rafe will be fine. I know she will."

"You can't know," cried Eden and leaned into Abby's shoulder. "Abby, why couldn't I tell her?" she cried. "Now I can't," she started and lost her breath and voice again.

"Eden, she'll be fine," said Abby as she rubbed Eden's back and head, trying to calm her. "You can tell her whatever you have to tell her when she comes out."

"Flynn..." Eden looked up at him. "Flynn, what am I going to do now?"

Flynn looked up desperately at the others not knowing what to say. He looked at Eden and focused. "We just have to wait, Eden. Be calm and wait."

Eden pulled back and looked at Abby with despair. "What's Bronte going to do without her?"

"She won't be without her. She won't." Abby hoped it was true as she held Eden again while she cried.

"I couldn't say it," she sobbed into Abby's shoulder. "I still can't say it. I don't know how I can."

14

Wednesday: 2:30 P.M.

JUDE ATWOOD FINALLY found Letty and Ephraim in an area between the circle of police and the news vehicles, stuck between the central command truck and a news van. They were anxiously waiting for more information from the police. As she waited with them, Jude heard a reporter in the news van next to them talking to a crewmember through his microphone and listening through his earpiece.

"You're a genius," the reporter said excitedly to whoever was talking to him through his earpiece. "No, it's great! I'll get the guys to set things up on this end." He looked up and smiled at his crew. "Okay, people, we're going with some live feed from Freddy's camera. He found a spot for his camera where he can see straight into the classroom. There's no sound, but we'll have a picture. Get us set up with the studio in case something happens, and we need to go live! Go, people!"

The crew worked fast and got the live feed up and playing on the screen mounted on the side of the van. A crowd had gathered around to watch with morbid fascination.

"Look," Jude said pointing at the video screen. "They have a shot of the classroom. Where's Rafe?" Everyone pushed through as they tried to see the screen better.

"He must have everyone up against the outside wall," observed Ephraim calmly as he watched the captor pace the room on his phone. "I wonder if he's on the phone with the police negotiator."

Letty held tightly to Ephraim taking comfort in his calm demeanor. "Ephraim, I wish I could see Rafe. I need to see if she's okay," she said fearfully.

Ephraim held her close to comfort her. "I wish the police would just shoot the guy so we can get her out of there."

"Why don't they?" said Jude anxiously.

"I guess he hasn't been classified as dangerous enough yet," reasoned Ephraim.

"Wait," said Jude as she pointed at the screen. "Look. There's Rafe. What's she doing?"

"She's giving they guy a wine bottle," said Letty in disbelief. "Is she trying to get him drunk?"

"How'd she get wine?" asked Jude confused.

"The guy ordered it for lunch," Ephraim drawled with a shake of his head.

"Is he some kind of drunk?" Jude asked outraged.

"I don't know," cried Letty. "He's just crazy, and I want all of this to stop."

"We should definitely keep Eden away from this van," said Jude with concern. "Seeing Rafe being held at gunpoint earlier really got to her, and she had an anxiety attack."

"We're all upset, Jude," Letty scolded angrily. Eden and her anxiety were the least of her concern. In her opinion, if Eden really cared about Rafe, she wouldn't have left her the way she had—twice. "I need to get more information. Come on, Ephraim. Let's see if we can talk to the captain again." She pulled Ephraim toward the command truck.

Jude made her way back across the grounds to report to Abby, Eden, and the others she didn't have any new information except she had found Letty.

After talking with Jude, everyone decided to go back to the police command center and demand more be done. Abby and the others convinced Eden to stay behind because she was still shaken up. Flynn volunteered to stay to keep her company and help her if he could.

"One of us will come back to let you know what we find out," said Abby gently as she ran her hand over Eden's shoulder. She shared a look of concern with Flynn as she left with the others to make their demands.

15

Wednesday: 3:30 P.M.

THE ACTIVITY AROUND the command truck looked chaotic to Letty Carver and her husband, Ephraim Holden. They fought through the turbulence around them and found the police captain and Clarice Biggalow standing under a tent nearby, the tent set up with computers and other communication equipment.

"We've stopped the live feed of the classroom from being broadcast, but we have it here so we can monitor the situation," the captain was telling the Conservatory president. "The negotiator is working on a resolution to the situation. All we can do now is wait."

"That's all?" interrupted Letty angrily. "He's working on something," she cajoled sarcastically. "Can't you just send someone in and take him out?"

The captain looked at her and shook his head. "It may escalate the situation. We can't take the risk with the hostages' lives at this point."

"Ms. Carver," Clarice said calmly, "they're doing the best they can. I'm sorry this is happening to you and to Rafe. She wasn't even supposed to be in there." She pursed her lips in disbelief and sighed. "Well, she was supposed to be there today. What I mean is she was just substituting." She looked past Letty, and her eyes widened in surprise. "Oh, no. This is unbelievable." She stepped past Letty. "What are you doing here? How did you get through?"

As Greer approached, Beth interpreted her words to Clarice. "I came early to meet with Rafe so she wouldn't have to drive to the airport. What's going on?" Then Greer voiced her own words, "Beth says people are talking about hostages."

Clarice looked up and sighed not wanting to deliver the discouraging news yet again. "Greer," she hesitated, "Rafe. She's in there. She's one of the hostages," she said as she pointed up to the classroom window, and Beth signed her words to Geer.

Greer shook her head in disbelief and looked to Beth to verify what was just said. She paled visibly and anxiously began her questioning. "Oh, my god, no! Is she okay? How long has she been in there? What does the guy want? What are the police doing?"

"Calm down, Greer," said Clarice sternly, trying to keep a professional composure in this time of uncertainty. "They've been held since about ten this morning. The police are still negotiating with the young man holding the class hostage. She seemed fine the last time they were in contact with her, but the police don't know how much longer it could be until they can resolve the situation."

Greer looked around, anxious about Rafe, and saw the classroom on the video screen and walked up to it. "What's this?" she voiced as she watched the activity on the screen.

"It's the room they're in," Letty said as she went over to stand next to her. "A cameraman found a spot where his camera could see directly inside. Don't worry. It isn't being broadcast live."

Greer watched the screen with Letty as the cameraman changed his angle until he found a subject inside the room. "There's Rafe!" she pointed excitedly.

"Oh, my god," cried Letty and she put her hands to her mouth.

"Captain, we have visual and motion in the room," said one of the officers monitoring the feed. "It looks like they're just talking."

Greer watched the screen intently.

16

Wednesday: 3:30 P.M.

INSIDE THE CLASSROOM, Rafe Salvaggio and the other hostages had been listening to Wade go on for hours on the phone about what he wanted and his demands for their release. It was grating on Rafe's nerves as she sat with her eyes closed listening to him. His wants were such mediocre and easily obtainable things.

Rafe knew she could get those things for him with a few phone calls. He wanted his art in some galleries, a teacher fired, his grade changed, money, his girlfriend to come back, his job back, but she knew he mostly wanted someone besides himself to blame for all of the problems in his life.

Rafe opened her eyes and looked at him. He looked too young to know just how hard life could actually get. She wondered what he would do if he had her life. She was sure he wouldn't be taking hostages—he would just use the gun on himself.

She wanted to shout and tell him how easy he had it with his insignificant problems. At least every important person in his life had not died horribly, and the woman he was in love with was not planning the total annihilation of his life and executing her plan like a military general, so precisely, so covertly, so coldly.

She knew Eden would push her out of her life forever, and out of Bronte's, except for possibly a once a year visit Jake said she may still be able to win—as long as she paid the price. She remembered Jake telling her how upset Eden was about seeing her will and the changes she had made to it.

She'll get what she wants, Rafe thought.

Rafe reinforced the walls around her heart and tried to forget the kisses and the smiles she thought were just for her and quashed the hope from continuing to fill her. It was all gone now.

Rafe's fury at the events in her life was tumbling and building inside her, and as she looked at Wade, she made a decision. Maybe she could help Wade and herself. Maybe she could end this so they both wouldn't feel pain anymore, or maybe he would break once he felt forced to make the decision.

Either way, my life is over.

Her breathing quickened as she searched for the final ounce of courage she needed, and she found it in the knowledge their pain might finally end and Eden would get what she wanted.

But not the way she planned it.

If she was upset about what she saw in my will, then just wait until she sees the changes. They all hated my father. Well, they can all hate me too and go to hell.

She looked at Wade again, and all of her thoughts could be read in her eyes, her face, and her posture. Seething with her own hurt and anger, she got up and approached Wade, hungry for an opportunity that could cause her own death and end the torment filling every part of her body. If her life were to end, she would be the one in control of when and how.

She took control for what may be the last time.

She walked determinedly up to Wade. "Wade, I thought you said you were an artist," said Rafe accusingly.

Wade swung around angrily to face her. "I *am* an artist," he growled agitated.

Rafe looked at him with contempt. "Then why the hell are you holding a gun and not a paintbrush or a chisel?"

"This way people will have to listen to me," Wade shouted and brandished his gun.

"Really?" Rafe laughed at him condescendingly. "Is that what you think? You think a gun will make people stop and listen to you, care about what you say, care what you feel?" She put her hands on her hips and cocked her head to one side. "Well, you're right. They will, for about fifteen minutes when they hear about it on the six o'clock news. Then what?" she asked with a raised eyebrow and sneered.

Wade scowled at her. "I don't know. Just shut up!" he screamed in her face.

Rafe stepped closer to him. "No," she said firmly as she stared into his eyes boldly, recklessly. "I'm not going to shut up. Do you think you're the only one in this room who feels pain? The only one who hurts? Well, if you do, you're wrong. Everyone in here feels pain just as much or even more than you do. The difference is they're not the ones with the gun." She looked him up and down disdainfully. "Just you."

"Shut up!" Wade screamed in anger. "They don't know what I am going through. They don't know how I feel!"

Again, Rafe took a step closer to Wade and blocked him from the students, who were watching the exchange in terror. Then she spoke softly but contemptuously. "You're right, Wade, they don't. And you know what? They don't fucking care how you feel. They're too busy worrying about their own problems and feelings."

Wade raised his gun and pointed it at Rafe. He moved to her side to press the gun into the side of her head. "Like you said, I'm the one with the gun," he reminded her. "I am going to fucking kill you!" he roared into her face.

Rafe turned her face slightly, feeling the warm metal of the gun press harder against her head. She looked at him defiantly then spit out her words. "Then kill me!"

17

Wednesday: 3:45 P.M.

BELOW THE CLASSROOM, on the Conservatory grounds, everyone had gathered around the news van, and they were watching the video feed as Rafe talked to Wade. Greer Noble was watching closely. Rafe's back was to the camera, but she could see what Wade was saying and knew Rafe was provoking him. Alarmed, she signed to Beth frantically. Beth went to get the captain and met Greer at the back of the van to keep the conversation private.

"She's provoking him!" signed Greer as Beth interpreted. "You have to do something. She's lost patience, I think. She's going to get herself killed."

The police captain walked around to look at the video as Greer and Beth followed. "Why would she do something so stupid?" the captain asked irritably. "She needs to give us time to talk with him." He pulled out his radio and spoke into it. "Call him. Ask him about his mother, anything to get his attention away from Dean Salvaggio. It looks like she may be escalating the situation." He turned back to Greer and Beth. "It's okay. We'll take care of it." He tried to reassure them and made his way back to the command area.

"I'll keep watching," Greer called out after him. She turned her attention back to the screen and saw Wade move to Rafe's side and raise his gun to the side of her head. She watched as

Rafe turned her head and clearly saw Rafe speak two terrible words. 'Kill me.'

"No!" Greer shouted out in horror. Frantically, she signed to Beth. When Beth understood what was happening, she ran after the captain. Greer looked back at the screen shaking with fear for Rafe's life. "Why is she doing this?" she voiced to no one.

18

Wednesday: 3:48 P.M.

ABOVE THE CHAOS of the grounds, Wade Delchus's phone was vibrating unnoticed on the desk where he had left it. He held his pistol to the head of the Dean, but she wasn't backing down from his threat to kill her. He didn't understand why she wanted to piss him off more than he already was. He worked to control his breathing and keep his muscles relaxed as his temper grew.

Rafe laughed and pulled away then turned to face him. "Go ahead and shoot me, Wade," she dared him. "Put a hole in my fucking heart, spray my blood all over the fucking classroom, and kill me. I really don't give a shit. Then they can put my body in a hole, and you in a prison cell and everyone will forget about us both by tomorrow morning."

Wade gripped the gun tighter and shoved it hard under Rafe's chin. "You're fucking stupid! You're a fucking steel-hearted bitch! I'll kill you!" he threatened.

Rafe stared heatedly, without fear, into his quickly shifting eyes. "You know what, Wade? You go ahead and kill me, but before I hit the ground, I suggest you put the fucking gun in your mouth and pull the trigger because, once the gun goes off, this place will be full of cops, and you won't have a chance to kill anyone else. Then both our bodies can be dropped into a hole in the ground and forgotten. How does that sound to you?"

Infuriated, Wade pushed the gun forcefully into her chest with each word he uttered. "Shut... the fuck... up!"

Not realizing everyone outside by the news van below was watching her and screaming frantically as her words were interpreted, Rafe took a step forward into the barrel of the gun.

"Or how about this," she spoke softly as the gun pressed into her chest, "the Chinese say you need three things for paintings: the hand, the eye, and the heart." She looked into his eyes. "With a gun in your hand, your eye only on yourself, and with anger in your heart, you can't say you're an artist, and I think it's really what you want to be." She felt him press the gun harder into her chest. "So you can give the gun to me and put all of these emotions and feelings into creating a piece of art people can't ignore or forget because it will be here, in the world forever, reminding them of you, your feelings, and your pain."

Regripping the gun, Wade kept it pressed against Rafe's heart. "Back off! I'm warning you!" he growled.

"No." Rafe looked unwaveringly into his shifting eyes. "Which is it, Wade? Will it be fifteen minutes of the world's undivided attention or immortality through your art? Are you going to destroy or create? What is it you want all of these people, who you think should care about your feelings, to remember about you? Do you want them to remember you for shooting some steel-hearted bitch of a dean in college because you can't or won't deal with your feelings like a reasonable person, or for being a great artist, like Caravaggio, who had his issues but sent his message through time by using his creative talent?"

Wade gave a short manic laugh and backed up a step then motioned to the presentation screen. "It says on the screen he was a murderer."

"He was." Rafe smiled knowingly. "But it's not what made him memorable. After he had died, he was completely forgotten about. The only reason we know anything about him is because his art was found and he was researched. As far as his crimes," she offered with a shrug, "he had the church to bail him out. You only have me." She let her words sink in. "Caravaggio didn't kill the church—he used it." She looked down at the gun then up at him and held out her hand as she spoke very softly. "Make your choice, Wade. Become someone who is forgotten in a moment or an artist who is immortalized through his works of art." With built up rage and animosity, Rafe urged him, "Fucking shoot me or give me the gun!"

Held by her gaze, Wade could see in her eyes she believed every word she had said. He saw no fear in her eyes and his own fear surfaced. He broke and could not shoot her, could not carry out his own threat, and he realized he had failed once again.

He loosened his grip on the gun and put it barrel first into her hand and whispered. "I'm sorry. I don't really want to kill anyone. Oh, my god, I'm sorry," he said as he began to shake.

Rafe took the gun from his hand and then he put the rifle slung across his back on the ground. Rafe lowered her eyes so he couldn't see her disappointment and spoke to him as well as to herself. "Never be sorry for being passionate, Wade. But never let your passion overcome your reason." She took a deep breath. "Sit down at the desk and give me your phone. I'll call to let them know it's over."

Sinking into the seat at the desk and holding his head in his hands, Wade looked up at her in desperation. "I guess I'm going to jail."

"A reasonable assumption." Rafe sighed as she picked the phone up off the desk. "Don't worry. I know you're not a bad person. Caravaggio was pardoned of murder by the Pope three days after his death. You didn't kill anyone, so let's see if we can do better for you."

Wade rocked back and forth with his head in his hands. "Thank you," he whispered.

Very calmly, Rafe turned to the girls in the class who were clinging to each other and looked up at her as if she were an ethereal being. "Okay, everyone. Just stay calm a little while longer." She looked at the student's faces as she put the phone to her ear. "I'll call and let them know we're coming out, and then I think class will be canceled for the rest of the month if it's okay with you."

Everyone nodded, and one girl barked out a short nervous laugh. Rafe turned her back on the students to talk on the phone, still holding the gun by its barrel.

19

Wednesday: 5:30 P.M.

POLICE OFFICERS SURROUNDED Wade Delchus as they brought him out of the building in a flak jacket and handcuffs. They took him away in a police cruiser followed closely by the press. After giving statements to the police, Dean Salvaggio and the other hostages were brought outside to cheers from the crowd. Parents and reporters dashed forward as the hostages were led to a cleared area for their release. Letty grabbed an emotionless Rafe and hugged her, crying with relief as others gathered around.

Clarice got Rafe's attention and pulled her to the side. "Dean Salvaggio, I need you to make a statement to the press. Just make the school look good."

Rafe gave her a halfhearted smile. "Okay, Clarice. Don't worry." Rafe stood on the stairs as the reporters gathered around and pushed microphones in front of her.

"First, I would like to thank everyone who gave support to all of us today," Rafe began as she looked out over the crowd. "This was an experience I know these students and I will not soon forget. It teaches us we are all fragile and need to be treated gently and, when impassioned, we should try our best to look for the reason inside us, so we are not overcome." She paused as she thought of her own impassioned moment. "One person's pain never justifies causing pain in another, but as humans, we are bound to make this mistake at some point in our lives. Fortunately, today, we all survived.

"Wade Delchus, in his despondency, did something he truly regrets and will regret for the rest of his life. So, when judging him, think of your own life, and be thankful you have the capacity to cope and deal with your problems without brandishing a gun, or giving in to the voice telling you to give up. We at the California Conservatory of Art and Design do not, and will not, give up on our students or on humanity. We hope Wade Delchus gets the help he so desperately needs." She stopped and looked around at the reporters and the crowd. "Now, I know people are waiting to be reunited so, thank you again." Rafe stepped back as the police captain stepped up to the microphones to speak to the press, and she looked around for a familiar face in the crowd.

A reporter began his live check-in with the studio, and his voice was broadcast over the airwaves. "We just heard from Dean Rafaella Salvaggio, who was the instructor held hostage along with eight students here at the CCAD by student Wade Delchus. As you could see, she was poised and stoic after the seven-hour ordeal. The students and police have told us her actions were responsible for ending the standoff and led to the gunman's surrender," he said and then paused to listen to the voice coming through his earpiece. "Correct, Bill. The students also reported she convinced the gunman to use her as a shield during the lunch delivery in order to keep them safe. She has refused interviews, but we are hoping she will make a more personal statement soon."

A crowd of people began to gather around Rafe and the other hostages. Greer watched Eden, who was standing apart from everyone, expecting her to go to Rafe to comfort her. But she was just looking at Rafe, her face showing a mix of emotion. Eden started forward and then hesitated. She then looked down, stopping herself from going to Rafe.

Greer saw Eden's hesitation and shook her head in disbelief. She couldn't stand seeing Rafe looking so miserable and her eyes without their passion. She didn't understand Eden's hesitation. She looked from Eden to Rafe and then dismissed Eden's presence and focused totally on Rafe who had turned and was watching Eden walk away.

Greer rushed resolutely up to Rafe and took her hands. She could see the surprise on Rafe's face Greer was there. Reaching up, she ran the back of her hands gently down Rafe's face. Greer gently touched Rafe's lips before lifting herself up on her toes, giving her an extremely deep and intense kiss. Some students cheered. When they broke apart, Rafe gave Greer a small smile and signed hello to her. Then, as her mind shut down and her body ran on autopilot, she gave into Greer's warmth and comfort, kissing her back to more cheers.

"Indeed," the reporter continued his conversation with the studio. "It's also interesting that the name of her company is *Eroina Conservazione e Design. Eroina* in Italian means 'heroine' and it is exactly what Dean Salvaggio was today. A hero." He paused dramatically. "This is Mark Marshall signing off." He waited for a beat and then switched off his microphone. "Are you getting the cheers and the girl's kiss?" he asked the cameraman with a grin.

"Oh, yeah," the cameraman said with a gruff laugh.

Hearing the cheers, Eden looked back and saw Greer and Rafe as they kissed. She turned around again and almost knocked down Abby and Julia. They looked up to see what had made Eden turn to leave and saw Rafe and Greer kissing on the stairs.

Abby turned to go after Eden. "Eden, stop!" she called. She caught up with her, and Julia was just behind her. Abby caught her arm to stop her.

"No, no, no," cried Eden unable to hold back her tears. "Abby, I have to get out of here."

"Eden, Greer might not know what's going on with you and Rafe," reasoned Julia. "It's just an emotional moment."

"No, Julia," Eden started then shook her head. "I'm sure she's the colleague Rafe was going to meet tonight. You were right. I've waited too long," she said in anguish.

"Eden, it's not too late," said Abby as she looked at Julia for help.

"You have to tell her if you love her," insisted Julia.

"You love her, Eden. Just tell her." Abby nodded encouragingly

"Abby, I can't. I don't know if I really do or not," she admitted and looked away from them, "and I've run out of time to figure it all out." She turned and walked away.

"Oh, my god!" yelled Abby in disbelief as she watched Eden walk away. "This can't be happening!" She looked at Julia. "What does she mean she doesn't know? What the hell has she been doing? I thought it was why she was spending time with Rafe and why she has been so upset with how Rafe was treating her."

"She was spending time with her to figure out her feelings," Julia said sullenly. "I think Rafe may have stopped waiting for her. I guess this means the infamous Salvaggio will be moving on to new pastures."

Abby shook her head in disbelief. "I've got to go talk to her." She took off to find Eden.

20

Wednesday: 6:30 P.m.

WHILE BRONTE PLAYED on the living room floor, Eden Kingsley was lying on the couch trying to hold herself together. Seeing Rafe with a gun to her head had shaken Eden to her core. The thought of Rafe dying was too hard to take in with all the other things happening in her life. Then seeing her kiss Greer had confirmed it was just too late for her, even if she did figure out all the feelings crashing through her. She didn't understand what had happened to make Rafe suddenly stop wanting to be around her. Now Eden thought maybe it was because Rafe had decided she would rather be with Greer. The sharp thought stabbed her hard in the heart, though she knew she probably deserved it because she had been keeping Rafe at arm's distance. But she needed to be sure, and now it seemed either she took too long, or she had her answer.

Abby had followed Eden home as quickly as she could and was at her apartment banging on her front door. "Eden, Eden, it's me, Abby. Let me in. Come on, Eden. Let me in! We need to talk!" Slowly, the door opened, and Abby pushed her way inside. "Eden, you have to tell me what's going on with you."

"I told you, I took too long figuring things out," she said dejectedly. She then went back into the living room and fell onto the couch.

Abby sat down next to her. "Eden, all this time I thought you knew you loved her, even if it was really deep down. What have you been doing? Thinking? I defended you to her," she said upset.

"I don't know," she said shaking her head. "I just wanted to make sure, you know?"

"No. No, I don't know," Abby said emphatically. "Rafe went from thinking you were out of your mind to telling you she loved you. I thought it was what you wanted from her! We all told her to give you a chance. We told her you loved her and she should be open to you. And you," she paused trying to control herself, "you've just been trying to figure things out? Eden?"

"Please," Eden begged. "Please, you just don't understand." How could she tell her, for a long time, every time she looked at Rafe, she imagined her touching and kissing someone else? Or how she felt the pain and humiliation caused by Rafe's affair all over again, and how she needed not to have those feelings anymore? How could she explain feelings of wanting to be close and actually being close conflicted with each other inside her mind and body? She couldn't explain to Abby all the things she was feeling about Rafe, Jake, and so much more.

"No, I don't," hissed Abby. "Explain it to me because I'm beginning to see why Rafe is acting the way she is toward you."

Eden fought to find the words to explain some small part of her feelings. They all thought it was just about her feelings of being with a man, but it was just one of a million things happening inside her. There was so much more— sometimes, it felt as if she were suffocating. "I just feel like," she hesitated and rubbed the hair on the back of her neck, "like whenever I'm around her, I lose myself. It scares me. I don't want to be lost," she said anxiously. "She's always in control and exudes this power, a power I just can't fight. I guess I was just trying to build up," she paused, "I don't now, some immunity to all of it."

She looked at Abby and could see she didn't understand. There was just so much. She didn't know if she could explain her feelings well enough. She closed her eyes and focused on just one thing she could explain.

"Okay, for example, when we started trying to have a baby, it seemed like I was slowly disappearing. She would always do something like describe my eyes, or she would start going off about her day or just disappear into a project. Sometimes, she would leave the country for undetermined amounts of time, and I would be left alone and wasn't able to talk to her. Then, what I needed to say or wanted to do would just become meaningless. Sometimes, I just felt emotionally abandoned by her." She paused and wiped her hands over her face. "Then we went through everything with the affair and finding out I was pregnant. I thought things would change after I moved back in with her and Bronte was born, but they didn't really. I was having other feelings and doubts about us, and myself."

She couldn't admit to Abby how she'd had a lot of her other feelings even before she was pregnant. She knew she wasn't explaining things well, but even if she were, she didn't know if Abby was the one she should be telling. Abby had good intentions, but sometimes, she made things worse when she blurted out things people had said in confidence.

"I don't really know how to explain it all. I guess I just still felt scared and lost. All I know is I don't want it to happen again."

Abby just looked at her in disbelief. "So, when you left her the second time around, you let her think it was all because you wanted to be with men and you went to Jake?"

"Abby, that's part of it," Eden tried to explain. "When I was with Jake, I wasn't just 'Salvaggio's Paradise' anymore. I was Eden Kingsley. Just Eden. I was with someone, and I had an identity. I felt stable and safe, and I knew who I was. I wasn't lost anymore." She felt lost right now, though, and could feel the tingling signal of pain on its way from her building anxiety. "There's so much more I just can't explain right now," she said softly. "But it's why I wanted to be sure of my feelings about men, and for her. I wanted to be able to hold onto myself, my identity. I knew I had to start out very slowly. I didn't want to make another mistake, and things were going fine until she got sick. I don't know what happened."

"Wow," Abby retorted sarcastically. "I didn't know you had it so rough being with Rafe. Why couldn't you tell her all of this?"

"I tried," Eden insisted. "It's just not very easy. We were making progress and talking. I thought things might work out, but there were so many things happening, and I guess I was just scared. Then, after today, I felt so terrible about what I was doing to her I just couldn't face her and cause her more pain after all she had been through. And now, she has Greer back," she said sadly and rubbed her arms hoping to postpone the pain because there was so much more than what she had told Abby. Eden had to be careful what she said because Abby was always compelled to tell what she knew, and it didn't always come out in the best way. She had to keep the information about Jake and the Stewards from everyone, as well as all of the things she suspected them of doing from vandalizing her car to filing the complaint with child services, and especially about getting the FBI involved.

Abby was fighting to stay positive and hopeful for Eden. "I don't think they're together. I think maybe she just came to see Rafe give her lecture on Friday," she speculated. "It's just been an emotional and scary day. Everyone's been caught up in it. Eden, you didn't even tell Rafe you were glad she was okay. You just left."

Eden put her head in her hands and shook it in shame. "I know."

"I know you're feeling bad right now, about everything," said Abby seeing it was true, "but right now, we need to think about Rafe. Thinking about someone else for a while can help you feel better sometimes, and she really needs her friends right now. You have to tell her you're glad she's okay, and do it tonight. Maybe you should take Bronte over for a while too. It may help her get through the rest of the night."

Eden looked up and wiped her tears away. She knew Abby was right. She wanted to let Rafe know she was glad she was okay and be there for her with Bronte. She did care about her, and it was an execrable experience for everyone to think they would lose Rafe. So it was not hard to imagine, for Rafe, the experience was even more harrowing.

"Okay," she agreed. "I'll take her. Let's go."

Abby leaned over and hugged her. "You have to find a way to tell her all of this stuff," Abby told her. Then she stood up as Eden started gathering Bronte's things. "Maybe you guys can still work it out together. I know you love her, and you know she loves you. If she knew all of this, she would do something about it. You can't just keep walking out on her."

"I didn't just walk out on her for no reason," said Eden as she picked up Bronte and put her on her hip. "And she's the one pushing me away now."

Abby shook her head at the whole mess. "I know," she said with a heavy sigh. "You guys can work through this," she declared and hoped she sounded reassuring.

Eden gave Abby a small smile and tried not to cry as she opened the door. "Maybe, if it's not too late."

21

Wednesday: 8:oo P.M.

THE PARTY WAS going strong at Rafe Salvaggio's house, and everyone was celebrating Rafe's release and survival of the day's events. Friends and students were scattered throughout the house and on the patio having a good time.

In the kitchen, food and drinks had been set up by Letty and were being enjoyed by everyone. She and Ephraim had brought a few staff members to help make sure the guests got tastes of all the food they were making, and the drink glasses were kept full.

A few people were in the kitchen sitting at the island and talking about what had happened earlier.

Stacey leaned across the kitchen island and laughed. "Can you believe Rafe was the one who ordered the steak and lobster?"

"Oh, and the wine," Jude said joining her laughter.

"I heard some of the students calling her Dean Steel-heart," said Lexi, one of Rafe's teaching assistants, as she grabbed a bottle of wine and headed to where her friends were waiting.

"Dean Steal-heart?" Julia repeated impressed as she poured herself more wine. "Well, she does have some nerve."

"She totally went Alpha on the guy!" said Flynn. He was in awe of Rafe and how she had handled herself.

"Yeah, I heard her blow off what she did and tell a reporter Wade was too relaxed to be a threat after drinking all the wine they had delivered," Erica revealed and popped a morsel of food in her mouth.

"The police captain really went off on her for provoking the guy," Jude added. "She just said, 'Well, at least I earned my lunch,' and walked away from him."

"Does nothing faze the woman?" asked Erica amazed.

"Rafe is a total rock star!" declared Stacey with a chuckle and held her glass up for a toast and they all joined in.

Jude looked over at the patio doorway. "Look, it's Eden and Abby. I wonder where they've been," she said as they approached. "I'd better go tell Rafe."

Rafe was in the living room on the couch lying with her head in Greer's lap. She was looking up into her laughing blue eyes and speaking to her without actually saying her words aloud so her words would be just for her.

Greer's hand was on Rafe's stomach and grasped in Rafe's hand. With her other hand, she was stroking Rafe's face and hair as she watched her lips closely not wanting to miss any of her words. She smiled as she watched her speak, and laughed, then kissed her for the sweet things she was saying.

Jude made her way to the living room, finding Rafe and Greer on the couch, and knelt down beside them. The couple was unaware Eden had already seen them and was standing in the entryway. "Rafe, Eden is here with Bronte," she said softly and pointed toward Eden.

Rafe sat up slowly and faced Eden who was holding Bronte as she stood watching her. She wasn't sure why Eden was here looking at her as if she had done something wrong. The only thing she had done wrong was *not* dying.

"Rafe," said Abby as she approached with a worried look. "Eden needs to talk to you. She brought Bronte. She thought you'd like to see her."

Rafe released Greer's warm hand and got up from the couch. She walked over to Eden and took Bronte from her, kissed the baby, and walked across the house and out on the patio.

"Hi, B Girl. It's good to see you. *Ti voglio bene,*" she cooed, kissing her again, and then she tickled her. Bronte wrapped her arms around Rafe's neck and kissed her cheek. She looked back at Eden who had followed her. "Thank you for allowing me to see her tonight."

Watching Rafe and Bronte, tears formed in Eden's eyes. "Rafe, I need to talk to you," she said shakily. She wanted to tell her she was glad she was okay, and she was sorry for whatever she did wrong. She wanted to let her know she understood if she took too long in figuring out her feelings, and she hoped they could still at least be friendly for Bronte's sake. She couldn't keep the tears from flowing, and it made it hard to think or talk. She just wanted them both to have some happiness in their lives.

Rafe saw her tears, but they didn't move her. She reached out, caught one, and then looked at it. "Tears of disappointment?" she asked dryly.

Eden looked at Rafe in confusion. "What?"

"I'm sorry things didn't turn out better for you today," said Rafe as she looked sadly at Eden.

"I don't—" started Eden as she tried to process what Rafe was saying.

"I tried to give you what you wanted," Rafe said cutting her off.

Eden looked at Rafe, and her mouth dropped open when she realized what Rafe was saying. She started to shake with outrage. "Rafe! I came here to try to talk to you! I can't believe you would say such a thing! I'm taking Bronte!"

Rafe let Eden tear Bronte from her arms. "I know you are," she said sadly.

"Abby! I'm leaving!" Eden yelled out, angry and crying, as she made her way out through the back gate.

Flynn and Abby ran out to see why Eden was crying. "What happened?" asked Abby.

"I couldn't give her what she wanted today," confessed Rafe as her shoulders slumped, and she walked back into the house.

"I'll go check on her," offered Flynn and went after Eden.

Abby followed Rafe inside. "Did she tell you?"

"Tell me what?"

"Rafe, she came over here to tell you how she feels about things, about you," exclaimed Abby.

Walking into the kitchen, Rafe went to the island and poured some wine. "I know exactly how she feels," she said evenly.

Beth was signing to Greer what was being said while Julia, Jude, Erica, and Stacey remained quiet and uneasy.

Abby looked at Rafe and tried to help Eden. "So, you know she feels lost and abandoned because she feels like she can't fight the power and control you have over everything?"

Rafe took a sip of wine and looked at Abby with pity. "Power and control? She even has you fooled."

"Fooled? Rafe—" stammered Abby.

Rafe cut her off angrily "Let me tell you a little something about power and control! Those are things you have to reach out and take! Once you take them, you need to be very careful about who you give them up to! I gave up a lot of power and control to Eden over many things. Believe me—she has mastered power and control like a military general! Now I'm taking it all back! It may be too late for some things, but I'm not giving anymore over to her!"

"Hey," Stacey interrupted a bit drunkenly, "Leave *Eroina* alone!" She laughed at repeating what the news reporters had been calling Rafe all day.

Rafe turned her scathing anger on Stacey. "Don't ever call me that!" she said in a fury as her face darkened with anger.

Stacey's eyes widened, and she shrank back as the others tensed at Rafe's explosion.

"Only two people call me that! One is dead, and the other is not you! Got it?" Rafe spat out as she stood over her threateningly.

"Yeah," Stacey squeaked out feebly.

"Yeah, Stacey. Shut the fuck up," said Abby trying to be on Rafe's side in something. "It's probably just Eden," she said and looked at Julia, "Or is it you?"

Julia's eyes widened, and she shook her head at Abby trying to send her a message to stop talking because she could see Rafe was about to combust.

Rafe spun her fury onto Abby. "It's none of you, and it certainly isn't fucking Eden!" she growled. "So stop it, Abby! I told you, it's fucking over!"

"Rafe, she just needs you to understand and be patient," Abby tried to make her see it didn't have to be over.

"Patience is something I've never had a lot of, and I've given her more patience and understanding than you can even fucking imagine! I'm going to bed." Rafe took Greer's hand and started leading her to the bedroom.

Greer pulled her hand away from Rafe. "No. No, Rafe. I'm not going into your bedroom with you like this," she said with uneasiness on her face.

Rafe looked at Greer and then at Abby. She could see Eden had them all fooled and on her side of things. She wouldn't allow Eden to pull her into the deception again. They always blamed her for all the pain and they were never on her side. "*Si può tutti solo andare all'inferno,*"[4] she said calmly.

Rafe grabbed a bottle of wine and went into her bedroom slamming the door. Inside, she sat on her bed and took a drink of wine from the bottle. She sat the bottle on the nightstand and saw the picture of her and Eden. She picked it up and looked at it, holding it tightly. Suddenly, she hurled it forcefully at the door shattering it. "*Perché diavolo ci fai questo a me, Eden?*"[5] she screamed in anguish.

---

[4] You can all just go to hell,
[5] Why the hell are you doing this to me, Eden?

In the living room, Beth signed what had happened to Greer, but she didn't know what Rafe had said in Italian. "What did she say?" Beth asked the group, and Greer looked at them with concern.

Julia cleared her throat. "She said, 'You can all just go to hell,' and then something about Eden I didn't catch." She saw everyone staring at her. "She taught me some Italian, mostly a lot of curse words, in our school days," she explained with a shrug.

Abby and Greer looked at each other with apprehension. "I don't know how they're ever going to make it back to each other," Abby said, distraught as the others just sat in stunned silence.

22

THE MORNING AFTER the hostage crisis at the Conservatory, Rafe Salvaggio was sitting at her dining room table where she had piles of photos of Eden in front of her. Some, she took just weeks ago, and others were much older from when they had first started to spend time together. She was drinking coffee, examining them closely one by one, and separating them into piles.

Greer came out of the guest room and saw Rafe at the table. She went to the kitchen and brought the coffee pot and a cup to the dining room. She refilled Rafe's cup, then filled her own and sat next to her. Observing Rafe over her mug, Greer could not help noticing the dark circles around her eyes and the drop in her shoulders. "Did you get any sleep last night?" She saw the slight tic of Rafe's lips and knew the answer was no. "What are you doing?" she asked curiously.

Rafe looked up at her with a frown so she could see her lips. "Looking for when all of the lies started and when she stopped loving me. They say a picture says a thousand words." She picked up one of the pictures and looked at it closely. "You would think I could see it in her eyes," she said not caring if Greer could understand or not, "but I can't."

Because of all the photos on the table, Greer was fairly certain Rafe's lack of sleep was because of what was happening with Eden. "Rafe, about yesterday," Greer started.

"I'm sorry about what I said to you," Rafe said cutting her off.

"Not what I wanted to talk to you about," Greer said calmly, "but your apology is accepted. Please don't cut me off."

Rafe looked at her, signed 'sorry,' and sighed. "What about yesterday?"

"Why did you do it," she asked remembering the way Rafe had provoked the gunman.

Rafe lifted her shoulders and frowned. "I couldn't let him use a student," she answered softly. "I couldn't let him put a gun against the head of one of those girls. What if they panicked and got shot over a stupid steak and lobster lunch?" She shook her head. "I couldn't let anything happen to them."

Greer looked at her evenly. "Again, not what I'm talking about, and you know it. Why did you..." she paused, "provoke him? Were you really hoping he would kill you?" Rafe looked at her silently, her answer in her eyes. Greer leaned very close to

Rafe's face and spoke forcefully. "Don't ever do something like that again." Rafe nodded to her. "I couldn't stand living in this world without you in it," she said softly.

"I won't," Rafe whispered. She leaned over and kissed her and signed 'promise' then smiled sadly.

She looked down at the table at all of the pictures of Eden and pushed them all back into one pile. She picked up her camera and took Greer's hand.

"Come on," she said and led Greer to the patio. "Morning light is the best for taking pictures. Sit here," she said pushing her down onto a pool lounger. "Let me capture you like you captured me."

23

AFTER CRYING ALL night, Eden Kingsley knew she would be worthless at work, so she had called in sick and called Lydia to say she was keeping Bronte at home. She woke up again when she heard Bronte playing in her bed. She got her dressed, made her breakfast, and then let her play. She knew Bronte was the only reason she made it out of bed this morning.

As she made a pot of coffee she hoped would help her through the morning, there was a knock on her door. She closed her eyes at the sound. She didn't know if she could take talking to anyone right now.

She unlocked the door and opened it, finding Abby looking at her with sympathy. She burst into uncontrollable tears. Abby helped guide her to the living room and sat on the couch.

"She thinks I want her dead," she cried in Abby's arms.

"I can't believe it," Abby said shaking her head. "It's just not the way Rafe thinks."

"I made her think it somehow. I should have known what I was doing to her when I saw she was changing her will." She sniffed.

"She changed her will? She has a will? Is she leaving me anything?" asked Abby overcome with curiosity.

"Abby, this is serious. I don't want her to die," she said through more tears.

"Of course, you don't," agreed Abby sobering herself as she held Eden and rubbed her back to comfort her. "Eden, last night, Rafe said you had everyone fooled. Is there something else going on? Do you know what she's talking about?"

Eden stiffened and hesitated. "She... she must be talking about the things I told you last night," she stammered. Immediately, she wondered if Rafe had found out about Jake or the other things going on.

"I don't know," said Abby doubtfully. "She seems to think you're the one with all of the control and power."

"I don't know what she means." Eden sobbed. "I feel totally out of control and powerless. She's in love with Greer," she said sadly.

"You don't know she loves Greer," said Abby trying to reassure her.

Eden pulled back and looked at Abby with despair. "I saw them last night. Rafe was lying in her lap. They were looking at each other so intently, whispering to each other and... and kissing."

"Eden, Greer is deaf," Abby explained. "Rafe never really speaks loud to her. She doesn't have to—she just talks, normal. Greer reads her lips, so she has to look closely at Rafe. They were just talking."

"While Rafe was lying on her lap and she was kissing her?" Eden scoffed.

"You seem to care a lot about what she was doing for someone who's not sure of her feelings. Are you jealous?" Abby asked pointedly.

"It's not jealousy," Eden said quietly while shaking her head denying Abby's words. She closed her eyes for a moment. "I'm just showing you I'm right. They love each other. I just... I took too long."

24

RAFE SALVAGGIO HAD taken the morning photo session with Greer Noble to the park for the afternoon. They had returned to the house after a couple of hours, and Rafe was in the kitchen making cold drinks. When she had the drinks ready, she took them to the patio where Greer was waiting.

They lay on the double lounger together on their sides facing each other sipping their drinks to cool off. Rafe took a sip of her drink and put it on the table behind Greer, and then took Greer's drink and put it next to hers. She pulled Greer's face to her and kissed her deeply.

Greer pulled back from Rafe. "It's been a wonderful day."

Rafe smiled at the auburn-haired woman before her. "Yes, it has." She moved to kiss her again.

Greer avoided the kiss. "I need to talk to you."

"I'd rather be kissing you," said Rafe looking disappointed.

"It's kind of what I need to talk to you about." Greer sighed.

Rafe stole a kiss. "Let's just kiss and not talk about it." She kissed her again quickly.

Greer put her hand over Rafe's lips. "Remember when I told you I didn't want to be the one you're with just because I helped you through things? I don't want you to stay with me out of some kind of debt." Rafe could only nod because Greer's hand was still covering her mouth. "Rafe, I know you're still in love with her."

Rafe closed her eyes and felt Greer remove her hand from her lips. She opened her eyes and could not stop her words. "I love you, Greer. I've loved you before I went to see you in Baltimore."

Greer laughed in surprise at the confession. "I love you too. I tried to tell you when you came to see me, but you have this terrible habit of cutting me off."

"If I would have known..." Rafe frowned at her words but loved the happiness she saw in her pale blue eyes, "things would have been so different."

"They would have been harder," she said, and Rafe looked at her puzzled. "Rafe, it would have made getting back with Eden harder. You were still in love with her. It would have confused things." She looked into her eyes and debated with herself. She wanted Rafe, but it was clear there was an obstacle only Rafe could decide to overcome. "You're still in love with her."

"Now I am confused," said Rafe with a furrowed brow. "Why are you telling me you love me now?"

"I don't know," said Greer as she ran her hand over Rafe's dark curls. "I guess because you said it first, and you deserve my honesty."

Rafe closed her eyes and rubbed her face with her hand. "What makes you think I'm still in love with Eden?"

"I can see it in your words," Greer started, and when she saw Rafe was about to cut her off, she put her hand over Rafe's lips again and continued. "I can see it in your expressions, your posture, and the little things you do like looking through all those pictures. It's as if you have stopped living inside for some reason. What happened? Abby told me you two were working things out. You've locked yourself up so you won't hurt when she's around. Then your eyes..." she sighed and ran her fingers lightly down Rafe's face and then covered her lips again, "your eyes were so empty yesterday when you watched her walk away. Why did she walk away?"

"Greer," Rafe said when she removed her hand, "she walked away because she doesn't love me." Rafe looked into her eyes pleadingly. "I want to love you. I know loving you will make everything go away."

Greer stroked Rafe's dark silky hair. "I can't make you stop loving her. I may help your pain for a while, but if you're going to stop loving her," she paused, "you have to do it on your own. But I don't think you want to stop loving her."

"I do want to stop. I have no choice. She's still with Jake," Rafe said, disgusted.

"What?" Greer exclaimed very surprised. "Are you sure?"

"Jake told me himself," said Rafe as she nodded.

"Have you seen them together?" Greer asked curiously.

"No," said Rafe annoyed. "I don't want to see them together."

Greer shook her head trying to make some sense of what Rafe was telling her. "It just doesn't make sense. Flynn and Abby are sure she just needs time and patience. She's having a hard time too, and she's feeling lost. They told me a lot of what's been going on last night. They didn't mention Jake at all."

"It's a secret she's keeping from me, from everyone," revealed Rafe. "I found out by accident right before I got sick. Greer, I opened up and jumped into hell," she said miserably.

Greer looked at her with sympathy. "Well, that proves my theory."

"What?"

"You're still in love with her," answered Greer. "You were lovesick, weren't you?"

"No," groaned Rafe, annoyed.

"You were," said Greer assuredly. She saw the uncomfortable expression on Rafe's face. "I'm sorry. It was painful, wasn't it?" Rafe scowled and didn't answer. "Poor thing. You're just too sensitive." She sighed and kissed her forehead.

"Don't make fun of me." Rafe pouted. She pulled Greer's face to her and kissed her. "I don't want to go into the darkness again," she said, not realizing Greer had caught her words. She kissed Greer again then put her leg over her and lifted up, straddling her on the lounger. "I know you can keep me here," Rafe said kissing her more passionately.

"Rafe," Greer pleaded, "we can't."

Rafe pulled back and looked deeply and intensely into Greer's eyes. "Greer, I do love you. I'm so happy you love me too. I want to make love to you, slowly, sweetly. I don't want you to think about Eden. I want you to close your eyes so you can't see her in mine. I want you to know I'm loving only you right now, not her. Please, please, close your eyes."

As Rafe watched, Greer considered her words.

Greer thought about how Rafe must truly be feeling like her life is full of darkness right now. She could see the pain in Rafe's eyes from being lovesick and from being in such a life-threatening situation. Her eyes softened with compassion and love for Rafe.

Greer slowly closed her eyes.

Rafe began by kissing Greer's eyelids gently.

25

AT A TABLE positioned perfectly in Club La Femme, Julia Hawthorn, Abby Van Falkov, and Erica Sunley were taking full advantage of the view. It was Thursday Theme Night, and the theme was Hot Jungle Nights. The penetrating beat of the music filled the bar and the voices of all the women who were laughing and talking surrounded them. The jungle theme had been embraced, and the sexual energy and carnal vibe thrummed through the air.

As she sipped her drink, Abby nodded to a girl clad in only a G-string and palm leaves. "Okay, now there is a jungle outfit," she said rakishly.

"Abby, that's not an outfit," proclaimed Julia with a laugh. "She's practically nude, and I for one am glad she has no inhibitions."

"Me too!" agreed Erica. She scanned the room for more skin, following the crowd with her camera.

"Well, look who's here," Abby said wolfishly. "Rafe and Greer and they brought Beth. You know, I'm beginning to like the girl. I think we really hit it off last night." She waved to them.

Julia rolled her eyes. "Oh, Abby! You always go after people who are so unavailable!"

Rafe, Greer, and Beth made it through the crowd and over to the table.

"Hey, guys," said Abby with a wink. "So you finally decided to leave the house?"

Rafe was holding onto Greer's hand and smiled at Abby. "What kind of hostess would I be if I didn't bring my guests to theme night at Club La Femme?"

"I hope you don't feel too out of place, Beth," said Abby overly polite.

"Never with you around, Abby," said Beth warmly.

Abby smiled brightly and winked at Julia. "Yes, I really do like her," she said under her breath. Julia and Erica looked at each other and rolled their eyes.

"I'll go get some drinks. I'll be right back," said Rafe. Greer waved bye as Rafe headed for the bar.

"So what've you guys been doing all day?" Abby asked Greer and Beth.

"Hanging out and talking mostly. Oh, and we went to the park," Beth interpreted for Greer. "I wish I could stay longer, but I have to be back at work Monday."

"Do you work in a dreary office too?" asked Julia trying to keep the mood light and glad it looked like Rafe was doing better.

"Definitely not dreary," voiced Greer. "I have a lot of colorful artwork on my walls from my patients."

"Maybe it's what I need, artwork. Something without a motivational quote in it. Maybe I should talk to Rafe about it."

"You work at your family's brokerage firm, right?" asked Greer as Beth interpreted.

"Yes, and it is boring. But I get to take a movie studio tour tomorrow. I went to a party with Eden, and I got a few good prospects there. One of them set up a tour for me," said Julia with excitement.

"I've never been to a studio, and I've lived in California off and on for years," said Greer through Beth.

"You should come by tomorrow and go with me. I'd love to have some company," said Julia, pleased to impress Greer with her contacts.

"I do have some time in the morning while Rafe's at work. I'd like to go," Beth interpreted. Greer smiled and continued. "I'm glad she got to stay home today, but she insists on going back to work in the morning to make sure things are ready for her presentation tomorrow night."

"I'm glad you were there for her," said Julia then took a drink. "I wish you could stay longer." She started to share her thoughts about Rafe but stopped when she saw Rafe coming back to the table.

Rafe returned with a tray of drinks. "Here we go," she said happily. "So what are you talking about?"

"I'm going to a studio tour tomorrow, and Greer is going to join me," Julia announced proudly. She purposely left out it was at the studio where Eden worked.

Rafe looked at Greer and smiled. "Sounds like fun."

"I'm sure it will be," Greer voiced and smiled back at Rafe. "Want to dance?" She didn't wait for an answer and dragged Rafe to the dance floor.

"They sure are smiling at each other a lot," Abby said suspiciously.

"I think they had sex today," observed Julia with a smirk.

"You think?" Abby looked at Beth inquiringly.

Beth raised her hands in surrender. "They don't tell, I don't ask," she quipped then laughed and blushed as she remembered when Rafe was in Baltimore visiting Greer. She almost showed up at the house too early—she knew because they had barely gotten out of the shower and dressed. It was the only time she had ever seen Greer blush so deeply.

"Look," Erica pointed to the dance floor where Rafe and Greer were kissing.

"Well, we know it's not because it was an emotional day," Abby quipped. "It's lucky Eden isn't here, or she would have more reasons for being upset."

"So she's made up her mind?" asked Julia curious about what Eden had told Abby.

"Not exactly." Abby sighed heavily.

"What did she say?" demanded Julia.

"She says she loses herself when Rafe is around like she has no identity," revealed Abby. "She wants to be Eden, not Salvaggio's Paradise."

"I don't understand. I thought she loved Rafe?" said Julia confused.

"We all did," said Abby dryly.

26

AT ASCESIS STUDIOS, Julia Hawthorn, Greer Noble, and Beth Westbern climbed into a golf cart sent for them. The movie studio was buzzing with morning activity, and they were only at the front gate. Whisked away from the gate to their special tour, their private tour guide drove them around.

Their driver honked his shrill horn to move through the crowd of people. As he maneuvered through the studio grounds, there was a constant flow of organized chaos filled with people and objects. Props were being moved, actors in costumes from street clothes to zombie makeup were rushing to sets, and even large equipment was being set up. Over the noise, the driver pointed out different places of interest to the important guests he was assigned to today.

"Down that way are props and costumes, to the right is our main studio, and in this building are our studio offices," he said as he finally stopped the golf cart. "Come on in," he requested as he sprang out of the golf cart, "and we'll get your VIP passes." They got out of the cart and followed him into the building toward the reception area.

"Ms. Hawthorn, I'm so happy you made it," said a smartly dressed woman walking toward them. "I hope they're taking care of you."

"Ms. Davidson, so nice to see you," said Julia in her most proper English boarding school accent shaking her hand. "Thank you for arranging the tour."

"My pleasure," Ms. Davidson smiled warmly. "Listen, I had to change some meetings around, and I was wondering if you would mind having our meeting before the tour."

Julia looked at Greer and Beth. "I'm sorry. Can you just wait in the lobby for a bit while I take the meeting now? It shouldn't take long."

"Sure, no problem," Beth interpreted for Greer.

"Thank you," Julia said and made her way down the hall with Ms. Davidson.

Greer watched the two women walk away and tapped Beth on her arm. "Do you think they're going to do it in her office or on a set somewhere?" Beth could not answer because she was too busy laughing.

While they waited, Greer looked at the company directory on the wall and saw Eden's name and office number. She signaled to Beth, and they made their way through the building and reached the desk of Eden's receptionist.

"May I help you?" asked the receptionist.

"I am here on a studio tour, and I thought I would stop by Ms. Kingsley's office," interpreted Beth. "Is she in?"

"Yes," said the receptionist looking from one woman to the other as one signed and the other spoke. "Just allow me to let her know you're here. Your name is?"

"Dr. Noble with Johns Hopkins Hospital," interpreted Beth.

"I see," replied the receptionist with a nod wondering if they were there for a special project. Maybe they wanted a medical expert for the zombie scripts. She picked up the phone and dialed. "Ms. Kingsley, there is a Dr. Noble here from Johns Hopkins Hospital. She says she is here with a studio tour. Of course." She hung up the phone. "She'll be right out," she said as she smiled and motioned them to the waiting area.

"Thank you," Greer voiced. She looked at Beth and signed to her. Beth looked at her concerned but nodded her head and signed 'yes' to her.

Eden's office door opened and a harried woman walked out complaining. "I hate Zombie movies!" she declared. "They've lost the costume budget and half the receipts for *Zombies in Mansfield Park*. They're over budget and lost everything on purpose," she fumed and made her way down the hall wondering what idiot wanted real blood and guts on circa eighteen hundred style costumes.

Eden followed the woman out of her office preoccupied with the papers in her hands. "How do you—" She stopped as she realized who was standing in front of her and froze in her tracks.

Greer smiled as she signed and Beth interpreted for her. "We're taking a tour and saw your name on the directory."

Flustered, Eden was not sure what to do. "Uh, come in," she said anxiously. They entered her office, and Eden was shaking nervously, but she fought to hide it before turning to them. "What can I do for you?"

Greer rushed up to Eden and slapped her ferociously in the face making her stagger back. "Stop hurting her! That's what you can do, you fucking bitch!" Greer voiced.

Eden cried out in shock. "I... I..." was all she could vocalize.

"She knows your secret!" Greer signed in Eden's face.

Shocked at what her boss had done, Beth hesitated but recovered quickly and spoke her words. She had never seen Greer this upset about anyone's situation as she had been about Rafe's, but she hadn't suspected she would resort to assault. She watched Greer signing angrily in Eden's' face and interpreted her words as expressively as Greer was signing. "If you don't love her, just tell her and let her go!"

"Stop torturing her this way!" Greer voiced with venom.

She looked at Beth then back at Eden and began signing in her face again, and Beth interpreted. "I don't understand how she can continue to love someone as heartless as you. Do you know you're taking her life away? Was she really so terrible to you that you have to play this game with her?"

Eden was shaking in pain. She looked up and tried to speak. "I don't—"

Greer slapped her violently again. This time, Eden went to her knees and cried while holding her face. "I don't know why I'm even telling you this, but Rafe deserves to be happy! And for some reason, beyond my understanding, she believes deep down she can find happiness with you," Beth continued to interpret Greer's quickly made signs. "So if there's even a small chance you love her like Abby thinks, you should do something about it now. You're losing her very fast because, for the record, just as Jake is her rival—well, I'm yours! If she comes to me again, you will never get her back. I'll make damn sure of it! Do you understand me?" she asked. "NEVER!" she voiced angrily.

"Jake?" said Eden in confusion, and Beth signed Eden's question to Greer.

"He told her everything!" Greer signed and moved toward her threateningly as Beth interpreted. Eden cringed before her. "Stop fucking with her life!" Greer voiced and stormed out of the office with Beth close behind her.

Through tears and sobs of pain, Eden took in what was said to her and began to shake uncontrollably. "Oh, my god! Jake. No, no!" She sobbed. "Jake, what did you say to her?" she asked the room in agony.

27

STUDENTS, STAFF, AND the public filled the art gallery inside the main building of the California Conservatory of Art and Design to capacity. In the lecture room, visitors were paying rapt attention to the beautiful dark-haired woman at the podium. Dean Rafe Salvaggio had been giving her presentation and was coming to her conclusion. Being projected and displayed on the screens behind her were works of the human figure complimenting her lecture, which included famous artwork in the form of sculptures, paintings, drawings, and modern imaging, including some of her own photographs.

"In conclusion," Rafe said, smiling confidently at her audience, "by looking at the human form, in all mediums, we can learn about ourselves and our nature. Within the human form, there is emotion, power, beauty, passion, and of course... sexuality. The human form, from ancient time to present, has always been the most beautiful thing, in my opinion, an artist can attempt to capture, interpret, expose, and reproduce." Rafe looked out at her audience and paused for dramatic effect. "Thank you for your time and attention."

The audience applauded her enthusiastically, and when the applause subsided, she spoke again. "Please stay and enjoy the food and drink, and of course, the student art in our Conservators Gallery. I'd also like to mention our former professor Doctor Greer Noble is here tonight. Please be sure to say hello to her as she is returning to Baltimore Sunday morning."

The crowd applauded again, and Rafe was approached by several students and other attendees who questioned her about everything from art, to classes, to the hostage situation.

Abby stood back with her group of friends and watched Rafe interact with the people around her. "I think we're going to be waiting on Rafe for a while," she said sarcastically.

"Wow. She's really popular, isn't she?" asked Erica, impressed as she set up to shoot a video interview with Abby.

"She's the best thing to happen to this art department in a long time," declared Clarice Biggalow proudly and made her way across the room.

"They all really love her," voiced Greer as she saw the looks of awe on many of the student's faces who were waiting for Rafe's attention. "It's amazing how she handles all of their attention and leaves no one out. That is true grace under pressure."

"No, it's just Rafe all the time," said Abby as Erica clipped a mic on her.

"She's really quite good at what she does here," said Julia impressed. "I've never seen her in this element before. I've always known her surrounded by the things and people from her former company."

"Remember her hard hat and her tool belt?" mused Abby with a dreamy look. " So hot."

Julia laughed as Beth interpreted for Greer who looked at Abby in surprise. "I'll have to ask her about those," joked Greer.

Stacey, along with Flynn and Jude, had been separated by the crowds milling through the gallery and finally found Abby and Julia. Stacey was looking up at the photos on the screens above the podium. "Wow. Her presentation was very..." she hesitated, "arousing. I don't think there is one pair of dry panties in the place." She snickered.

"Stacey," chided Flynn, "don't say such rude things."

"What? It's a good thing," declared Stacey. "Who knew an art lecture could be so sexy?"

"I heard some students saying her presentation was shot on video. They want to broadcast it on their website and charge for viewing it to raise money for the department. They seem to think they'll make a lot of money," Erica relayed.

"I'd pay to see it again," Stacey affirmed with a laugh.

"I know I'll be getting a copy of her presentation for my blog," said Abby. "I may keep a copy for myself, as well. I don't remember anything like this when I went to college."

Beth was interpreting the conversation, and Greer laughed at Abby's comment. "You must not have hung out in the art department. This would be considered pretty tame. We artists are a very passionate group."

"Really? I thought it was just Rafe. I need to get to know more artists. Maybe I'll take a class," Abby mused.

"It's a class, not a night club, Abby," Julia said drolly.

Rafe was finally free from her audience and made her way to Greer and the group. "Well, what did you think? Too much? Too boring?"

"Oh, my god, Rafe. You mean too over the top sexy!" Stacey giggled as her wild red curls bounced around her.

Rafe looked at Stacey as she shook her head and wrinkled her brow. "The art club was a little upset I didn't use any more

Bernini, but I only had so much time. They did appreciate that I included Canova's *Cupid and Psyche,* but they feel Bernini's work is more alive with feeling."

"The *Saint Teresa of Avila in Ecstasy* would have been a nice addition for your passion or sexuality portion," Greer pointed out.

"Ecstasy? Who?" stammered Abby. "I definitely need to look into this art thing more."

"Abby, I think you would like the *Ecstasy of St. Teresa,*" said Rafe with amusement. "She was a woman who had claimed one night an angel had appeared in her bedroom. She told the story about an angel who took his arrow and plunged it into her over and over again until her body filled with a fiery ecstasy making her body tremble and weaken with rapture so intense, she felt as one with God. Bernini captured the moment in marble and placed it so the golden rods arranged behind it would capture the sunlight. It would look like it was on holy fire with the golden reflection on the marble. It's a beautiful sculpture and very dramatic when the sun hits it. Photos don't do it justice."

"So," Abby dragged out the word, "she had sex with an angel?"

"Something like that." Rafe chuckled, not surprised Abby ignored everything else she said.

"It's one of the most erotic pieces of art you'll find in a church," added Greer. "They almost didn't allow it to be seen at all."

"It's in a church?" Abby exclaimed in shock.

Rafe nodded. "It's is a religious piece depicting a saint."

Abby was astounded. "She became a saint for having an orgasm?"

Greer touched Abby and explained. "The description of her orgasm led to Bernini's vision of his sculpture. I'd say it has to be one of the best, most intense orgasms ever recorded in history."

"Well, if I could get an angel to give me an orgasm, I might have a different outlook on religion," proclaimed Abby as Rafe and Greer laughed. She looked at Erica. "Are you getting this on video?"

"Rafe, can I get copies of a couple of those works for my office?" asked Julia. "I've never seen some of those pieces, and I would love to sit back and *really* look at them in my free time."

"Sure." Rafe chortled. "I'll see what I can do for you."

Clarice Biggalow appeared smiling in front of them. "Rafe, Greer, come with me. There are some people I *must* introduce to you," she said and began gently pulling them away.

Greer looked at Rafe with a humorous glint in her eye. "Must she?"

Rafe gave a short laugh. "She must!" She waved to Abby and the others. "Well, we have to go mingle." She smiled at Greer. "Come on. Let's do this."

Julia watched as Rafe and Greer walked away very close to each other and as Greer reached out to touch Rafe's back. "They really are great together. Would it be so bad if she didn't get back with Eden?"

"She does seem happy," admitted Abby. "She's laughing again."

"They look good on camera," said Erica as she snapped the viewer closed. "We can set up again when she comes back."

"So now you're okay with her age?" Stacey teased, and Julia gave her a look and shook her head.

Abby did her best to ignore Stacey. "Maybe Greer doesn't mind being Salvaggio's Paradise."

Flynn looked at her friends and frowned anxiously. "Eden loves her. I know she does deep down. Greer's okay, but Eden and Rafe are meant to be together."

"Flynn, you don't know what you're talking about," snapped Stacey. "Eden has joined me as a total hetero now."

Abby sighed. "I remember when she said men are boring and gross."

"Guys, Eden's just having a rough time," Jude said as she tried to keep the peace. "We shouldn't judge her."

"One thing's for sure, I don't understand her anymore," grumbled Abby. "I can't believe I actually helped her hurt Rafe."

"What are you talking about?" asked Stacey. Rafe had always been nice to her and made her feel welcome, and it meant a lot, so she had a soft spot for her. She let her use the house for a zombie movie night, and they talked about zombies with each other for a month. She felt they had connected over their time together.

Abby looked at her friends knowingly. "Yeah, all this time, we've been telling Rafe to give Eden a chance," she paused and looked over at Rafe, "and Eden was just was trying to figure out if she loved her or not. She says she has to build up immunity to Rafe's powers or whatever."

"Well, Abby, you're the one who thinks Rafe is a wildling with strange powers." Jude chuckled. "Maybe Eden can't handle her wildling soul-stealing powers," she said wiggling her fingers dramatically.

"What's Rafe going to do after Greer leaves on Sunday?" Julia asked rhetorically interrupting Abby's chance to rebut Jude's comment. "I think we should try to get her out and help her have some fun." Everyone nodded in agreement and vowed to help Rafe out on the fun front.

28

EARLY SATURDAY MORNING, Eden Kingsley and Flynn Ogden were sitting in Flynn's dark blue Chevy truck in front of Jake's apartment building. Eden was desperate to find out what Jake had said to Rafe terrible enough to make Greer resort to violence against her. She put her hand to her cheek remembering Greer's message. Her face still stung with the memory of everything that had happened yesterday from Greer's visit to suffering another anxiety episode causing her to have to leave work early.

Focusing on the fact Rafe was not leaving with Greer tomorrow helped. She felt it meant she had more time to figure things out when it came to her own inner turmoil. She knew Greer's threat was real, and Rafe could change her mind and decide to go to her, and if she did, it would be the end. Thinking about it like that made everything inside her feel like chaos mixed with physical torture.

It was a strange relief Rafe had changed and would not speak to her because of Jake's words and not because she was going to Greer. Jake was a problem she thought she could handle. She had to keep Rafe out of the problems with Jake and the Stewards, and she hoped by doing this, she could keep it that way. She could hear Flynn talking and forced herself into the present. It was time to carry out their plan. It was time to confront Jake.

"I think this is a bad idea," Flynn said very worried about the possibility of getting into another fight with Jake and his friend.

"I have to know what he said to her," said Eden anxiously preparing herself to face Jake again.

"Maybe we should just ask Rafe," suggested Flynn. "I have a bad feeling about this."

"Rafe won't talk to me right now." Eden sighed and rubbed the back of her neck. She could feel the layer of nervous perspiration that had broken out over her body. "I've tried calling her, and she doesn't answer my calls or return my messages." She had to do this now, or she knew she would lose her nerve. She grabbed the door handle. "Just give me an hour.

"No way," objected Flynn. "I'm not giving you an hour! He could do anything to you in an hour!"

"Okay, thirty minutes then," Eden compromised nervously, wishing Flynn hadn't made her feel more dread.

"Fine," agreed Flynn reluctantly. "Try to make it as short as possible. You can't let him know you have information about him," he said fearfully. "If he knows, he may really hurt you—or kill you!"

Eden shook her head and touched Flynn's arm to reassure him. "Jake has done some bad things, but I doubt he's a killer." She opened the truck door. "Thirty minutes," she said as she got out and then walked into the apartment building.

Flynn leaned over and opened his glove box. He took out his gun and held it tight in his hand. In his opinion, Eden was fooling herself about Jake. They had no idea what he and his group were capable of, and it wouldn't surprise Flynn if they had killed someone. He wished he could have convinced her somehow not to go and to talk with Rafe instead.

Eden approached Jake's apartment with hesitation. Questions were burning in her mind, and she needed answers. Had Jake already found out about the information she had about him and the Stewards? Had Jake told Rafe lies? Or does she know what they were really keeping from her? Either way, how will she face Rafe and fix things? Was it even possible anymore?

At the very least, could they still get along for Bronte's sake? Would Greer allow it if Rafe went to her? Could she use the one chance she had left to find the answers about her own feelings and make things work with Rafe or was she putting Rafe and herself through more torment by even trying? Why couldn't she just know like Julia, and Jude, and Rafe exactly what she wants, who she wants? Does Rafe really love Greer?

Shaking her head to help rid it of all her cluttered thoughts, Eden mumbled to herself. "I really don't know if I can blame her." She felt like she was trying so hard. She just didn't understand what was happening to herself anymore.

She looked at the door to Jake's apartment, braced herself, and knocked.

"Eden!" said Jake with surprise as he opened the door and looked around the landing. "Is everything okay? Come in. I'm so glad to see you."

"I'm not staying long," said Eden trying to hide her anxiety. "I just need to ask you something."

"Come in, please. You can ask me anything." Jake smiled as he took her arm and led her into the apartment and then to the living room. "Sit down, please," he said politely motioning to the couch. "What is it you want to ask me?"

Eden sat down, and Jake sat next to her. She decided directness was her only course. "What did you say to Rafe?"

"Rafe?" said Jake looking confused. "What are you talking about?"

"I know you said something to her, something about Bronte or me," said Eden sternly. "What did you say?"

"I just told her the truth," Jake said sincerely.

"The truth? What truth?" Eden asked worriedly.

Jake looked at her longingly. "I told her I still love you, and you and Bronte would better off with me." He saw Eden was about to protest, so he cut her off. "Eden, I know you haven't gone back to her, and I can't help thinking it's because you still have feelings for me. I told Rafe I'm sure you're still in love with me. I think maybe she's come to the same conclusion."

A sickening feeling washed over Eden. "But I don't have any feelings for you. None at all. I don't love you," she said emphatically.

"Are you sure?" he asked looking at her with sadness on his face. "Eden, I miss you. I want you back in my life. I can't believe you don't love me anymore. I want us to be a family again."

Eden shook her head in revulsion. "I could never be with you again, Jake, not after what you've done."

Jake took Eden's hand in his. "I'm sorry," he said desperately. "I got involved with the wrong people. I know it now," he said remorsefully. "I was just, so hurt, and I wanted you back so badly I would do anything—anything to make you come back. I didn't really want to take Bronte. I just wanted to talk to you. I thought those people could help me get you back. It was crazy and wrong. It just pushed you further away," he said sadly. "They tricked me into thinking they were helping me, us." He pulled Eden's hand to his lips to kiss it.

Eden pulled her hand away from him quickly. "Stop! Just tell me, is that all you said to her?"

Looking at her with disappointment, Jake shrugged. "I told her Bronte deserved the same kind of life she had growing up, with a mother and a father in her life." He saw Eden frown but continued. "We talked about how Bronte deserves to be able to make the same choices she did with her life. And I told her you deserve to know your feelings mean something and you matter," he said solemnly, "and what you want and think are important. You deserve to be okay with your choices. And Rafe, well, she just makes it so hard for you to follow your true feelings, and she's just never really there for you. When we talked about it, she didn't disagree. Eden, why are you asking me this?" he asked with concern. "Did Rafe do something or say something to hurt you again?"

"No," said Eden reeling at those very familiar words. "Rafe hasn't hurt me." She needed to know more. "What did she say to you?"

"She really didn't say much," Jake insisted. "She just listened. She agreed you should feel okay with whatever choice you make. She promised she wouldn't stand in the way if you chose me. She agreed to pull back and not pressure you into having feelings for her." He looked into Eden's eyes pleadingly. "Eden, please come back to me. I love you," he whispered, leaned in, and kissed her cheek.

"Don't Jake!" Eden pulled back in shock. "I don't want that from you!"

"What do you want from me, Eden?" asked Jake sadly.

"I don't want anything from you except answers."

"I want to be your answer," confessed Jake as he embraced her and kissed her deeply, then kissing her neck and shoulder. "I want to give you everything—a home, safety, my love," he whispered.

Eden pushed him back and looked away from him. "I have to go," she said softly fighting her building panic. "I can't do this."

"Stay, Eden," Jake begged and held her arm and pulled her closer. "Stay with me." He pulled her toward himself.

Eden resisted his pull. "No, Jake! Let go of me," she hissed and jerked her arm away.

Jake caught her arm again and pulled her into his arms. "I can't. I can't lose you again. I know I'm who you want, what you want. Even Rafe knows you want a man. You want me. I'm the man you want."

Eden broke out of his arms and stood. "You're wrong, Jake! You're not who I want. It's a fact I'm very sure of. I have to go!" She walked quickly to the door. Fighting her need to run, she turned to face him again. "Please, leave me alone. And leave Rafe and Bronte alone too."

Jake followed her and stepped around her blocking the door. "I just don't believe you. I can't," he said as he looked at her longingly.

"Move, Jake. I have to go," she said as her heart beat hard in her chest with fear. "I want to leave now," she said fearfully.

"Eden, you're making a big mistake," Jake insisted not getting out of her way. "Please, come back to me. I can give you the life you've dreamed of having. I want to give you that life."

"Please, let me out," insisted Eden holding down the panic building inside her.

"Okay, okay," Jake relented. "Just think about it. I'll wait for you. I won't go into the arms of another like Rafe did." He opened the door. "I love you so much."

Eden stepped outside the apartment. "I don't love you, Jake," she said firmly and walked quickly down the hall as Jake watched. She could feel his eyes on her back, and it took everything in her not to run and show her fear.

Jake walked back into the apartment smiling. He picked up his phone and pressed the *Stewards* phone contact. The phone dialed, and Jake listened to the ringing until there was an answer on the other end.

"Guess who just stopped by." Jake laughed into the phone. "You got it! She wanted to know what I told Rafe. Of course, I didn't tell her the truth. I don't know how she found out. Rafe must have told someone. No, no, I just planted more doubt and reminded her how Rafe fucked around on her. I just hope it was enough. Yes, she may be wavering, but it won't stop us. Rafe has cut her off and has already found someone else. No, I'll just keep up the surveillance and keep my eye on things. Don't worry. Rafe is turning out to be the type who just delivers things to us on a platter. My mistake was trying to serve her the meal instead of giving her ingredients to make one for me! We'll just keep concentrating on her for now. Yes."

Jake went to his window and peered out through a small gap in the curtains. He watched Eden as she walked toward a familiar truck and wished it were Rafe he had to convince to leave with him. He hated dealing with Eden and didn't want to be saddled with her and her issues. "Oh, yeah, the gay boy she's been spending time with is still doing his nightly patrol. Never happen. I just change cars, and I'm never spotted. Yeah, talk about stupid. Fine, I'll stop by next week. Bye." Jake ended the call and went back to his breakfast still smiling. God was with him.

Outside the apartment, Eden was relieved to be away from Jake again and rushed to make it to Flynn's truck. She felt sick Jake had told Rafe those things. Eden knew the only reason Rafe believed Jake was because she still didn't have a handle on the chaos of feelings inside herself.

Flynn watched Eden walk out of Jake's apartment building with relief and quickly put his gun away before Eden made it to the truck. "What did he say?" asked Flynn as Eden got inside. He started the engine and took off quickly as soon as Eden had on her seatbelt.

"I think he may have convinced Rafe I still love him somehow." Eden sighed and tried to control her shaking hands. "He said more to her. I know it. Rafe would have never acted the way he described if he really told her those things. She would have come to me, and she would have been very, very angry. I know he was lying but," she confessed, "some of the stuff he said really hit home."

"Eden, you can't trust him or listen to anything he says. You have proof he can manipulate people very well. Don't let him do it to you," advised Flynn anxiously.

"I won't," Eden assured him. "It's just," she hesitated, "he knows exactly how I'm feeling and what I've been thinking. How can he know?"

"You know how," Flynn said. "He's been through this with other people. He knows what to say and do to get what he wants. You have the proof."

"Flynn, I think you should hang out with Rafe just in case he tries to talk to her again." She rubbed her temples frustrated with what little information she got. "What did he say to her to make her think I would want her dead?" she asked herself with trepidation. "Maybe you can get her to talk with you so we can sort out the truth from the lies."

"Eden, please," begged Flynn. "Let's just tell her."

"Not yet. I can't," said Eden in a panic as she trembled. "I have to try to fix this myself. I'm the one who caused it. I have to fix it. We can't tell her yet. You promised, Flynn."

"Okay," he reluctantly relented, "but we have to tell her soon." He could see she was upset and afraid, and he wanted to put her at ease. "So what do we do now?"

"I have to call Abby and see if she can take Bronte to Rafe for her art lesson." Eden sighed. "I don't think I should go today."

"Why not?"

Eden put her hand to her face. "Greer will be there, and she's made no secret about how she feels about me," she said in misery as she shook with the anxiety of ever seeing her again.

29

AFTER TAKING PART in a fun and successful art lesson in the new studio with Bronte and the other children, Rafe Salvaggio and Greer Noble had invited Abby and Beth to stay for dinner. After enjoying dinner, Abby and Beth were in the living room hanging out together and talking. Rafe got Bronte all cleaned up and dressed while Greer was helping gather her things together so Abby could take her back to Eden's apartment.

Rafe carried Bronte into the living room with Greer close behind her. "I can't believe Eden didn't come to the lesson," Rafe said as they sat down. "I wonder if this is the first step to try to stop the lessons. I hope not. They're for Bronte, not for her or me."

"No, I don't think that's why," said Greer as she gave Beth a look and put a finger to her lips telling her to keep her thoughts silent. Beth told her directly how disappointed and shocked she was she had slapped Eden. Greer admitted she let her frustration get the better of her, but she didn't regret what she had done. "I'm kind of glad she didn't show up," she voiced. "It gave me the opportunity to spend time with you and Bronte. I loved watching her learn today. She's come so far." She brushed her hands down Rafe and Bronte's faces. "You two are so adorable together."

Rafe smiled at the compliment. "I'm glad you got to be with us too. I guess she's ready to go," she said to Abby. "Thanks again, Abby. I'm sorry you're being put in the middle like this."

"I'm glad to help out." Abby smiled brightly. "Plus, I got to spend some time with Beth." She took Bronte and started out the door.

Beth followed Abby to the door. "I'll see you in the morning," she signed as she spoke to Greer and Rafe. "Call if you need anything." She picked up Bronte's bag and followed Abby out the door.

When the door closed, Rafe turned to Greer and smiled. "So what do you want to do on your last night here?"

"I have some ideas." Greer grinned with laughing blue eyes as she reached up, put her arms around Rafe, and kissed her.

"Mmm, I love your ideas," whispered Rafe and returned Greer's kisses as she ran her hands over her body.

Greer pulled back and held her hands up for Rafe to stop. "Wait," she said. "Wait here."

"Where are you going?" Rafe laughed as Greer made her way to the guest room quickly, but she didn't answer because she couldn't see the question on her lips. Rafe shook her head, went to lock the doors, and then sat on the couch to wait.

Greer came back into the room with one hand behind her back and found Rafe on the couch. She took Rafe's hand, pulled her up, and led her to the space in front of the fireplace. She took her other hand from behind her back and gave Rafe a pen.

"This one is for you," she said with a sly smiled.

Rafe looked at the pen mystified. "Why are you giving me a pen?"

"It's a body marker for marking on skin." Greer laughed. "I want to teach you a game."

"I always get into trouble when I play games." Rafe frowned.

"You can't get in trouble playing this game," Greer assured her. She looked at Rafe and smiled at her doubtful face. "Here's how it works," she began. "We use three letters—T for touch, K for kiss, and L is for lick," she said and signed the letters. "Wherever I write a letter is where I'll do what the letter stands for. Get it?"

"Okay," said Rafe slowly as she looked at her pen. "You're sure this isn't permanent?"

"I'm sure," voiced Greer with a laugh. "I'll start. Oh, one more rule," she grinned, "you can't move. You have to let me do this and stay as still as you can. Okay?" Rafe looked at her and nodded. "When I'm done, then it's your turn."

Greer unbuttoned Rafe's shirt slowly and slipped it off her. She took her pen and wrote a small K on the cleavage thrusting from her bra. She looked up at Rafe and smiled. Next, she made a T on Rafe's ribs. Then she unfastened Rafe's pants, slipped them down, and made an L on her thigh.

Rafe watched as Greer bent and licked up her thigh and over the L.

"Oh, god," she gasped and reached down for Greer.

"No, Rafe," Greer chided her gently. "You have to stay still." She waited as Rafe took her hands away from her. Then she reached out and ran her hand up Rafe's ribs over the T slowly and lightly. She then kissed her breast where she had made her K. She looked up at Rafe, who had her eyes closed, fighting to control herself, and touched her face. "Okay, it's your turn." She smiled slyly.

Rafe opened her eyes and looked at Greer. Her clear blue eyes were filled with humor. She looked at the pen in her hand then signed. "T, K, L?" Greer nodded. "Okay," she said. Rafe pulled Greer's shirt over her head and helped her slip out of her pants. She pushed Greer gently to the floor and laid her back so Greer was leaning on her elbows. Rafe leaned over Greer and began writing feverishly on her body.

"Rafe? What are you doing?" Greer said because Rafe was taking much too long for one letter. She sat up, pushed Rafe's hand to stop her from writing, and looked at what she had done. "Rafe, no," Greer complained. "You can't do that!"

"Why not?" Rafe grinned. She looked at Greer and at what she had written on Greer's body. The letters ran from Greer's breastbone, down her body, past her stomach, very neat and close together.

Greer shook her head. "Just one letter at a time," she said exasperated but smiling.

"That wasn't a rule," countered Rafe as she laughed. She then ran her warm hand down Greer's body and began to kiss and lick the marks she had made.

"You're not playing right." Greer laughed as she pushed Rafe back. She looked at her and shook her head exasperated. "I'll bet you drove all of your teachers mad in school, didn't you? "

"No," Rafe said innocently. "My teachers all loved me, including you," she joked and kissed her stomach again.

Greer sat up and picked her pen up again. "Okay, new game," she said. "I'll make an X or an O on my body, and where there's an X, you kiss and an O, you lick. Got it?"

"Got it." Rafe smiled innocently.

Greer took her pen as she looked down at herself and made an O in the space between her breasts and then looked at Rafe. Rafe looked at her and then at the mark on her chest. She took hold of her and began licking her. "Rafe! Rafe, stop." Greer laughed. "What are you doing?"

Rafe stopped and looked at Greer smiling. "You made an O so, I'm licking you," she said slowly.

Greer took a deep breath and sighed. "You're supposed to lick inside the circle."

"You didn't say that," Rafe chuckled, "so I chose to lick everything on the outside."

"Rafe," Greer laughed, "you really are incorrigible. I should have known you would be one of those people who give their own interpretations to the rules. I guess I have to be more specific with you."

Rafe gave Greer and impish grin. "I'll make up the game this time."

Greer looked at Rafe and wondered just what she had planned behind those beautiful eyes. She nodded slowly and agreed. "Okay." Rafe smiled then took her pen and wrote a letter over Greer's heart. Greer looked down at what she wrote and looked back up at Rafe. "R?" she said and raised her eyebrows. "Okay, what are the rules?"

Rafe bit her lip and smiled. "The rule is whoever has a name starting with the letter gets to do anything she wants to the person it's written on," she winked, "and said person can't do anything about it. Except enjoy it," she said and took Greer back down to the floor and began kissing her hungrily.

"Rafe," Greer said between kisses, "that's not... a real... game." Rafe reached down and touched Greer between her legs. "Oh, god," she moaned, "not, fair."

"I know," said Rafe as she looked into Greer's eyes pretending to be sorry. "I told you, games just get me into trouble." She kissed her again, and then she moved down her arching body... touching, kissing and licking.

"Oh, yes," Greer moaned then gasped at Rafe's touch, "there's my wildling." Then she lost herself in in the sensations Rafe was creating in her.

30

SUNDAY MORNING SUNLIGHT streamed in through the bedroom windows as Rafe Salvaggio woke up to the sounds of Greer Noble in the shower. Rafe rose to put her robe on and caught the image of herself in the mirror over her dresser. She laughed as she saw Greer had gotten her revenge with the body markers while she was asleep. She heard Greer opening the bathroom door, so she continued to slip on her robe and went to stand in front of the door.

Wrapped in her towel, Greer opened the door and looked up in surprise. "Rafe!" she yelled. "You scared the shit out of me! What are you doing standing here?"

"Waiting for you," she said and opened her robe. "A little late night artwork?" She smiled ruefully as she displayed her body and the art Greer had applied like graffiti in the night.

Greer laughed. "No, very early morning," she said and gave her a quick kiss.

"What's it mean?" asked Rafe as she admired it again in the mirror.

"It's just something I made up," said Greer as she walked past Rafe to get her clothes.

Rafe grabbed her, sat her on the bed, and kissed her. "Tell me. It's a pictogram. Tell me what it means."

Greer pulled back, looked at the drawing on Rafe's stomach, and traced it with her finger. "It's a hand making the sign for I love you," she said and looked at Rafe holding her hand up to show her the sign. "Because I do."

She leaned toward her and kissed her then looked back at the drawing. "These middle knuckles I've made into pyramids to represent time, longevity. Something I wish we had," she said sadly. She took a breath and continued. "The R filling the index finger is for you." She gave her a small smile. "The G filling the little finger is for me."

She traced the letters and moved her fingers up to the eye she drew between them. "The Egyptian eye of Horus between them represents healing. Something we both will need," she said softly feeling the pain of having to leave here without Rafe again.

She touched the middle of the drawing. "This larger ornate G in the middle of the hand is my mark, my claim to you, which will only last as long as the pictogram is still on you." She looked at Rafe and smiled. "You have to take a shower some time, and I know my claim is fleeting."

She looked at the drawing again. "The paisleys and organic forms filling up the thumb and the rest of the hand represent the nature of love as a living thing that grows and dies but is always born again." She looked at Rafe again. "Something we need to always remember."

Rafe looked down at the drawing and then back at Greer.

"It's silly, I know," said Greer and lay back on the bed.

Rafe shook her head slowly. "No, it isn't silly at all." She smiled as she looked at her face. "It's beautiful. You're beautiful." She leaned over Greer and kissed her. "You're very talented," she said softly and kissed her neck and shoulders as she pulled open Greer's towel to continue her way down her body.

Rafe," said Greer as she put her hands on Rafe's face and pulled her up to make her look at her. "Beth is out there waiting. We have to leave for the airport in a little while." She kissed her and then twisted out of Rafe's embrace. She got up, leaving Rafe surly. "Come on, get dressed," she encouraged Rafe as she started putting on her clothes.

Rafe got up and stood in front of Greer as she dressed. When Greer got her shirt on, Rafe pulled her back onto the bed. "Now that I think about it..." she growled playfully and kissed Greer's neck then looked back at her, "it was always the teachers who drove *me* mad." She kissed her on her collarbone and put her hand up her shirt teasingly.

Greer squirmed away from Rafe laughing. "You're just bad!" she told her and kissed her back. She took her face in her hands again and kissed her forehead. "Thank you," she said softly. "Thank you for bringing me into your bedroom. It means a lot to me." Rafe just looked at her, into her soft blue eyes. Greer could see Rafe was about to say she loved her again. "Hurry and get dressed," Greer commanded with a smile before Rafe could move her lips. She kissed her quickly, untangled herself, and then went out the door.

Rafe watched her leave and sighed. "I wish we could just stay in my room and never leave," she said to herself. She looked down at the pictogram on her stomach and touched it lightly.

31

FINALLY APPEARING FROM her room, Rafe Salvaggio went into the kitchen for her morning coffee. She had thrown on some shorts and a t-shirt after brushing her teeth and washing her face. She decided she would take a shower later. Greer and Beth were sitting at the table drinking their coffee and signing to each other as Rafe sat down with them. Greer looked across at her and took a deep breath. "Rafe," she said cautiously, "I want to talk with you about Eden and your rival Jake."

Rafe looked at her sadly over her coffee cup and then at the suitcases, a reminder Greer was leaving. "No," she said softly, "I don't want you to think about my problems your last hours here."

"It's almost all I've been thinking about since I got here," she admitted. Rafe looked at her and then tilted her head down. Greer decided to try a different approach. "Do you know why I love you?"

Rafe looked up and smiled. "No, tell me."

Greer looked at Beth and signaled her to interpret then began signing. "I love you because you aren't afraid to question me, challenge me, and push me. I love you because we have a lot of fun when we're together and even more fun when we have sex." She grinned at the spark in Rafe's eyes. "When you touch me, I can literally feel your touch for days, sometimes weeks. Almost every time we make love, you leave your mark on me, and I'm reminded of you constantly." She pulled back the edge of her pants and showed Rafe a small bruise on the top of her hip. "No one has ever touched or held me as roughly or tightly as you do."

Rafe frowned at the bruise. "Greer, I'm so—" she started, and Greer stopped her.

"Don't you dare say you're sorry," she voiced. Greer glanced at Beth and continued. "Everyone I've ever been with who is hearing and even some who are deaf like me have treated me like I'm this breakable thing because I have a disability or because they think I'm fragile. I may be small, but I'm anything but breakable." She smiled and gave a firm nod. "Beth was going to come over and take you out when she saw the bruise on my shoulder from the first time we had sex. It's very hard to hide things from someone who is constantly around you."

Beth nodded her agreement and continued revealing the words Greer signed. "She had a very tough time letting me be alone with you." Greer looked at Beth and smiled, and Beth blushed but continued interpreting. "But I was so happy to find such an intense and confident lover. I always felt so relaxed and warm after we made love like all my cares and worries were taken away. I thought I was going to have to teach you how to make love to me, but instead, you took control without thinking I might be fragile. It was my fantasy come to a very real reality with evidence anyone could see if I chose to show it. They were never big, thumb size, except for the bruise from the vanity which, by the way, lasted for a little over two weeks," she complained playfully. "But I could feel them, and touch them, and along with them was always a vision of you."

Rafe bit her lip fretfully. "I'm not sure what to say," she said and held tightly to her cup.

"You never even realized you were doing it, did you?" asked Greer. She laughed as she realized the truth.

"No, I knew." Rafe smiled with a glint in her eye. "I knew I was holding you tight. I wanted you to hold on longer." She grinned at her as certain thoughts filled her mind. "I had more things I wanted to do to you. But I didn't realize, you know. I guess you're more fragile than you think."

Greer looked at Rafe and realization hit her, and she laughed and started signing. "It's part of your so called technique, isn't it?" she asked with a laugh of sudden realization.

"What are you two talking about," asked Beth in confusion, "some kind of S and M?"

Rafe chuckled as Greer blushed. "No," said Rafe with a wink. She knew Beth was waiting for more, but it was all she was getting.

"My god, it just makes me love you more." Greer sighed and became somber. "But then there was the other afternoon," she paused, letting Beth refocus and catch up with her signs, "when you confessed you loved me, and I told you I loved you. You said you wanted to make love to me slowly, sweetly. I didn't think anything of it. I just thought it was going to be the same intense fun moments we always had. But it wasn't. It was different. Very different!"

Greer saw the worried look on Rafe's face and laughed as she signed for Beth. "It was good different. You gave me another thing I had never experienced before. I don't know if you realize what I felt—what I experienced. I want to tell you." She smiled at Rafe. "I closed my eyes," she paused, "and I could literally feel you overwhelming my senses. I could feel your body heat rise, and your kisses were making it so hard for me to breathe even though they were so, so very gentle.

"You stripped off my clothes and your hands, your hands are usually very warm but this time," she paused and wet her lips then signed, "they were burning. I could feel the heat of them penetrate my muscles. They just all gave in to you—there was nothing I could do to stop it, and I didn't want to, either. I felt myself open up to you, and you had barely touched me. I think you knew, but you just kept going. I forgot where we were. I'm sure I wanted to tell you 'we can't do this' again, but I lost the thought.

"As you made your way down my body, so achingly slow, I could feel your breath, and I couldn't keep any thoughts in my mind. I couldn't even think about what I wanted to do to you. I forgot everything but the feeling of the moisture of your breath contacting my skin and your tongue licking slowly over and down and into my body. It was as if you were pouring your essence inside me and taking control of my soul and my mind, and there was nothing I could do about it.

"You brought yourself up to kiss me again, and I still couldn't look into your eyes. It was like a command I couldn't break. I had to close them again when my face was so near to yours because I knew I would be totally lost to you no matter what—or who—I saw in them. I was already lost in what you had done to me, were doing to me. I had become so vulnerable

I had no choice except to trust you—trust that you would keep me safe until I could find control of myself again.

"It felt like you kept me on edge for hours. Just when I was going to beg you to release me, my world imploded. I could only see orange and yellow colors behind my eyelids as I felt my body tremble with release as shock waves ran through me. Then I felt your kiss on my mouth, deep and soft, as I breathed in your breath again. You moved your kisses to my neck and shoulder, and I felt you sigh, and your breath as you spoke next to my ear. I knew you were telling me you loved me. I desperately wanted to say it back, but my mind was still not in control of my body.

"You pulled me close and just held me there for a while with one warm hand in the middle of my back. With your other hand, you took mine and kissed it, and then you placed it on your heart. I couldn't do anything but rest my head on your shoulder. I swear I could feel your heart beat skip to match mine. I felt tears forming uncontrollably in my eyes, and I could only take short, shaky breaths because your touch was still echoing inside me. I kept my eyes closed so my tears wouldn't fall.

"After a while, I felt your breathing as it slowed and became regular, so I slowly opened my eyes and saw you were sleeping. I got up and went inside and into the bathroom. I couldn't stop the tears anymore when I got there," Greer said as she looked at Rafe for a response.

Rafe looked down at her hands then up at Greer, and then flicked her eyes up at Beth and back to Greer, who was looking at her intensely. "Wh—" she cleared her throat, "why were you crying?"

Greer saw Rafe look at Beth and realized she was uncomfortable. "Rafe," she voiced softly, "don't look at her, just look at me. Try to pretend she isn't here. This is a private conversation, okay?"

Rafe nodded her head only looking at Greer. "Okay." She was used to Beth interpreting, but they had never had a conversation like this with her there.

With sadness in her eyes, Greer continued, "I was crying because we weren't just having sex and just having fun anymore. This was something different," she said and looked into Rafe's eyes. "I was crying because no one had ever made me lose control over myself like that before and feel so helpless. It was scary, freeing, and thrilling all at the same time. I've never had to trust someone so completely with my heart and my body. It was like you transferred part of yourself inside me and took part of me back with you, and I knew there was no way I was going to deny you that piece of me."

Rafe shook her head and smiled. "I seem to remember you doing some pretty thrilling things to me," she said and winked.

Greer knew Rafe was trying to be funny because she was still feeling a little uncomfortable. She held her gaze until Rafe stopped smiling and understood she was not going to let her sidetrack them and waste the little time they had left. "You caused that spark in me to burn for you, to want you," she voiced then signed again for Beth. "It was a trade of love I've never experienced with anyone. Then I realized you hadn't left one mark on me I could see because," she paused, "the bruise was on my heart this time. I cried because I wanted to keep all your love for myself, and I wanted more, but I knew in my heart, even though you said it was for me, it didn't really belong to me." She looked at Rafe sadly. "It belongs to Eden."

A tear threatened to break away from Rafe's eye as she saw the sadness in Greer. "No, it belongs to you," she swore and blinked away the tear because tears were not allowed. "I want it to belong just to you."

Greer took Rafe's hand in hers sorrowfully and spoke for herself. "Rafe, you can't give me something you've already given to someone else and who you still truly want to have it."

Rafe pulled her hand away, suddenly cold and shaking. She knew what was happening, but she didn't want to face it again. Someone else was leaving her, and she had no real control over anything.

"I..." she shivered, "I don't know what to do." She held on to herself as she looked at Greer in anguish. "I'll stop loving her. I will... I have to. I promise," she said in torment wondering if she was making herself a liar now if she couldn't keep her promise. But she had to have something to hold onto, something to feel like she was not falling into the darkness of despair alone again. If she just focused, she could stop loving Eden. She could convince and negotiate herself into a corner where she would have no choice except to stop. Then she could keep her promise. Then Greer would stay, and she would not be alone and have to face all the pain again.

Worried about Rafe's distress, Greer got up and went over to her. She straddled Rafe over her chair, hugged her, and then kissed her. "Rafe, it's okay. You don't have to make me that promise." She brushed her hair back and looked into her marvelous gray-blue eyes. "I don't want you to put your love for Eden on a shelf for me. If you do, I know someday, you'll be tempted to take it down again, and I couldn't bear that kind of pain. I can hardly bear the pain I'm in right at this moment."

"I never want to hurt you," Rafe whispered knowing Beth could not hear, but Greer could read her lips.

"If I felt just a fraction of what you've given to Eden," Greer voiced and shook her head. "Rafe, you've put so much of yourself into her. I couldn't understand before that moment why you felt the way you do, but now..." she hesitated and closed her eyes for a moment.

"I'll take it back," Rafe said softly. "I have to. She..." Rafe couldn't say the words Jake had said—*Eden didn't love her back and only wanted to hurt her.*

Greer took Rafe's face in her hands and put her head against hers. She sighed and sat up so she could sign again, and Beth could relay her words. "You need to follow your heart to the end of this. I want you to be happy. You put so much passion into everything you do. From your restoration work," she laughed. "I mean, just look at this house," she pointed around, "to your art and photography, to the way you love someone. She has to have given part of herself to you too like I did." She paused. "How could she not? You do love her. You need to fight for her."

"Won't you fight for me?" Rafe pleaded in a desperate whisper.

Greer and Beth exchanged a quick look. "I am fighting for you, Rafe, in my own way." She paused. "I am." She looked into

Rafe's eyes considering whether or not to tell her about her encounter with Eden. She decided it would be better just to stay silent about the matter. "I love you, and I want you," she continued to sign. "But I can't take you knowing I'd be taking you away from everything you're living for until you're really sure about everything. I know how much being a family with Eden and Bronte means to you. And how much it hurts you not to be whole for Bronte. I can't take your chance for happiness away from you before you've had the chance to be sure you really can be happy with a different dream."

Rafe sighed and leaned into Greer's chest feeling the comfort of her warmth. "I just don't know where to start anymore," she said into Greer's chest knowing Beth would sign her words to Greer. "She's..." Rafe leaned back, "she's pushing me completely out. Jake said if I go over unannounced or do anything else, she'll..." she swallowed, "she'll file a restraining order, and I'll lose Bronte for good. I don't want to lose them both," she said softly. "I thought I could just choose one," she said and looked away.

Greer got up from Rafe's lap and went to sit back in her own chair. She looked at Rafe and saw her hopelessness. "Oh, Rafe. You're listening to your rival, you're following his rules, and you're following Eden's rules too. You proved last night you can make your own rules. What is it about them that caused you to change from how you were last night to how you are right now?"

Greer looked at Rafe for an answer, but Rafe just frowned and said nothing. Greer knew if Eden really were with Jake, Rafe would need to go through the process of dealing with

Eden. She would finally need to let her go if she decided to fight for her and then lost. And if Rafe were wrong, then hopefully, Greer's conversation with Eden would certainly make her take action to talk to Rafe.

"You really have given them control, haven't you?" she signed with a frown as Beth interpreted. "In your mind, they control everything. Rafe, they don't control you. They don't control anything unless you let them. You're the one who said control is something you have to reach out and take. Go out and make your own rules and take it." She looked at Beth, who nodded her encouragement, then back at Rafe. "Abby talked to Beth last night," she paused, "about Eden. She said Eden was very upset about Wednesday night."

"Good," Rafe said tersely. "She should be upset."

Greer watched Rafe's body visibly stiffen at the mention of Eden being upset and knew she was forcing herself not to care about her. "I've been thinking about what Abby told Beth. If she's really with Jake," Greer hesitated, "why wasn't he the one with her at the Conservatory or the one comforting her when she was so upset? He wasn't there. Abby was. Abby didn't even mention him and no one, including you, has seen her with him."

"It's because they're keeping it a secret," Rafe said in frustration.

"Possibly," Greer voiced, "or he could be lying. Eden told you she wasn't with Jake. Who are you going to believe Jake or Eden?"

"Why would he lie? What would be the point?" asked Rafe with a heavy sigh as she shook her head.

"I don't know," said Greer. "Maybe he's still in love with her and wants her back, or he's angry and thinks if he can't have her, no one can. Who knows why some people do the things they do."

"Well, I don't trust either one of them," Rafe frowned because Greer just didn't understand what was happening. She didn't know about the fact Eden had told Jake details of their private conversations, or the fact she had caught Jake coming out of Eden's apartment after fucking her, or about the plan Eden had behind getting close and filing the injunction. She fought down her frustration and pushed away the feelings those words and images evoked. "She can't even look me in the eye anymore," she said through her clenched jaw knowing Greer could not read her lips.

Beth signaled the time, and Greer got up from the table. "Rafe, I have to go to the airport now." Rafe stood, and Greer wrapped her arms around her lovingly for what she knew could be the last time. "I just have one more thing to tell you," she voiced softly into Rafe's ear.

Rafe pulled back and looked into her eyes desperate for her to know she did love her but knew she couldn't say it again. "Tell me."

She kissed Rafe sweetly and then touched her lips with the tips of her fingers. "You can't make love to me again." She looked into Rafe's hurt and questioning eyes and couldn't hide the pain she felt at the loss of her love. "The next time we're together..." she paused, "I'm keeping you—no matter what."

Greer pulled away from Rafe. It was one of the most difficult things she had ever done when it came to her feelings for another. Beth opened the front door, and they headed out to their rental car.

As they pulled away, Greer watched Rafe wave. Before they made it to the end of the block, Greer lost control of her emotions and was in tears. Beth did her best to console her boss and drive them to the airport. It was going to be a very hard and emotional trip home.

32

ALONE IN THE house once again, Rafe Salvaggio had been lying on the couch feeling numb since Greer and Beth had left earlier. She had been thinking over Greer's words about Jake and Eden trying to figure out what to do and not getting anywhere. She got up and went to her room to take a shower. She took her shorts and shirt off and saw Greer's artwork on her stomach. She ran her finger over it, tracing the symbol of Greer's love again.

She put her robe on over her bra and underwear and walked into the living room and set up a small backdrop then set her camera up on the tripod. She set up her lights, made some adjustments to the camera, and took some light readings with her light meter and made a few notes. She liked how detailed photography could be. She would meticulously record and detail all the information on the shots she would take and would do the same when she made her prints. When she was ready, she set the auto-shutter and took off her robe then went to stand in front of the camera. The camera beeped its warning, and the lights flashed.

After allowing herself to become engrossed in her photo session until she was happy with all the possibilities she had thought of on her film, Rafe put her robe back on and put the camera and lights away. She took a beer outside and sat on one of the loungers by the pool to try to relax and think some more.

Seeing the pain in Greer's eyes as she let go, and not chasing after her, was one of the hardest things Rafe had ever done. Another loss adding to the weight already crushing her beyond tolerance. But Greer was right. It would be selfish to go with her, especially if she had suspicions or fears she would leave her for Eden someday. Greer had to feel that way for a reason. Rafe thought Greer was intuitive and selfless and knew she wanted all of her and didn't want to compete with Eden for her love.

Rafe knew she was still in love with Eden. She would never deny the fact. She never denied it to Greer, and it was probably the main reason why she was gone.

The problem, though, was the person Eden loved. Eden was telling Jake she loved him, and she was sleeping with him. Apparently, now, she was spending time with Abby too, for some reason.

Rafe clenched her fist tight around her beer bottle. Eden wanted something from her too, and if it was what Jake said she wanted, she was ready. At least, she hoped she was ready. She didn't know if Jake was telling the truth or not. When she found out the truth, then maybe she really could break away. She swallowed down the old pain for Eden that was always there threatening to swell up and pull her back down into heartache.

Another half-hour went by, and Rafe heard a car pull up. Julia, Abby, and Jude walked into the yard and spotted her by the pool. "Hey, Rafe," Abby greeted her. "We came to keep you company."

"Yeah, we brought wine," said Julia as she held up a couple of wine bottles.

Rafe gave them a sad smile. "Thanks."

"I'll get some glasses and bring the party," Julia quipped and went in the house.

"Of course, you will," said Abby forcing cheerfulness for Rafe as she and Jude sat down next to her.

Jude saw Rafe's empty beer bottle and wished she had told Julia to bring her one of those instead of the wine.

After turning on the music, Julia came back outside with wine glasses. "Here we go," she said and handed everyone a glass and filled it with a very good red wine. "So, what should we toast to?"

Jude looked at Rafe as she sat silently. "Are you okay?" she asked her with concern.

Rafe turned and looked at her and the others. "I'll be fine." She held her wine glass up in salute. "Healing," she said softly.

Abby and the others looked at Rafe and then at each other before making the toast. Abby leaned forward and looked at Rafe's leg. "What's that," she pointed, "on your leg?"

Rafe looked down at her leg and smiled as she looked back up at Abby. "It's an L," she said remembering Greer's games.

"I can see it's an *L*," said Abby sarcastically. "Why do you have an L on your leg?"

Rafe let out a small laugh. "Greer was trying to teach me something." She winked. "I'm her most incorrigible student." She took a drink of her wine and then looked out at nothing, silent in her own thoughts.

"Rafe," said Abby breaking the silence, "Eden wanted me to ask you if you want Lydia to bring Bronte over Tuesday after you get home from work."

The thoughts she had of both Greer and Eden in her mind and the love for them clashed in her heart and was too much for Rafe. A tear tried to escape, but she blinked it back with practiced ease. "Yes," she whispered.

Abby saw Rafe's eyes about to tear, so she moved over to sit down next to her and gave her a hug. "It'll be okay, Rafe. I know it will."

Rafe pulled away from Abby and wiped a traitor tear making its escape down her face, but another quickly replaced it, and she felt herself on the verge of losing the control she had fought so hard to maintain. "Abby, Greer loves me," she confessed and shook her head. "Eden is hurting me so much." She swallowed back the sound her pain wanted to release. "I do love her but... I'm just not sure what to do anymore."

Abby looked away and sadly whispered to herself between her teeth, "I can't believe I'm saying this." She looked at Rafe and took a breath. "Rafe, you should talk to Eden."

Rafe blinked another errant tear away, took a drink of her wine to fortify herself, and smiled sadly at the three faces looking at her. "I think I'll have to do more than talk."

She took another drink of wine and stood up. She walked to the edge of the pool and took off her robe revealing her body and her black lingerie. She looked down at Greer's art on her stomach and touched it. She closed her eyes, took a breath, and dived into the pool washing away Greer's claim over her as her friends unknowingly witnessed it from their places by the pool.

33

PILES OF BOOKS with sticky notes protruding from their pages surrounded Rafe Salvaggio as she sat on the living room floor. She was leaning back against the couch reading a book while three other books lay open beside her and her wine glass sat on top of a small pile. Every once in a while, she stopped and made a note in one of her notepads in her neat handwriting.

She was so engrossed in her reading she didn't hear the tentative knock at her door. When she finally heard it, she looked up and frowned at the interruption. She put her book down and picked up her glass of wine, carrying it with her to answer the door.

She opened the door and looked at her visitor with confusion. "Flynn," she said surprised. "What are you doing here? Is something wrong with Jude or Stacey?"

"Um, no," said Flynn as he shifted nervously. "They're out tonight with everyone." He hesitated. "It's Thursday."

"Oh, what's up?" she asked and took a sip of her wine.

"Well," he started apprehensively, "I just didn't feel like going out, and I knew you were here by yourself so," he looked down at the porch, "so I just thought I'd come over to see if you wanted some company." Flynn was keeping his promise to Eden. He would spend time with Rafe and hope he could learn something to help Eden figure out what Jake said to her. What he really hoped was he would find a way to convince Eden to tell Rafe everything happening with Jake and the Stewards.

Rafe looked at him with a frown and chuckled. "So you got picked to be the one to check up on me. I don't need Julia and Abby to send me a babysitter."

"Oh, no," Flynn said nervously. "I mean, I'm not here to babysit. I just thought maybe, since I live right next door, I could come and talk, or whatever," he paused, "since we're both home alone." He fidgeted with his nails. "You know, so we could get to know each other as neighbors." He looked up innocently. "Why do they think you need a babysitter?"

Rafe sighed regretfully. "I'm sorry, Flynn. Come in." She closed the door behind him. "It's just those two have been hounding me to get out, and I have things I need to do."

Flynn looked at the piles of books spread out over the room. "What are you working on?"

"I'm studying war," she said as she moved some books. "It's really very fascinating." She saw Flynn's concerned look and laughed. "I don't mean the actual killing part. I mean the strategy behind it. There are so many facets," she said as she picked up a book. "I was just reading about military rank. Do you know how someone becomes a general?"

Flynn's mind went blank at the question. "No," he managed.

"Well, in ancient times, they had to show their battle skills and just survive," Rafe explained. "Now they have to survive intensive training, paperwork and promotion reviews, and for those sent to war, they're knocked back into that ancient tradition," she said and smiled at him, "and they still have to deal with the paperwork and politics. Of course, education and family can make a difference sometimes too. You know the type of war I find most fascinating?"

"What?" asked Flynn as he picked up a book and looked at the title, *The Art of War,* and opened it.

"The cold war," she said musingly. "The cloak and dagger wars of intrigue, strategy, and spies."

Flynn was suddenly worried Rafe had somehow found out why he was visiting her. "Are you working on this for a class you're teaching?"

"Something like that," said Rafe absently and took the last sip of her wine. "Do you want something to drink? I have wine, and I have beer."

"I'll have a beer, thanks," said Flynn relieved she was letting him stay so he could keep his promise to Eden. He watched as Rafe went to get him a beer from the kitchen and refilled her glass with wine. "So why do you like the cold war stuff?" he asked when she came back.

"I think it's the strategy part of it mostly," said Rafe as she handed him the beer. "Being able to anticipate and think several moves ahead of the enemy and putting yourself in control of information and actions ultimately allowing you to achieve your goals."

"Kind of like chess," observed Flynn.

"Exactly," said Rafe and looked thoughtfully at Flynn. She thought about the night they admitted him into the hospital after protecting Eden and Bronte. She felt bad for not showing him enough appreciation. He was a good guy. "Can you keep a secret?"

"Sure," answered Flynn nervously wondering what else he would have to keep to himself.

"Follow me," she said with a smile and led Flynn out to the garage. She picked up a crowbar and handed it to him. "Help me open this," she said as she indicated the large wooden crate sitting in the empty car space, and picked up a blue wrecker bar.

"Okay," said Flynn and helped her pry open the front of the crate.

As the front of the crate fell away, Rafe looked inside and smiled. She got some wire cutters and cut the bands holding the piece inside in place and had Flynn help her pull it out of the crate.

"Well," she said as she brushed her hands on her pants, "what do you think."

Flynn looked at the dilapidated piece of furniture and all the small pieces wrapped in plastic. "It looks like it's in rough shape," he observed.

Rafe laughed. "It's a restoration project," she told him. "I've been looking for a project to do, and I found this online. I don't think the people even knew what they had."

"Well, what exactly is it?"

Rafe looked at the pile of wood she knew looked worthless to Flynn, and it was practically worthless to the people she bought it from. "What you're looking at are the remains of a nineteenth-century mahogany Empire chaise recliner with open scroll work edging and ornate carvings and feet. In its present state, it is worth less than what I paid for shipping to get it here." She smiled at Flynn. "But after I restore it, I think it may be worth a bit more." She chuckled softly.

"So why do I have to keep this a secret?"

"I just want this to be something I can do and not have a lot of opinions being thrown at me. You know the girls. They'll come over and start telling me I'm wasting my time or it's a hopeless project. But I don't think it is."

Flynn looked over the battered ornate pieces and the dirty, torn upholstery. "Well," Flynn said with uncertainty, "if you think you can restore it, then you should. It looks like it was really nice at one time."

"Oh, it was," Rafe assured him with a smile, "and it can be again." She started taking the rest of the crate apart. "I'll tell you what, if you want to help, I'll teach you a little about restoration."

"Sounds cool," he said and began helping her break down the crate.

"Great," said Rafe excitedly. "While we work, let's play a strategy game."

"Okay," agreed Flynn happy he had been given another reason to stay and keep his promise to Eden.

As Rafe worked, she went into lecture mode. "Say you're stranded on an island, and you find out there are two more people stuck there with you, but they're the enemy," Rafe said as she thought of Eden and Jake. "You're not sure why, but they've decided to let you join their camp, and you're all getting along to survive. One day, one of them," *Jake*, thought Rafe, "comes and tells you the other one, a person you really trusted," *Eden*, thought Rafe, "is planning to kill you. What do you do? Do you trust the messenger?"

"I guess," said Flynn as he picked up nails from the crate, not realizing what the game was about.

"Really?" said Rafe. "Why?"

"He's being nice," Flynn suggested tentatively, "and helping me to survive."

"Possibly," said Rafe thoughtfully as she started to pry off the back of the crate. "But why would he suddenly become a traitor to his countryman? Why..." she grunted and pushed down on the wrecker bar, "would he help you survive over his comrade? If they want you dead, why even include you in the camp? Why don't they just leave you on your own to survive or die?" She watched Flynn think about her questions as he pulled his side of the crate apart. "What if you believed the traitor, you killed the other guy you like, and later, you found out you were lied to and killed an innocent person? What does the traitor have to gain from it?"

"I don't know," said Flynn stopping to take a swig of his beer.

"There's the problem," Rafe said with a smile as she carried a piece of the crate and sat it against the wall of the garage.

"There's always a reason why. Figuring out the reason is what's difficult. So you have to make some hard choices. Eliminate them both immediately and remove all risk, and at the same time, make it more difficult for you to survive. Or use the information you have to find out the truth and eliminate either the traitor or your possible killer, or both if necessary, at a later time. You have to think these moves through carefully."

Flynn nodded and thought about the scenario as he helped move the crate pieces. "Well, if I'm their enemy anyway, why would he tell me? Isn't the point of war to kill the enemy?"

Rafe smiled encouragingly. "Now you're thinking. So how do you find out the answers? You could just go up and ask the person if they're planning to kill you, but how would you know if they were telling you the truth? They aren't going to admit it to you unless they're ready to kill you right then. Can you take the chance?"

"No, I can't ask," reasoned Flynn, getting into the game and taking the broom Rafe handed him to sweep up the debris. "So what do I do?"

Rafe smiled and looked at him intently. "You have to ascertain the disposition and intent of your opponents by strategically and covertly infiltrating their defenses to enable your survival and the ultimate annihilation of your true enemy."

"So how do I start?" asked Flynn smiling at Rafe's eloquent words and hoping for another chance at receiving praise from Rafe.

Rafe put her finger to her lips and paced around the chaise lounger contemplating it and Flynn's question. "First, you have to decide which person is most trustworthy strategically, the traitor or your possible killer?"

"The traitor, I guess," said Flynn.

Rafe looked at him and frowned. "The traitor? But you already know he has turned on someone." She paused. "What's to stop him from doing the same to you?"

"But the other person is planning to kill me," Flynn said defending his answer.

"You don't know it for a fact, and you like the person," argued Rafe. "You've been given information by a questionable source. For all you know, he wants you to kill the other guy so he doesn't have to. Maybe he has some unknown grudge against the guy or has something the traitor wants."

"So I trust the other guy?" asked Flynn confused.

Rafe grinned and winked at Flynn. "Strategically," she said as she unwrapped pieces of the lounger.

Flynn looked at her not understanding. "What do you mean?"

Rafe went over to her workbench to mix some cleaning solution. "You can't really trust him because he really might be planning to kill you," she said, "but you have to get close so you can watch him. You'll need to gain more information and find out what his plan is so you can save yourself. If he is innocent, maybe he'll come to trust you, and you can have him as an ally against the traitor."

"But won't the traitor know what you're doing?" Flynn reasoned out as he took the rags he was handed.

"Yes," agreed Rafe. "Good thinking," she said as she began showing him how to clean the old wood. "This is why it's so tricky. You have to get them separated somehow. Just clean with the grain of the wood."

"Well," said Flynn slowly as he followed Rafe's instruction, "we're on an island, so how can I separate them?"

"You think about it for a while and see if you can figure it out," said Rafe as she began cutting off the old upholstery.

"Okay," agreed Flynn liking the idea of having an assignment, "so what's next?"

"Next, you have to evaluate your own defenses and assets," Rafe informed him as she went into her lecture mode again while working to pull out horsehair stuffing and putting it in the trash. "In this scenario, you have yourself and the information the traitor gave you," she paused, "information that may or may not be true. Then you have to evaluate the enemy. They have two people," *Eden and Jake*, thought Rafe, "a knife, a machine gun with ammo, and grenades." Rafe pulled out more old stuffing and thought about the kisses Eden had used to cut her with, the abuse charges, threatened restraining orders, and the injunction to stop the adoption. "They also have life sustaining water," *Bronte*, Rafe thought, "without it, your life could be cut short.

Flynn looked at Rafe disheartened. "There's no way to win," he complained, "because they have everything."

Rafe nodded understanding his frustration. "Well, maybe you can convince them to let you carry the knife, and then you'll have something. Sometimes, you have to start small, and a knife can be more valuable than the other weapons in the long run."

"How can a knife be better than a gun or a grenade?" Flynn laughed as he picked up another small piece of the lounger to clean.

"Well," Rafe reasoned, "you don't need bullets for it to function and you can use it more than once."

Flynn shook his head in defeat. "I don't think I would survive this. I would've picked the gun," he said thinking of the gun he had in his truck.

"The gun could be useful too if you could get the enemy to part with it and you knew how to use it," explained Rafe. "Don't underestimate yourself," she encouraged Flynn and looked to make sure he was not putting too much water on the old wood. "You have a mind to put together information, your strength to fight, and your knowledge to help you use what is readily available."

"Anything else?" he asked eagerly.

"No," said Rafe somberly as she went to get a tool to pry out the old staples. "Now you need to find the courage to step into the line of fire, take the pain, and go to war." She looked at Flynn's face and saw she had his full attention. "Did you know you can declare war without telling anyone?"

"No, I didn't," said Flynn, intrigued.

"In some cultures, all you have to do is announce it to the stars or the gods," lectured Rafe. "When you do this, it gives you a kind of power over your enemy, and an advantage, because mentally, it puts you on the offensive side of the battlefield. And if you use your strategy to plan your attacks, they will never know what hit them. You can also declare war on anyone or anything."

"I don't know if I really like the idea of war," said Flynn. "It seems like mostly innocents get hurt."

"Yeah, I know what you mean," said Rafe. "But war can be over anything from politics to love. It isn't always something fought with bullets," she explained. "There's a war on poverty, drugs, hate, disease, and more. War can be declared by countries, companies, families, or individuals." She looked at Flynn challengingly and saw he was soaking up this information like a sponge. "Do you have something or someone you would like to declare war on? Someone from work." She paused. "Maybe a company or something?"

Flynn hesitated, thinking about Jake and his friend in the park who had put him in the hospital. They were definitely his enemy. "Yeah, I have someone," he said boldly. "I definitely have someone I want to declare war on."

Rafe nodded and smiled at him as she wondered if he might be a kindred spirit in the need to declare war. "Me too," she revealed. "Come on." She wiped off her hands and walked back into the house through the kitchen, then out onto the patio through the patio door as Flynn followed. "Okay, you don't have to say who or what you're declaring war on out loud. You just have to think of them and say the words 'I declare war on you' loud enough for the stars or gods, whichever you prefer, to hear you. Let's do it. Ready?"

Flynn smiled and felt empowered by Rafe and was ready to declare war. "Yeah, I'm ready."

"Okay," said Rafe, "you go first."

Flynn looked up at the stars and thought of Jake and the other guy. He thought about what they had done to him and what they were doing to Eden. He finally felt like he had some real power. "I DECLARE WAR ON YOU!" he proclaimed to the sky.

She smiled at Flynn and looked up at the stars with him thinking about her own war. "I DECLARE WAR ON YOU!" she yelled out at Eden and Jake.

Rafe was taking back control.

"So what now?" Flynn asked, feeling powerful.

"Now we learn about strategy and build our strength. Come on." Rafe led him over to the side yard where she had a weight rack and a multi-functional lifting bench set up on the deck. "About six months ago, I saw I was losing tone in my body, so I decided to get back into shape and ordered this set. Since I don't work on a construction site anymore, I don't get as much exercise on the job. So I started doing weight lifting and getting into my running again. We can talk about strategy while we lift weights and work on the chaise lounge."

"This is great," said Flynn as he admired the equipment. "I've wanted to bulk up my muscles." He picked up a weight and liked the idea of being stronger in case he had to deal with Jake.

"Good," said Rafe and smiled at Flynn's enthusiasm. "You can come over and help with the chaise and use the weights anytime, but I like to run alone," she told him and picked up a weight. "Let's get started." They began to plan their workouts, and as they lifted weights, they began their lesson on strategic warfare.

34

Together with
My Baby and my baby
My Love and my Life
Having you both
Makes me complete
Our family is so beautiful,
I love you both
With all of my heart
     ~ Rafe

EDEN KINGSLEY HAD spent her Tuesday morning reading and rereading the same few pages in a script, unable to focus. The things that had happened with Rafe at the school and then when she let Abby talk her into going to Rafe's house were on her mind. Coupled with confronting Jake and the encounter with Greer, it made focusing on work difficult. The lack of sleep didn't help either. She couldn't turn her mind off at night, and when she woke, she felt like she was living in a daze of pain and chaos.

The only thing giving her any hope was she now knew Jake was the reason for Rafe's sudden change and she hadn't found out about his ties to the Stewards. She hated the fact many of the things Jake told Rafe were not far from the truth. Eden was sure most of the things Jake knew about were from when they had talked about them when they were together, but there were still some things she wasn't sure how he knew. Jake always talked about how Bronte deserved a mother and a father, and Eden felt guilty she hadn't contradicted him. At the time, she thought she was doing the right thing, making sure a man was in Bronte's life. She had messed up so many times, she wasn't sure anymore if she would ever find the right place for herself and Bronte.

Eden put her elbows on the desk and leaned her head into her hands. "I don't know what I'm doing," she said softly to herself. It seemed like she was reminding herself of her failures a lot.

The fact Jake somehow knew certain reasons why she was having difficulty with figuring out her feelings for Rafe had been surprising. She didn't remember talking with him about how Rafe treated her at times as if her feelings and opinions weren't important, and how it made her feel. She was sure she never mentioned the fact she wanted to make decisions and choices for herself, and Rafe seemed to always be the one making decisions. She hadn't even talked to Rafe about those things.

Eden knew she had to tell things to Rafe, many things, but she felt like she couldn't yet. She didn't want to hurt Rafe. She had convinced herself hurting Rafe wasn't what she was doing. She was just trying to figure things out so neither of them would be hurt again.

The threat Greer would take Rafe away, and she would never see her again had shaken Eden to her core, and it was still on her mind. She didn't know what the 'never' Greer talked about meant. Did she mean physically or emotionally? Would she let Bronte see her? Would they try to take Bronte? She shook her head to stop those thoughts. She knew Rafe would never do anything to hurt Bronte. She only knew she didn't want to find out what 'never' meant.

There was a quick knock on her office door, and the receptionist popped her head inside. "Ms. Kingsley, a courier just delivered a package for you."

Eden pulled herself together as she looked up. "Oh, okay,'" she said as the receptionist brought the package in and put it on the desk.

"Another admirer or all business this time?" she asked light-heartedly. It seemed like the executives got packages all the time. Sometimes they were gifts or promotional items they shared with the staff. If it was something like that, the receptionist wanted to have first dibs.

"I'm not sure. I'm not expecting anything," said Eden and used her envelope opener to slice the package open.

Eden pulled out the paper-wrapped items and could see right away it was something framed. She wondered if it was an award or a framed photo of a star or a movie still. The receptionist waited expectantly as Eden pulled off the paper wrapping.

"Oh," raved the receptionist when she saw the photographs. "They're wonderful!" She was disappointed the delivery turned out to be personal, but she was glad she was the first to see the photos. "Well, I'll let you enjoy them," she said and made her way out of the office.

Eden barely registered the receptionist had left the office. It was taking everything inside her to try not to cry or show the emotions overwhelming her as she looked at the photos Rafe had sent. She remembered the day Rafe took them at the carnival. One was from Rafe taking photos when she and Bronte were on the carousel riding on the blue horse. For the other, Rafe had set up the timer so all three of them could stand in front of a colorful carnival poster.

The memories of that day flooded her mind. The three of them had so much fun on the rides and just being together as a family. The guilt she felt when she couldn't return Rafe's confession of love sliced through all the good memories of the day. She still couldn't bring herself to say those words to Rafe. She had to be sure, absolutely sure before she said them to her.

Looking at the photos, she fought the tears as they threatened to fall. She thought she had time to figure things out since Jake was the reason for the change in Rafe. Now the evidence sitting in front of her made her doubt time was on her side. The thought of her running out of time clawed its way up through the chaos in her mind, and Eden could feel a migraine headache was edging closer.

Rafe's smile turning into an angry scowl slipped into her mind's images. Then the images flicked quickly from memories of her time spent with Rafe to one of Rafe kissing Greer on the steps of the school. The image of Rafe held at gunpoint and all those emotions it evoked washed over her again causing her body to shake. Jake's smug face telling her what he had told Rafe. The mistakes she had made with Michael. She felt herself falling farther away from Rafe, but she wasn't sure if she should be happy or terrified. Flynn. It was the reason he was spending time with Rafe. So she would know what Rafe was doing, what she was thinking, if she were leaving, and if she was out of time.

She turned the framed photos over to try to stop the train of thoughts. Then she saw it. Rafe had attached a poem to the back of one. Her eyes roamed over it and, as the words were taken in, her hand flew to her mouth to stop the sound of her cry. Her heart hammered in her chest, and the weight of her emotions and guilt pressed in on her, making it hard to breathe.

Eden could feel the warning pain rake over her body. She knew her anxiety was trying to push through. She fought it by trying to stop thinking. She covered the photos with the paper then leaned over in her chair and breathed deeply.

"No," she said softy. "I'm okay. Everything is fine. I'm going to be fine," she told herself. The problem was her body knew it was a lie. She was not fine.

Her vision began to darken at the edges, and Eden knew it meant her migraine was about to be unleashed, bringing even more pain. She could feel the creeping itch forming on her arms and neck as they grew and were turning into the angry, fiery bumps of hives. Once those feelings got to a certain point, Eden knew no amount of willpower could stop the pain and agony that would scourge her.

Almost working on autopilot, Eden felt herself use the desk to help her stand. She grabbed her briefcase and rushed out of her office without a coherent word to anyone. The itching had already begun deep inside her ears, and she knew she had to get help. She had to get to the hospital again.

By the time Eden got to the hospital, her throat had closed up, and she had broken out in red welts across her body making it feel like her body was on fire.

She was lucky when she got to the hospital. One of the nurses on duty knew what to do for her right away. She had been on duty several times when Jake brought her in. She led Eden into an exam room to wait for the doctor to okay the treatment. The nurse turned off the lights and gave her an icepack to help prevent Eden from scraping off her skin with her nails. Another wave of pain thrust through Eden. She thought, after leaving Jake, she wouldn't need to get help like this again. Tears streamed down Eden's face from the physical pain raging through her body.

It was all too much. She cried in agony and tears leaked through her tightly closed eyes as she clawed her fingers into her skin.

Hours later, after finally getting treatment, her body was covered in red welts and claw marks on her neck and arms where she had scratched the raised hives. Her migraine was still hanging on, but she was able to drive home. The doctor recommended she see a psychiatrist since this was happening again. She knew if she didn't get help, this scenario would repeat, so she took the doctor's advice and made a call to the psychiatrist she had talked to when she had issues with coming out and dealing with her parents. She hoped he could help.

35

AS SHE MADE her way through The Kiki Bistro, Letty Carver carried hot plates holding Ephraim's latest addition to the lunch menu. She was so proud of her talented husband. She felt lucky they were able to work with each other every day in a place that made them both happy, even though it was hard work sometimes. She went up to the table by the window and put the plates down in front of Abby, Erica, and Julia.

"I think you're going to like this," Letty said enthusiastically as she joined them.

"Thanks," said Julia as Abby nodded and dug into her plate.

"Ephraim is such an amazing chef!" said Erica as she enjoyed her bite of food.

"So did you convince Rafe to get out with you tonight?" inquired Letty hoping Rafe would get out of the house.

Julia sighed and put down her drink. "No, I got the same answer as last week. She says she's still not ready. Last night, I found her reading a pile of books and drinking beer. I think she has literally buried herself in her work."

"Well, it's Rafe," said Abby as she chewed. "We just have to keep trying until she gives in out of annoyance with us."

"She does tend to isolate herself when she's hurt or unhappy," agreed Letty. "But at least she's doing something productive. Since the day before yesterday, Eden has apparently been absolutely useless," she revealed, repeating the gossip she had heard.

"What happened?" said Abby her interest peaked.

"Well," Letty leaned into the table to repeat everything she knew, "Eden's receptionist came in and was talking about her," she said in a low voice so as not to be overheard. "Apparently, Rafe took some photos to be framed a while back, and the frame shop just couriered them to Eden's office Tuesday. The receptionist said Eden had to leave the office, and since she got them, she's been a total mess."

"What were the pictures?" asked Erica with curiosity as she ate.

"I think they were from when they went to the carnival on the beach front," said Letty. "I saw copies at Rafe's house. One was of Eden holding Bronte on a blue carousel horse, and the other was of all three of them in front of a big carnival poster. But I think what really set her off was the note from Rafe. The receptionist said was taped on the back of the picture of them all together. She didn't get a chance to read it, but whatever it said, it apparently hit Eden hard."

"Good," said Abby as she wiped her mouth with her napkin. "Maybe it'll make her wake up and make up her mind about Rafe."

Letty nodded in agreement. "I also heard the reason she left yesterday afternoon was to go see her shrink again, the one that gave her the Xanax when she was going through her episode with her anxiety back when she was dealing with her parents."

"Yeah, Dr. Cathcart," said Abby knowingly because she got his name from a friend and gave it to Eden. "I hope he can help her figure things out. I can't believe I told Rafe to talk to her," she took a drink, "but she hasn't done it yet. Where is Eden today, anyway?"

"She's still at the office, I think," said Letty. "Like I said, the receptionist said she was a mess, and it seems like everything she touches right now falls apart. She had a takeout order picked up for her earlier."

Julia pointed at Abby with her fork. "Why *did* you tell Rafe she should talk to her?"

"I talked to Greer and Beth before they went home," she confided. "Greer seems to think Rafe has to resolve this before she can really move on, even if it means Eden and Rafe don't get back together. She said Rafe couldn't live her life always wondering 'what if' and living with regrets."

"I really like Greer," admitted Julia, "even though I still think she's too old for Rafe."

"Don't go knocking us older women," scolded Letty good-naturedly. "Love doesn't care about age."

"Yeah, you're probably right," Julia conceded. "You know, I think Greer may be hurting over this whole thing too. I wonder if Eden knows just how many people are in pain because of her."

"I don't think she does," said Abby as she looked up. "Oh, shit," she said. She slid down in her chair. "Look who has the nerve to show her face in here."

Julia followed Abby's eye line. "Who is it?"

"It's Starla," she hissed. "She's coming over!"

"Isn't she the girl who—" Julia started and was cut off.

"Yeah, yeah, yeah," hissed Abby, who was now almost under the table.

"Well, I'm not hanging out for this." Letty chuckled and headed for the kitchen.

"Yeah," said Julia, "I can't handle any more drama. I'll see you later," she said and slipped away.

"I think you better handle this one," said Erica with a cringe and followed Julia quickly.

Starla Samuels walked up to the table smiling and confident. "Hey, Abby.

"Starla," said Abby suspicious of Starla's motives and mad at how good the buxom, dark-haired woman looked.

36

OVER THE LAST two weeks, Eden Kingsley had spent her time waiting for news from Flynn. Now she was also dealing with her chronic anxiety problems again. She was still recovering from the serious anxiety attack she'd had Tuesday. She was lucky she had managed to drive herself to the hospital from work before it became debilitating.

After she had recovered enough, she started seeing Dr. Cathcart. Luckily, he was available for an emergency meeting. She was still in a lot of pain and had broken out in hives again, so he had given her Xanax. She was feeling better, but she still needed to figure out many things in her mind. Dr. Cathcart was able to fit her in his schedule, and now she would start seeing him every Monday after work.

Waiting for Flynn to give her news had made her sick with worry. She was anxious to talk with him about Rafe. Now he was finally here sitting at the table after having dinner with her and Bronte. He had helped clear the table, and Bronte was happily moving all of her toys from the living room into the kitchen for Flynn to see.

"So you didn't find out anything at all?" asked Eden as she picked up a pill off the table and swallowed it with a sip of water. "You've been hanging out with her almost every night for over a week."

Flynn looked Eden over with worry. She looked pale and tired with dark circles around her eyes, and they were red and puffy from crying. Her face was puffy too, and she had some blemishes around her hairline. He frowned at the red marks and depressions on her arms from her nails being raked across or pressed into her skin because of the pain from the welts raised from her anxiety. He shook his head. "No. We just talked about a project she's working on. Then, sometimes, we would play a kind of game. Was that your Xanax?"

"You're playing games with her?" asked Eden, irritated and ignoring his question.

"Yeah," said Flynn proudly. "It was a mind exercise where you had to use strategy to figure out how to solve a problem. She's really smart." He took a toy Bronte had handed him, and the baby went to get more.

"So you didn't ask her anything?" Eden looked at him frustrated.

Flynn looked away wishing he could give her something to help her. "I didn't exactly get a chance to ask her anything."

"So she just took over the whole conversation as usual," complained Eden upset she was getting no information.

"I don't know if she took it over," said Flynn uneasily. "I wanted to hear what she had to say, and it was kind of fun helping her."

"Flynn, it's important we find out what happened," said Eden in desperation. "What we need to know is important. You can't let her take over and make you feel like you don't matter."

"She didn't make me feel like I didn't matter at all," insisted Flynn as he was handed a moist plush mouse. He grimaced, put it on the table, and wiped his hand on his jeans as Bronte went to get more toys. "Actually," he said as he recovered from the drool-covered mouse, "she made me feel powerful and important and smart like I could do anything." He took a breath and decided to take a chance to see if she would change her mind. "I think we should tell her everything that's going on." He looked at her earnestly. "I've been assessing our situation like Rafe taught me. I think by not telling her what's going on, we're giving Jake too much power over us. If she's with us, it takes his control away, and we won't have to worry about it if he tries to tell her more lies."

"I told you we can't tell her," stressed Eden angrily. She looked at him ready to cry but tried to hold herself together as Bronte wondered back in with another toy. "I have to make my last chance count, for both of us. I have to figure everything out," she choked out, and a tear streamed down her face despite her effort. "I feel like my life is ending because I can't cut through all these feelings and thoughts." Eden looked at Flynn through a new wave of anxiety-driven tears, and she knew the only thing stopping the pain was the pills as her body shook. "Why can't I just know? I did once."

"Why is it so important to keep this from her?" asked Flynn desperately trying to understand.

Eden couldn't stop the tears from streaming from her eyes. She wiped them away from her face and was angry she was crying, feeling as if she had no control of her feelings. "Flynn," she snapped in a half sob, "she thinks I want her to die! She thinks I'm still in love with Jake! I need this chance. I need it! If she finds out about everything and how it started because of me before I can fix it, I'll lose my chance! Don't you understand, Flynn? If she finds out," she paused in misery, "then it's gone! If I hurt her again, she'll go to Greer!"

Flynn watched as Eden cried and was at a loss. He didn't know how to help her or how to make her feel better. He didn't know how she was going to fix anything. What he could see was she wasn't doing well, and she needed support. He wished she would let him tell Rafe everything. But he knew she depended on him and was giving him her trust. He knew from experience breaking a trust, especially when someone was in crisis, could be devastating. So he would just do his best to watch out for her and help her as much as he could.

He decided he would learn all he could about strategy from Rafe and hope it helped win the war he had declared on Jake and would help Eden fix her problems with Rafe. He hoped Eden's doctor could help her fix the problem she was having with the anxiety taking such a toll on her.

Flynn looked down as he felt something land on his lap and saw Bronte smiling up at him as she gave him her stuffed orange cat that must have gone with the soggy mouse from earlier. He picked up the tiny dark-haired girl and sat her on his lap so she could reach all her toys on the table. Then he looked at Eden. "I'll keep helping however I can," he promised, "but Rafe isn't going to just start telling me things."

"I know," said Eden softly. "It'll just make me feel better knowing you can tell me what she's doing and you're watching to make sure Jake doesn't do anything to her."

37

GATHERED TOGETHER AT The Kiki Bistro for Saturday brunch, Abby Van Falkov and Julia Hawthorn watched Rafe with frustration as she read a book and didn't join in the conversation. Since Greer left, they had been badgering Rafe about getting out of the house and doing something with them. Because of Rafe's stubbornness, they hadn't been as successful as they had hoped but they kept trying. She finally agreed to meet them, and now they were having their coffee practically in silence.

The waitress delivered their food, and Abby took one of the plates from the waitress and put it in front of Rafe. "See, isn't this better than just having coffee at home?" she said pushing Rafe's book aside.

"It's nice, Abby. Thank you for bringing me," she said and smiled as she put her book and notepad away.

"What's all this stuff you're reading?" asked Julia amused at Abby's antics.

"It's research," said Rafe with a shrug. "Nothing you'd be interested in."

Abby put her fork down. "Rafe, we need to talk to you about Eden."

"I knew this was coming," Rafe scoffed. "You brought me out so I would feel obligated to listen, right?"

"No, no," Julia swore. "We just thought it would be good for you."

Rafe put down her fork and crossed her arms. "Okay, I'm listening. Talk away."

"It's time you and Eden talked," Abby declared. "It's been practically a month."

Rafe just glared at Abby. "I see."

Julia could see Abby was sinking so she came to her rescue. "Rafe, you're not returning her calls, and since she got those pictures and your note, she's been a mess. You should know she's started on her Xanax again."

Rafe frowned trying not to show her concern for Eden. "So you're telling me I'm causing her to need it? Remember, she's the one who's not sure of what she wants. She's causing herself stress and anxiety."

"No, no," Julia tried to explain and not make Rafe angry. "I'm not saying you're causing her to need it."

Abby looked sternly at Rafe. "You've done some things that make it look like you don't want her around anymore. You accused her of wanting you to die, you stopped wanting to be around her, you went to Greer," she hesitated as she saw Rafe's scowl. "Why did you do those things?"

"She was really upset when she thought something was going to happen to you," interjected Julia.

"You know what?" asked Rafe sadly. "Eden knows the answers to all of those questions already."

Julia sighed and looked at Abby. "Tell her the identity thing, Abby."

"Yeah, okay," nodded Abby hoping this bit of information would help Rafe. She started out cautiously this time. "Eden told me whenever she's around you, she feels like she loses herself," she revealed, "like she's not Eden. Oh, and she feels emotionally abandoned by you sometimes."

Rafe squinted and looked at Abby, holding back her anger. "*She* feels emotionally abandoned by *me*?" she scoffed. "Interesting since she is the one who did the abandoning." She stopped herself and took a breath for control. "I'm not pouring my heart into this again just to have it brushed aside. I have to be sure too. She's not the only one feeling abandoned and confused."

"She doesn't want to hurt you again, Rafe," said Abby, exasperated at how Rafe could twist everything around. "It's why she wants to go slow. She wants to make sure... you know... she won't leave you for a man again."

The heat of anger rose inside Rafe, and she took a sip of her water to calm herself before looking back at Abby. "Abby, from where I stand, she only has to ask herself one question, and the answer to the question will be the answer to all of the other questions she has."

"What question?" asked Abby thinking maybe this was the moment everything could move forward.

"Does she love me?" said Rafe calmly. "There are only two possible answers, yes or no. And she really does already know the answer."

"Rafe, she doesn't know," Julia said in sympathy. "You have to let her be around you so she can answer that question. You need an answer figured out as much as she does."

Rafe looked up and gave a half smile because she already knew how she felt. It was Eden who she doubted. "Okay, you win," she said strategically. "She can be around me as much as she wants as long as someone else is there. We'll see how things go. But she has to remember," she paused and looked both of them in the eye, "I'm not hers yet either and," she added, "she has to tell me what she wants."

38

EARLY SUNDAY MORNING, Flynn Ogden was at Rafe Salvaggio's house still keeping his promise to Eden. For the last few weeks, the time he had spent watching over Rafe consisted mostly of talking about strategy, working on the chaise lounge project, or doing strength training. He came over this morning for his daily weight training routine he started the first night he had come over. Flynn was already feeling stronger and found he really enjoyed his time with Rafe. They were out on the patio finishing their weight lifting session when Abby and Erica came through the back gate to talk to Rafe.

Abby took in what Rafe and Flynn were doing and was surprised. "Wow, weight lifting? A little sexual frustration, Rafe?" she teased, and Erica laughed with her.

Rafe gave them both a 'piss off' look as she strained to put the weight back in its holder. "No, Abby."

"I just wanted to spend some time with Rafe, and you know, get to know her better since I live next door," said Flynn thinking he had to explain his presence. "We just thought weight training would be fun."

"Fun?" Abby laughed mockingly. "Weight training?"

"I like it," Rafe said smiling at Flynn to reassure him. "I feel better after and look at this." She pushed up her sleeve and flexed her well-defined bicep for Abby. "Isn't it great?"

"Whoa!" blurted Erica impressed.

"I've been lifting for a few weeks and can feel the difference," said Flynn proudly.

"You started with good muscle tone, and you do it almost every day," said Rafe. "You should be pretty ripped soon."

"Just don't get too carried away," said Abby not impressed. Muscles were not her thing. She sat down on a patio chair and got straight to one of the reasons she was there. "It's been a week since our talk, and you haven't been spending time with Eden like you promised."

"I'm here," said Rafe with a quirk of her lips as she put another weight away. She sat next to Abby while Flynn showed Erica weights and how to lift them. "I go to The Kiki Bistro and other places. She knows where I am. Did you tell her our conversation?"

"No, I didn't tell her, Rafe!" Abby said frustrated. "You're supposed to tell her."

"Oh," said Rafe acting unconcerned. "I thought you or Julia was going to deliver the message since you negotiated the deal."

"Fine." Abby sighed, exasperated. "I'll tell her." She refocused herself for the real reason for her visit. "Listen, I have something I need to ask you and before you say no like you have to everything else, just hear me out.

Rafe looked at her suspiciously. "Okay, I'm listening."

"There's this thing happening at the beach on Saturday," she paused cautiously, "and I kind of said I had a team."

"Abby, I don't want—" Rafe began, but Abby cut her off.

"You said you'd hear me out," Abby reminded her.

Rafe sighed and crossed her arms. "Okay, go on."

"It's Starla and some of her friends," Abby started.

Rafe shook her head. "Oh, Abby, not her again."

"Rafe, what could I do? I had to! And now I've waited until the last minute to ask you because you've been so," she stammered, "you!" Abby sighed and continued. "She challenged me, us. I had to!" she said again.

"No, Abby, you didn't have to," Rafe said annoyed.

"I already have most of the team," she pushed. "We just need two more, and I was hoping you and Flynn could help out."

"What will we be doing?" asked Flynn happy to be invited.

"It's the Lesbian Beach Obstacle Course Competition," Abby revealed.

Rafe laughed hard and shook her head. "I'm not doing it."

"You have to!" Abby said desperately. "I've got Jude, Julia, Stacey, and me. I just need you and Flynn, and we have a team. Please, I can't let Starla think I chickened out. Please, Rafe. We only have to challenge one team, I swear!"

"It sounds okay to me," nodded Flynn then shifted nervously. "Will they let me be on your team?" He was worried since he was a gay man, they wouldn't want him there.

"Of course!" said Abby. "We can make up our team with anyone we want as long as there are at least four women on the team. Plus we're challenging Starla's team," she rolled her eyes. "It should be a piece of cake!"

Flynn beamed with excitement. "Okay, I'm in!"

"Oh, thank you, Flynn!" She hugged him then turned and looked at Rafe. "Rafe?" Rafe just looked at her. "Rafe, please," she begged with a slight whine.

"What about Erica?" Rafe pointed at her.

"I have to film everything," Erica said with a shrug as she put a weight back on the rack.

Rafe shook her head at them warily. "Why do you always get yourself into these things?" asked Rafe knowing there was no answer. "Who cares if she thinks you're a chicken? She's a nightmare."

"I know, I know," Abby agreed. "I need you to help me, Rafe. Please. It's for a good cause. I think it's like for homeless lesbians or something."

Rafe looked at Abby as if she were crazy and laughed at her. "Homeless lesbians? Abby, that's ridiculous!"

"Well, I don't know what the cause is, but it has to be a good one! Please, Rafe. I need you on the team," Abby pleaded again.

Rafe looked at Abby and then at Flynn who shrugged. "Okay," she sighed, "but after this promise me you'll stay away from Starla."

"Thank you, Rafe, thank you. I will. I promise," Abby said relieved. "I gotta go turn in all the forms. See ya! Come on, Erica, before she changes her mind!"

Flynn watched Abby scamper away with Erica close behind her. "Do you think she'll stay away from her?"

"I make her promise to stay away from Starla every time." Rafe sighed. "So, no."

39

LATER THE SAME evening, Flynn Ogden made his way over to Eden Kingsley's apartment to talk with her about his time with Rafe and to keep her company. It was also his excuse for being there to watch over her. Eden still had no idea he was sitting out in his truck at night watching for Jake. He knew Jake and his group would show up sometime to try to hurt Eden or try to take Bronte again, and he was ready.

Flynn was on the living room floor playing with Bronte while Eden cleaned the kitchen. He laughed as he watched Bronte drag out all the toys from her toy box and off the little shelf Eden had set up for her in the living room. It was a huge difference here at Eden's house than at Rafe's house when it came to Bronte's toys. It seemed like it was clear there was a kid who lived here, but at Rafe's house, you would never know it unless Bronte was there. But then Rafe always packed everything up and sent it home with Bronte when she left. The only thing Rafe really had at her house was a trunk filled with over a hundred old hand carved blocks she said were hers when she was a kid, some pool toys, and a few gifts Greer had bought for Bronte. Flynn didn't really know why she kept so few toys. Maybe it was because Bronte was not there as much.

When Eden was finished in the kitchen, she came into the living room, sat down on the couch with a glass of water, and took her pill. "Anything at all today?" she asked hopefully.

"Not really," said Flynn as he made a toy horse gallop around the floor in front of Bronte. He looked up at Eden and was glad she seemed to be doing better and looked much better too. Going to the doctor and taking her medicine was helping. "Abby came over and talked her into doing an event at the beach on Saturday. It's an obstacle course," he said with excitement.

"I wonder why she didn't ask me," she said feeling left out.

"I think she can only have six people on a team," explained Flynn and saw her disappointment. "She probably thought you weren't up to it. Are you feeling okay today? You look really good."

"Thanks, yeah," she said as she smiled self-consciously and nodded. "Talking to Dr. Cathcart again on Monday helped." She turned the conversation back to Rafe. "I don't know how she keeps everything locked inside her. She doesn't talk to anyone. She just cuts everyone off."

"She's been reading a lot for work, and she still goes out to take pictures and to run," Flynn informed her, leaving out the secret restoration project in the garage. "Maybe I can find out where she's going to take photos next time and see if I can go." Flynn looked down and built up his courage. "Eden, I'm getting tired of keeping things from her. It's getting harder now since I have to hang out with her. She's so nice to me. It makes me feel guilty for spying on her."

Eden waved Flynn's words away. "What did she say when you asked her about us doing things together again? The only time I see her is at Bronte's art lesson," she said warily. She didn't take Bronte inside the house anymore. She just took her home, or when someone would stay, Rafe kept Bronte and Eden would leave. Rafe was still concerned someone might accuse her of something and cause child services to make good on the threat of taking Bronte and stopping the adoption.

"Nothing," admitted Flynn. "But Abby came by and asked Rafe why she wasn't spending time with you like she promised. I think you should talk to Abby."

Eden looked at Flynn with surprise. "She promised Abby she'd spend time with me?"

"That's what it sounded like," Flynn nodded releasing the toy horse to Bronte who put it in her mouth. "Maybe you should talk to Abby and go do the thing on Saturday. I'll call and say I have to work or something; then you can be on the team."

"Flynn, it's a great idea!" she said with hope on her face for the first time in a long time.

40

FROM HER SPOT on the beach, Abby Van Falkov was watching the crowd of teams along with Jude and Julia as they waited for the rest of their team. The other teams taking part in the Lesbian Beach Obstacle Course Competition were forming up and taking stock of each other too.

Abby looked over at Starla's team and sized them up. "Those girls don't look so tough," she said confidently.

"Except the the big one." Julia pointed doubtfully. "She looks like a Green Beret or something. Do you think she's a ringer?"

"I hope not," Abby said with suspicion. She perused the crowd as if she were shopping for new clothes or a new girlfriend. "Wow. Look at her!" She poked Julia. "Skin!" They all looked in the direction Abby was pointing.

A stunning woman was walking toward Abby and Julia's spot on the beach and talking on her phone. She had her dark hair pulled back, dark sunglasses covering her eyes and carried a small mesh beach bag with a beach towel. She was dressed in camouflage boy-cut bikini bottoms and a dark green sports top revealing her glistening, finely etched muscles and tanned body shimmering and glowing under the sunlight. She walked casually but with confidence and grace even though she was walking on sand. Her body motion was fluid and uninhibited as she talked on the phone, or touched her hair, adjusted her sunglasses, or swung her arm as she walked.

As she approached, a trio of women got up their nerve and moved to intercept her. She continued to walk and talk on the phone as they came into her view. She held up her hand to the women, showing them her first two fingers, and waved to them in a cut motion as she gave them a 'not interested' look. The women stopped in their tracks at the motion and the look the beautiful woman gave them, mostly involving just a slight twitch of her lips. Their body language and faces told the story of their utter disappointment as the woman passed by them. Seeing the dejection of the three discarded women, others hesitated to approach her, but they continued to follow her with their stares, along with Abby and Julia.

"Oh, fuck!" Abby drooled. "Did you see what I saw? Look at her walk! She can run my obstacle course anytime," she joked bawdily. "She's got it going on, and she knows it!"

Julia looked at the woman with her mouth hanging open. "My god, there should be a law," she quipped and licked her lips involuntarily.

Jude started laughing hysterically. "Guys, it's Rafe."

"No, it isn't," Abby screeched. She looked closer and watched as the woman removed her sunglasses. "Oh shit! It is Rafe!" She gasped. "But she's... she's..." She couldn't finish her thought.

"I know," agreed Julia as soon as she could speak as she stared with disbelief. "I haven't seen her dress quite like that since our school days. I didn't think she dressed like that at all anymore." She blinked her eyes to be sure of what she was seeing. "She's usually so—" she stopped in mid-sentence, the word she was about to utter turned to mist.

"All put together," helped Abby. "I've never seen her looking so, so..." she lost her words as she watched Rafe walk.

"Down and dirty," interjected Jude helpfully as she smiled and shook her head at the two women.

"Down and fucking dirty," wisecracked Julia. "She's back," Julia declared with a knowing laugh, "and I think the temperature out here just went up."

Laughing, Jude waved at Rafe. "Hey, Rafe. Over here."

Rafe waved back at Jude, ending her call and dropping her phone in the protective pocket of the mesh bag. She walked over, tossing her bag on the beach blanket next to the girls, and stood close to Abby with her hands on her hips.

"Well, I'm here," she proclaimed.

Abby pretended to fan herself and laughed. "Yes, yes you are. What *are* you wearing?"

Rafe looked at Abby confused. "Clothes. What was I supposed to wear?"

"You call those clothes?" squealed Abby. "I've never seen so much of your skin exposed in public at once."

Julia reached out, touched Rafe's arm, and felt her muscle. "I never realized you had muscles under your clothes. What's the stuff on your skin?"

Rafe looked down at herself. "It's just sunblock."

Abby ran a finger over Rafe's sunblock. "Very shiny sin—I mean sunblock," said Abby mesmerized.

Jude and Julia laughed, and Rafe shook her head ignoring Abby's antics. It was not like they had never seen her in a swimsuit.

At the intruding sound of a quad runner, they all turned as it pulled up beside them and the driver cut the engine. "Hey, everyone!" Erica called out as she pulled off her helmet and jumped off the quad. "How do you like my set up?" She had her cameras mounted in various places on the vehicle so she could cover several angles.

"It's great," said Abby with excitement. "Did you get us the GoPros?"

"Yeah." She opened up a box on the back of the vehicle, pulled out some rigged up helmets with cameras attached, and passed them out. "These have built in mics and dual cameras to get all the action."

"I'm not wearing a camera," said Rafe as she shook her head. "I don't want to be on your blog or any other place you might publish."

"Come on, Rafe. It'll be fun," said Abby as she put on a camera helmet featuring one camera pointing at her face and another pointing forward.

"No, Abby," Rafe said firmly. "You don't have permission to use images of me anywhere. I mean it. I don't want to do anything that might make me look bad for my job at the school." She looked at Erica. "The warning goes for you too." She looked back at Abby. "Promise me, or I walk."

"Okay, okay, I promise," said Abby disgruntled. "You're just no fun anymore."

"Rafe, we have to figure out our strategy," said Jude with a smile because Rafe was the one person Abby could not push around. "Have you seen Flynn?"

"No, he'll be here, though," said Rafe confidently. "Come on. Let's go look at the course." Jude followed her to walk the course, and many pairs of eyes followed them with interest.

A spunky, spiky-haired girl approached Jude. "Hi, Jude. Who's your friend?"

"Hey, Marti. It's Rafe. Rafe Salvaggio," said Jude, smiling because it seemed Marti couldn't take her eyes off Rafe. Jude kept walking to catch up to Rafe when Marti ran back to her friends. As they walked together, others stopped in their tracks to watch the striking pair make their way through the course.

Rafe pointed to a group down the beach. "Is that Starla's team?"

"Yeah. We think the big one is a ringer," said Jude using her chin to point her out.

Rafe looked the team over carefully, and at the same time, a cute bikini clad redhead from Starla's team looked Rafe over openly. "Well, I think we can take them," declared Rafe. "So what are the rules?"

"The rules are pretty much anything goes short of major bloodshed," answered Jude. "All the team members of one team have to cross the finish line before the other team to win. It gets rough."

"Let's walk the rest of the course," suggested Rafe, and they continued along the beach.

After assessing the course, and getting to know the obstacles, Rafe and Jude were getting excited and had transformed into their competitive mode. "I think we should put Stacey and Flynn together, Abby and Julia together, and you and I should be cleanup. It won't stay organized long, but it will give us a good way to start," said Rafe with barely controlled excitement.

"Sounds good," Jude agreed, feeling Rafe's mood. "Let's go tell them."

As they walked back and joined Julia and Abby, someone called out. "Jude, Salvaggio! Looking good, really good, but you'll never win! You should give it up! We have Big Rosie!" It was Starla, and she was pointing at the big woman who was leaning on the cute redhead.

Rafe looked past Starla and at the big woman and the cute redhead who was staring back at her. "I think we'll do fine, Starla." Rafe smiled wickedly.

"How about we put some money on it?" Starla asked full of confidence.

Julia joined in. "A wager?" she said excitedly. She looked at Rafe who was still staring at the cute redhead. "What do you think, Rafe?"

Rafe squinted and pursed her lips in thought. "Julia, I think you would be a fool not to take her money." She walked over to Abby and grinned. "Julia is betting on us to win."

"What!" Abby said frantically. "Stop her! I can't find Flynn!"

"Well, you better go find him," ordered Rafe with a laugh and watched her take off in a rush.

"I've gotta get to the starting line," said Erica and took off on her quad runner across the sand.

Julia walked back over with a swagger. "I got great odds. Where's she going?" she asked watching Abby run down the beach.

"To find Flynn," Rafe said and looked at the piece of paper Julia had handed her outlining the wager.

Jude looked up, saw Stacey, and waved her over. "Stacey, have you seen Flynn?"

"No," said Stacey panting, her face almost as bright red as her hair from dragging a cooler and another big box over the sand. "Here are some drinks." She handed everyone a bottle of water. "And here's the lock box for our things. Abby said they would have it for us at the finish line." Everyone began putting cellular phones, keys, sunglasses, and other loose items into the lock box.

Rafe rubbed her hands together excitedly. "Okay, Jude and I have come up with a good strategy. Julia, you and Abby will work together, Stacey, you and Flynn. Jude and I will be cleanup."

"What's cleanup?" Stacey asked naively as she spread more sun block on her pale skin.

Rafe smiled mischievously and winked at Jude. "Cleanup is if you get stuck on a wall," she paused, "we push you off."

"What!" screamed Stacey scandalized. "No!"

"Yes," said Jude as she nodded and smiled as she put on one of Abby's camera helmets, "if you want to win."

Rafe looked at them with the fever of competition burning in her eyes. "And we *are* going to win!"

Shaken by Rafe's fervor, Stacey looked around uneasily. "I don't know if I like this," she wavered. "Abby didn't tell me any of this."

Jude laughed as Rafe's fervor infected her. "Stacey, it's no holds barred—anything goes short of bloodshed!"

"But a little blood is okay." Rafe smiled evilly.

"Blood?" Stacey swallowed her pale skin going a shade lighter. She liked horror and zombie flicks, but the thought of real blood made her queasy.

Julia looked at Jude and Rafe with apprehension. "Should we be worried?"

"No, Julia," said Rafe enthusiastically. "You're a *dragon,* remember?"

"Right," said Julia slowly her tone filled with worry.

"What am I?" asked Stacey, wanting Rafe to give her an animal name too, as Jude helped her put on her helmet.

Abby ran up panting heavily. "Flynn," she heaved, "can't come. Problem at work. But," she panted, "I found Eden. She can substitute. She's coming," she pointed back where she came from then ran off to bring back Eden.

Rafe watched Abby run down the beach. She shook her head and smiled at Jude. "We have to rework our strategy." She looked at Stacey. "Stacey, you're a lioness," she said, animated in her response. "You just have to claw your way through the course." She looked at Julia and held her shoulders. "Julia, it's you and Stacey. I want you to throw her over the walls if you have to, got it?"

Julia looked at Rafe uneasily. "Uh, I don't think I can do it," she protested feebly.

"Julia, you're the dragon! You can do it!" she encouraged her. She pointed at the other team and said angrily, "You know what those girls over there told me?"

Julia looked at the other team. "What?" she asked weakly.

"They said you would never be able to get laid if it weren't for your accent," said Rafe pretending to be outraged.

"They," she started flustered, "what?"

"I know!" said Rafe indignantly. "They said you have to open your mouth and shoot off a couple of pip pips and cheerio's before anyone will even think about looking at you, let alone fuck you!"

Julia's mouth opened in shock, as she was extremely offended. "Well, fuck them!" she said angrily. She looked at Rafe innocently. "It isn't my fault I lived in England in my school days! My father moved us there! It's not like I had a say in the matter." She pouted as Jude handed her a helmet.

"Yeah," said Rafe. "It's not your fault you have an accent all the girls like," she said. Rafe looked at the other team then back at Julia and clenched her fist in front of her. "So, fuck them! You'll show them. You'll throw Stacey over those fucking walls and show them!"

"I don't..." started Stacey fearfully, "I don't like the sound of that."

Rafe frowned and looked at Stacey with concern. "Well, Stacey, they said you are like an insipid self-indulgent ginger child, and they wouldn't let you do any of your make-up artwork on their asses with those pale death claws you call hands."

Stacey jumped up with outrage, her pale skin flushing with anger against her curly fire-red hair. "Fuck them!"

"Yeah!" yelled Rafe raucously. "Fuck them! Go! Get to the starting line, and let's see those claws!"

41

PACING AND KICKING sand, Abby Van Falkov was anxiously waiting for Eden to show up and join the team as Flynn's replacement. All she had to do was have a team so she could save face in front of Starla. Now everything had been made worse because Julia made a wager with them. If they lost, Abby would never live it down. Starla would make sure it was all over the blog-o-sphere, and it would be Blog-Gate all over again.

Abby couldn't believe she had actually dated and liked Starla! She almost didn't recover from all the shit Starla pulled when she started her own blog after their break up. Now their relationship was ground down to just a series of competitions whenever they saw each other.

Eden finally found Abby in the crowd of people. "I'm here," she announced and gave her a hug.

"Thank god!" said Abby in relief. "Let's go!" she said as she pulled her along toward their group.

Eden looked down the beach and saw the scantily clad woman standing next to Jude whose back was to her. She stopped Abby in her tracks, almost pulling her over. "Wow, Abby! Who's she?" she pointed toward the stunning woman next to Jude. "Is she Jude's new girlfriend? Where does she find those women?" she asked blushing at the fact she had noticed the woman's body and forced herself to look away.

Abby laughed out loud. "I can't wait to tell Julia you didn't recognize her, either! Eden, it's Rafe."

Eden looked over at Rafe in surprise. "What? Oh, my god! She's—" she shook her head at seeing her body so exposed out in public. "What's she wearing?"

"I know!" said Abby excited and couldn't stop talking about Rafe. "She's so fucking hot, like a half-naked Amazon, and she's back to being herself! I almost didn't recognize her, either. She's all shiny too. I thought she would never leave her house! I don't know if it's the bare skin or the new muscle definition she's got going on, but she's getting some tonight for sure. I think the group over there is voting on who gets to take her home. I overheard a few ladies say they're thinking about mud wrestling for her after the competition." She looked at Eden, who just stared at Rafe, and she cautioned her. "Remember what I told you—she's not yours yet and all the other stuff."

Still looking at Rafe in disbelief at how much of her body she could see, Eden nodded. "I—" She shook her head. "Okay, fine. I know, I know."

Abby looked at Eden's face and laughed again. "That's right," she said and couldn't hide her smile, "you haven't seen her body for quite a while. Close your mouth," she said as they approached Rafe. Abby turned around revealing her amused smile to the others. "We're here," she announced.

As Eden and Abby stopped in front of her, Rafe put her hands on her hips and cocked her head to one side. She looked Eden up and down with her impish smile. She winked at her and watched Eden's face flush red. She then looked at Abby. "Abby, you're with Eden. Jude and I are cleanup."

"Cleanup?" said Abby confused.

"Yeah," confirmed Jude with a laugh as she handed Eden a camera helmet. "We make sure you make it through the course," she paused dramatically, "no matter what!"

"She'll make it. Won't you Abby?" asked Rafe encouragingly. "You'll win! You're not a chicken, are you?"

"Uh, no," said Abby wearily not sure what Rafe meant.

"Right. You're our leader, our president!" said Rafe excitedly and animated. "You can't let her call you a chicken! Starla says you're nothing! She told everyone she'd wipe your face all over the course then blog about it for the next year." Rafe paused and looked at Abby with fiery eyes. "Are you going to let her mess with you?"

Abby was mad at what Rafe said Starla was saying about her. "Hell no!" she said angrily. "She said that?"

Rafe looked at Abby seriously. "Yes, she did," she paused and looked over at Starla then back at Abby, "and she laughed at you and said everyone knows you only blog because you're hard up, desperate, and frustrated because you haven't had sex in so long."

Abby stomped her foot outraged. "The bitch!" Her lip quivered because even though it was not the reason she blogged, the truth was she hadn't had sex in a while, and the reminder stung.

Rafe turned and looked at Eden sternly. "And you're a general," she said with a wink.

Eden shook her head in confusion as Jude turned on the camera attached to the helmet on her head. "A general? What does that make you?"

Rafe gave her a smirk. "I'm the private who's going to save the general's fat ass," she said and turned on her heal, walking with confidence and attitude to the starting line, leaving both Eden and Abby looking at her in shock.

When Eden recovered from her shock, she was pissed. "Screw you, Rafe!" She looked back at her own ass then looked at Abby angrily. "Is my ass fat?"

Abby looked at her ass considering her words carefully. "Nope," she said warily under Eden's angry look. "It looks... fine," she stammered.

Jude laughed. "She's just trying to get you worked up, get your adrenalin flowing."

Eden frowned, and then looked down the beach at Rafe, still boiling inside. "Well, it worked," she growled. As they followed Rafe to the starting line, Eden watched as Rafe walked over to the other team. "What's she doing now," she asked bewildered. "We have to get in our places."

42

WITH A CONFIDENT, swaggering stride, Rafe Salvaggio approached the opposing team heading for the cute, bikini clad redhead who had been staring at her since she arrived. When she stood in front of her, Rafe gazed intently and seductively into her eyes and smiled with her mouth partly open. She reached out and touched the girl's hair then leaned in slowly, kissing her deeply while putting her arms around her and sliding her hands down her body. She moved her hand from the girl's nearly bare ass around her slowly and eased it between her legs.

The redhead was entranced and fully engaged in Rafe's kiss, and she put her arms around Rafe's neck, letting her have her way until Rafe was pulled off roughly by Big Rosie.

"Keep your fucking hands off her!" screamed Big Rosie, enraged and holding her huge fist in front of Rafe's face. She towered over Rafe, and her bulk of muscled mass was tinged red with vein-popping anger.

Rafe stood close to Big Rosie and looked up at her menacingly. "Oh, I will, just as soon as she keeps her eyes off me." She turned back to the redhead and ran her hand down her face and chest as the girl looked into Rafe's smoldering gray-blue eyes. "Just keep your eyes on my ass, beautiful, and everything will be okay." She turned and flashed Big Rosie a mocking smile and slowly strode back to her team as Big Rosie yelled at the cute redhead.

Eden looked at Rafe as if she had lost her mind. "What are you doing?" she asked as Rafe rejoined them.

Rafe grinned at her with a wicked glint in her eyes. "I'm winning."

"But," Eden said confused, "the race hasn't started yet." Rafe just arched her brows and walked over to Julia.

Jude fell down on the sand laughing. She pulled herself up using Abby as support. "Eden, Rafe just started the race!" She laughed again and shook her head. "It's anything goes," she reminded everyone.

Abby watched Rafe spinning up Julia and Stacey and was not amused. "I think Rafe is redefining *anything goes*."

43

THE TWO RIVAL teams lined up at the starting line and looked at each other with venom, each wanting to destroy the other. Abby Van Falkov couldn't hide her desperation to win or her annoyance as Rafe Salvaggio winked at her like it was going to be a walk in the park. The announcer made her speeches and introductions, and then the starter shot sounded.

"*Vincerò!*"[6] Rafe called out with fervor to spur on her team as the teams tore off determinedly for the first obstacle.

The competitors each dived under the mesh 'barbed-wire' and crawled through the wet sand to the other side. Starla kicked sand in Abby's face making her slow down as she spit and sputtered sand from her mouth. Rafe and Jude screamed at her to keep going. When she finally made it out, she took off running, and they quickly followed. They all ran for the next obstacle, the balance beam, and Rafe pushed the cute redhead off onto her ass as everyone else tried to cross.

"I said you have to keep your eyes on my ass!" Rafe yelled at the redhead. "It means stay behind me!" She pushed the girl back down as she tried to stand and pointed her finger at her. "Don't get up!"

Big Rosie came screaming after Rafe and pushed her away from the redhead ferociously. Rafe stumbled back and just caught herself from falling before taking off over the beam. She was gaining on the others and saw another girl was on the cargo net wall with Eden. "Stacey!" she yelled. "Stacey, there's

---

[6] I will win!

the girl who said your masks weren't worth wrapping her shit with! Pull her off the wall!"

Stacey ran to the cargo net wall screaming. "Fuck you! Bitch!" She grabbed the girl by her shirt and ripped her off the ropes, making her fall hard to the ground, and then the fiery redhead started pummeling her. "Fuck you! Fuck you! Fuck you!"

Rafe saw Stacey was falling behind as she thrashed and slapped the girl she had down in the sand. "Climb, Stacey, climb! Julia, get her up!" Julia pulled Stacey off the girl, and Rafe looked up and saw Abby was sitting on the top of the wall with Jude coaxing her to go over as girls from the other team passed her. "Jude, push her off!"

Jude saw Stacey and Julia coming, and without warning, pulled Abby off the wall as she screamed out in fear. Julia pushed Stacey up and over as Eden landed on the other side of the wall.

Rafe made her way up the cargo net wall. Big Rosie pulled Rafe down, pushing her hard against the ground and shoving her into the sand. Rafe recovered laughing and jumped up as she brushed sand from her arms. She looked up at Big Rosie and saw she was on the wall pulling herself up the net.

"You won't pass me again!" Rosie promised with animosity.

Rafe jumped on the cargo net wall and climbed quickly, passing Big Rosie as she used the large woman's shoulder as a ladder. She made it to the top, jumped down, and went into a roll as she landed. She looked back as she stood to see if Big Rosie was over yet. Rosie was still on the wall, so Rafe took off running and caught up with Eden. *"Vai! Corri!"*[7] she screamed into her ear from behind.

A dark-haired girl pushed Eden forward, and she made a sudden stop in anger. "Dang it, Rafe. Stop pushing me!"

Girls from the other team were breathing down their necks, and Big Rosie put her leg over the wall.

"It wasn't me!" Rafe yelled in her face. "Just run!"

Eden turned in frustration and ran for the next obstacle, a huge sand dune with a water pit on the other side. She could feel Rafe behind her.

"Vai! Run!" Rafe screamed. They made it to the top of the dune, and Rafe pushed Eden and Stacey down the hill and rolled down with them. Rafe was able to land on her feet in the water pit. "Now that was me!" Rafe laughed manically, having a lot of fun.

"Dang it, Rafe!" Eden shouted as they tried to climb out of the water pit with all the other drenched and sand-covered women.

A girl pushed Stacey under the water, and she came back up looking like a drowned red rat as she tried to pull herself out. She coughed up water and cried out in a small voice. "I can't do it! Help! Help me!"

"Up and out!" shouted Rafe as she threw Stacey up over the edge of the pit and onto her ass as Jude did the same to Abby. Eden and Julia helped each other out and started toward the next obstacle. "Jude, we have to slow the other team down!" yelled Rafe.

---

[7] Go! Run!

"Go, I got it!" yelled Jude as she started laughing and pushing the other team members back into the water pit until Big Rosie showed up. "Oh, Shit!" said Jude with a worried laugh as she took off for the next obstacle.

Rafe looked up the course and saw Abby on the rock wall with Starla right behind her. "Abby, push her down! Push Starla down!" she screamed.

Abby saw Starla start to pass her. "No, you don't!" she screamed. Abby shoved her sideways, causing Starla to lose her grip and fall. "Yeah! I did it!" she celebrated then slipped. "Oh, no!" she shrieked out in fear but caught herself and clung to the wall.

Rafe looked up at Abby with frustration. "Abby, climb! Climb, or we'll lose!" She ran and climbed up the wall passing Abby then straddled the wall. "Grab my hand!" She grabbed Abby's hand and pulled her up so she was facing her. "Are you going or do I push you?"

"I'm going! I'm going!" screeched Abby, and she whimpered as she slid over the edge of the wall to the other side.

"Come on, Julia!" called Rafe. She grabbed Julia to try to pull her over as a girl on the other team pulled Julia back to the ground. Rafe shoved the girl off the wall and Julia finished the job pushing her to her knees, making her eat sand. Rafe turned her attention back to Stacey. "Stacey, give me your hand!"

Jude saw Julia and Eden starting the rock wall and ran to help them go faster. "Move! Hurry!" she yelled and pushed Eden up the wall as Rafe pulled her over. "Go, Rafe!" yelled Jude. Rafe jumped down and followed the others as Jude pushed Julia over the wall. Then Jude jumped down, and they all ran to catch up.

Rafe pushed Eden and Stacey forward. "They're right behind us! Run! *Affrettatevi!*[8] she screamed at them. One of the other team members caught up with Rafe and tried to shove her. Rafe swerved causing the girl to miss and take a face dive into the sand as Rafe rushed to the next obstacle. She looked up and saw Eden being taken down by a brunette from the other team.

Stacey was trying uselessly to get over the top of the log beams. "I can't make it over. I'm too short!" she cried out. A girl shoved her ruthlessly off the beam and climbed over.

Blocking a girl from the other team, Rafe looked over and saw Stacey on the ground. "Julia, throw her over!" The girl from the other team grabbed Rafe in a tight hug trying to take her to the ground. Rafe whispered seductively into the girl's ear. "Hold on any tighter, and I'll have to marry you," she said and smiled wickedly. The girl looked at Rafe in surprise and loosened her grip. Rafe laughed and broke free, causing the girl to fall backward into the sand where she pounded the ground with her fists in frustration.

"Abby, come on!" yelled Jude. "Put your foot here!" Jude put her hands together for Abby to step into and launched her over the logs as Abby screamed in fear. Julia did the same for Stacey and then pushed a girl from the other team off the logs.

"Don't rip my shirt, you jerk!" screamed Eden. She pulled the hair of the girl who had been holding her back and escaped

---

[8] Hurry up!

from the brunette. She kicked sand at her and headed for the log beam.

"Go, Jude!" screamed Rafe. Jude hurled herself over the log beams just as Rafe and Eden made it to them. Eden jumped up and over as Rafe pulled a busty blonde off the log and then went over it herself, heading for the next obstacle.

"Jump off, Abby!" Julia screamed, "Jump! Jump!"

In fear, Abby held onto the rope as she hung suspended over a mud pit as it swung her back and forth. "I can't!" she screeched.

"Julia, push her!" screamed Jude.

Julia pushed Abby, and she fell into the mud pit. Abby came up covered from head to toe in mud. She spat out mud from her mouth and wiped her face with her hands. "I'm okay, I'm okay," she told herself frantically. "Do you think this is good for my skin?" she asked Julia hopefully.

Julia stood speechless at Abby's ridiculousness.

"Go, Julia!" Jude screamed.

Julia snapped out of her daze, grabbed the rope, and swung over Abby as two members of the other team passed her up on the other rope.

"Run, Julia. I'll get her!" yelled Jude. Julia ran, and Jude jumped onto the rope, swinging over and then jumped down. Jude grabbed Abby and pulled her out of the mud pit, causing the mud from Abby to transfer to Jude, covering them both.

Abby looked down at herself holding her arms away from her sides. "Fuck, look at me!" she cried and pouted.

"Run, Abby. They've passed us!" Jude pushed Abby to get her started. "Come on, Stacey!" Stacey swung over, and Jude caught her. "Run!" Jude yelled at Stacey.

"Go, Ede, Go, *vai, vai!* She's right behind us!" Rafe screamed. Rafe stopped to give Eden time to get to the rope and to see if she could slow the other team down. The brunette tried to get around Rafe, and Rafe tackled her, taking the girl to the ground knocking the wind out of her.

"Fuck," the brunette tried to speak and caught her breath again, "you!"

Rafe laughed close to the girls face. "Only if you ask nicely!" As Rafe got up, Big Rosie appeared out of nowhere and took Rafe's legs from under her. Rafe hit the ground hard. *"Merda!"*

She got up again, shoved Big Rosie back down at the same time, and then ran for the rope obstacle. Rafe saw Eden was just then pulling the rope back. She sped up and made a running jump for Eden and the rope. She grabbed them both, and they swung over the pit. Rafe let go of the rope and took Eden down with her. Eden hit the ground hard, and Rafe rolled into her fall.

"Dang it, Rafe. Just stay away from me!" Eden screamed at her. "You're hurting me!"

Rafe grinned mischievously. "It could be worse—we could be in the pit!" She laughed mirthfully. "You're fine, run! She's coming!" Rafe yelled, and Eden ran. Rafe turned and pushed Big Rosie back on the rope, so she fell into the mud pit.

"You're dead!" screamed Big Rosie furiously as she came up from under the mud.

Rafe laughed and ran to the next obstacle. The others were halfway through the long muddy water trench. Rafe jumped in and made her way through. "Jude, Julia," she yelled, "don't let them pass you!"

Julia grabbed a girl by the hair and dragged her back from the edge of the trench. "Fucking cheerio bitch! Do you have a problem with my accent now?" She shoved the girl down into the mud and pushed herself forward using the girl as a step stool to get out. Julia then dragged Abby with her. "Come on, Abby!"

"Come on!" called Jude. She reached down to pull Stacey and Eden out of the trench. A girl grabbed Eden and yanked her back by her shirt, ripping it more, and passed her.

Eden threw a mud clod at the girls back, and the girl cried in pain but kept going. "You owe me a shirt, peahen!"

Rafe caught up and pushed Eden roughly up and out of the trench from behind. "Peahen?" She laughed at Eden's attempt to cuss then yelled, "Go! Last one! Run!" yelled Rafe.

They ran to the last obstacle, a big wall with just a rope to help climb up and over. Julia and Abby were trying to get each other over the wall, but the mud and water they were covered in made it difficult. Jude was on top of the wall waiting to pull Stacey up. "Come on, Stacey! Hurry!" Jude screamed at her.

"Stacey, get up the rope!" screamed Rafe. "Ede, help me hold them off!"

Eden pulled Starla off her rope, pulling Starla's shoes off as she fell. Eden looked at the shoes surprised and threw them as far as she could.

Starla ran across the hot sand after her shoes.

Abby finally made it over, and Julia followed her, landing almost on top of her.

Eden looked back over her shoulder. "Oh, crap! Rafe, here comes Big Rosie!"

"Get up the rope!" yelled Rafe. She ran toward Big Rosie, and Big Rosie went after Rafe as she led her in the opposite direction. Jude pulled Eden up as Starla recovered her shoes and climbed the wall after her.

"I'm gonna ring your scrawny neck!" screamed Big Rosie, determined to catch the laughing Rafe.

"Rafe, let's go!" Jude yelled and jumped off the wall. She looked back at Eden. "Jump, Eden! Come on!"

Rafe made a sudden direction change, and Big Rosie went off balance for a second giving Rafe time to make a break for the rope. She jumped up, grabbed the rope, and pulled herself up. Big Rosie was seconds behind her. Rafe jumped down almost on top of Eden. She pushed Eden toward the finish line. "Move your ass, General!"

Jude crossed the finish line. She turned and saw the other team only had one member still out, and they had two. "Come on, Rafe! Don't let her pass you or we lose! Run, Eden!"

Everyone was screaming for them to run and cheering them to the finish line.

Rafe was breathing down Eden's neck. "*Corri*, run! Go, go, *vai, vai!*" She ran pushing Eden forward. "She's right behind us! She's catching up! Go! Move your ass!" She pushed Eden forward hard. Eden tripped and fell over the finish line as Rafe jumped over her.

"Dang it, Rafe!" Eden screamed as she recovered from the fall.

Abby, covered in mud, looked around them astounded and started jumping up and down. "We did it! Rafe! Fuck-n-A! We did it!" She jumped into Rafe's arms and hugged her. "We win! We win!"

A sand-and-mud-coated Rafe held Abby up, swung her around, threw back her head, and laughed. "*Vittoria!*[9] Victory is ours!" she cheered.

Stacey was still trying to catch her breath with her clothes clinging to her and fell to her knees. "We..." she gasped, "we win, you fuckers!"

Julia was bending over holding her side. "Yeah, now," she puffed heavily, "pay up!" She stood up a bit and limped her way over to Starla.

"Oh, my god." Jude smiled as she made an effort to brush off the sand and mud from her arms. "I can't believe we just did that!"

Stacey held her leg and sat down. "I..." she cringed in pain, "I don't like playing with Rafe. I think I'm going to have a bruise on my thigh." She groaned. "She's so fucking pushy!"

Eden was on her knees catching her breath, her ripped shirt gaping open on the side. "I know." She panted. "I know what you mean. It was crazy!"

Rafe pulled Stacey up and shook her excitedly. "We won!" she shouted. She let Stacey go back down to the ground like a ragdoll. She turned and grabbed Eden up and put her face so close, Eden could feel her breath on her lips. As Eden leaned

---

[9] Victory!

into her, Rafe laughed and pulled herself away and saluted her and winked. "I told you we'd win, General!"

Eden staggered back breathless. "Rafe!" she yelled miffed.

Rafe laughed and turned to shake hands with Big Rosie. "Great race!" She smiled and patted her back.

Big Rosie frowned then shook her head. "I want you on my team next time. But there's something I owe you," she said with her hands on her hips. "Which one is your girl? Is it her?" she pointed at Eden.

Rafe looked at Big Rosie, smiled, and nodded her head toward Eden. "Her? Not yet. Come with me." She led her over to Abby. "Big Rosie, this is my funny girl Abby."

"Abby," said Big Rosie. As Abby looked up at the women, confused, Big Rosie grabbed her and kissed her deeply as she put her hand on her crotch then let her go abruptly. Big Rosie looked at Rafe justly. "Now we're even."

Rafe chuckled and brushed some sand off her. "Now we're even," she agreed with a grin. "Okay, who wants to celebrate? I say we need beers all around. Let's go!"

"What was that?" asked Abby recovering from Rosie's kiss.

Rafe gave Abby a wicked and grinned. "Your reward for winning the race."

Julia made her way back from Starla. "Look at this. Five hundred dollars for each of us!"

Abby looked at Rafe then Julia in amazement. "Well, all right then. Let's go celebrate!"

Jude laughed and smiled at Abby. "You do realize Julia bet if we'd have lost, we would have had to pay them three thousand dollars, right?"

Abby realized how close they were to having to come up with so much cash and exploded. "Julia! No more betting!" she shouted at her. "It's a good thing Rafe and Jude saved your ass!"

44

THE MUD AND sand-covered competitors were drinking beers and celebrating at the Sand Bar. Abby Van Falkov was watching Jude Atwood and Rafe Salvaggio, who were sitting at a table with Big Rosie and the cute redhead, as well as a couple of other hangers-on. Rafe was celebrating enthusiastically with a couple of girls who were doing their best to get her to go home with them. It looked like Rafe was flirting with them shamelessly, and Jude was her partner in crime.

"I think the competition has gone to her head," said Abby dryly as she watched the girls gush all over Rafe.

"You may be right," said Eden trying to look anywhere but at Rafe. "She kissed Big Rosie's girlfriend, the redhead, but now it's like she's Big Rosie's best friend."

"It was just a tactic," Julia said waving it off. "I can't believe she told us all that stuff just to get us riled up. I almost yanked a girl's hair out."

Stacey looked at her scraped up fists. "I think I gave a girl a black eye." She frowned. "It was really mean of Rafe."

Abby held up her beer in salute not wanting to bring down the mood. "But we won," she cheered.

"True," said Julia, "and we each got five hundred dollars." She grinned as she held up her cash.

Stacey laughed. "Okay, don't tell her I said it, but..." she looked over her shoulder and back, "it was worth it. I need the money."

"And I got some really good shots even if we can't use the ones with Rafe," said Erica with an excited smile.

"Why can't you use the ones of Rafe?" asked Eden.

"Oh, she's being a spoilsport," complained Abby and shook her head. "I can't wait to see the helmet cam action."

"Abby, don't ignore what she said," Julia warned her. "You saw how high profile her job is now. If you fuck things up for her, she'll murder you."

Erica laughed. "Abby can't stand it when she has such hot material she can't use."

Abby glared at the other table. "You know what I really can't stand?"

"What?" Eden asked. She took a drink of her beer and thought how glad she was pictures of Rafe in her skimpy outfit weren't going to be all over Abby's blog.

"Just look at them and then look at us," Abby said. They all looked over at the other table. "Rafe and Jude look fucking hot all covered in mud and sand, and we look like shit."

"Speak for yourself," said Julia, looking down at herself and the mud clinging to the ends of her silver hair. "Oh, I do look like shit!" She looked back over at Rafe and Jude. "How—" she stammered, "how is that possible?"

"It's their confidence," Eden said, sure of her answer. "They don't care about the sand and mud, so no one else does, either."

"Confidence?" said Abby and shook her head. "No, no, that's not it. Look at Rafe. When she walked out on the beach, all clean and glistening, most of the girls were following her with their eyes. Now they are all literally following her," she complained. "Jude too. It's because they look so, so," she couldn't find the words.

"Down and dirty extreme version?" suggested Julia.

"Close enough," conceded Abby. She looked at Rafe, and the whole situation irked her. "Eden, it is imperative you take her back off the market for the sake of fairness. Jude is enough competition for the rest of us. If Rafe starts hanging out with Julia at the bars again, or with Jude, there'll be no hope for us, or for you."

"I've been trying to get her to go out to the clubs for the last few weekends," said Julia with a knowing nod. "This is the first time she's been out since—" She stopped herself and looked at Eden awkwardly.

Eden looked down at her beer. "Since Greer?"

"Yes, since she took Greer to girls' night at *Club La Femme*," admitted Julia as Abby kicked her under the table, and she tried to hide her pain.

Abby looked over where Rafe was standing. "Eden, I think Rafe's looking at you," she said as she looked away quickly.

"She is," Erica confirmed. "Here she comes."

Rafe walked up and brushed a spot of sand off her bare stomach as the girls all watched. She smiled at them. "Do you need more drinks over here?"

"I'm fine," said Julia taking a sip of her drink so she could tear her eyes away from Rafe's abs.

Me too," said Stacey with a grin as she watched the girls in the bar drool over Rafe.

"I'm cool," Erica smiled then quickly looked at Abby.

"I'm good," said Abby annoyed at Rafe for showing off.

"No, thanks," said Eden softly feeling herself flush under Rafe's gaze.

Rafe looked away and brushed some sand from her leg. "Okay." She looked at Stacey. "Hey, Stacey, don't worry about what was said about your masks. You're very talented, and anyone would be lucky to have you do their make-up," she said and smiled charmingly.

Stacey looked at Rafe warily. "Thank you. It's fine. I know it was just part of the game."

"Good," said Rafe with a nod then looked at Abby and Julia. "Abby, you were a great president, and you are definitely not a chicken." She winked. "Julia, your accent is very sexy, and anyone who says differently is just jealous."

"Of course, they are," said Julia with a smile as Abby looked at Rafe suspiciously.

Rafe turned and looked at Eden. "And, you, General, your ass is the nicest one I've ever pushed over a finish line." She winked and grinned as Eden just looked at her then looked away.

"Okay," said Abby. "What's going on? Why are you saying those things?"

"Yeah," agreed Julia. "We know you were just spinning us up."

Rafe ignored their questions and smiled at Julia. "Julia, I think I'll take you up on your offer next weekend."

"You'll go to the club?" Julia said excited, immediately forgetting her questions to Rafe.

Rafe looked at Eden and watched as she took a nervous drink of her beer. "Yes, how about The Kiki. Letty says they're having live music Friday night."

"Sounds great," said Julia. "Wear something like you have on now. Then it'll be an interesting night." She chuckled as she thought of the possibilities.

Laughing softly, Rafe bent over Eden and smiled as her eyes twinkled. "Now you'll know where I'll be," she said softly then stood back up. "Well, I have to get home. I have some reading to do. Bye." She walked out, and many eyes and a couple of girls followed her.

Abby grabbed Eden's arm. "Are you going?"

Eden looked at Abby, her emotions a cross between frustration, anger, and fear because she had not figured out all her feelings yet. "Dang it!"

"What?" asked Julia not sure why Eden had a sudden outburst.

"Nothing," said Eden in frustration. "She's playing a stupid game with me."

"What do you mean?" asked Abby. "She's doing what she promised."

"Did you see her look?" Eden said angrily. "It's like she's enjoying this now and putting on a show for everyone by swaggering around half naked. I bet she wore it just to throw her 'she isn't yours yet' line in my face."

"Eden, she didn't even know you were going to be here, so you can't say she dressed like that to upset you," said Abby in confusion.

"It doesn't seem like she's playing a game to me," Julia said concerned. "It seems like she wants you to make up your mind once and for all and tell her exactly what you want while she keeps her options open at the same time. She's not leaving you any room for gray area and not stopping herself from living. You have to admit she does look good."

"Yes, she does," agreed Abby and took a swig of her beer. "So, Eden," she looked at her curiously, "what are you going to do?"

Eden looked at Abby and Julia anxiously. "Tell her I said I'll be there. I have to go home," she sighed and left the table.

Jude walked over and sat down with them. "Where did Eden go? She looked upset."

"Apparently, it makes her mad when Rafe tells her where she'll be," said Stacey and took a sip of her beer

Abby frowned at Stacey. "Don't be stupid." She looked at Jude. "Rafe was just over here giving us all compliments, what's up with her?"

Jude laughed. "Well, we were talking about tactics, and it was mentioned Rafe might have hurt your self-esteem. I guess she just wanted to make sure she didn't."

"What?" Abby screeched. "Like she could ever affect my self-esteem!" she said indignantly.

"I think she just wanted to tell Eden she had a nice ass," said Julia with a smirk.

"Well, she does," affirmed Jude and chuckled. "She looked hot in her torn shirt too. Rafe kept looking over at her."

"Really?" said Abby slowly then looked at Julia knowingly.

Erica looked around at the crowd. "What happened to all the excitement in here? Everyone is suddenly acting like their dog died or something."

Abby took the last sip of her beer. "Rafe was the excitement in here, and she left."

"I have to know how she does it!" said Julia jealous. "Let's get out of here."

45

EDEN KINGSLEY HAD just arrived for her Monday appointment at Dr. William Cathcart's office after work. She had started seeing him about a month ago, not long after the incident with Rafe at the Conservatory and after receiving the photographs she had taken at the carnival. The photographs included a poem by Rafe that had sent her anxiety and guilt over the edge. Eden had revealed *almost* everything going on to the doctor with the hope he could help her understand her feelings and what was going on with Rafe. He had prescribed her Xanax because of the anxiety she was exhibiting, and he knew she had been on it previously without known side effects.

She felt like she couldn't tell him everything about Jake and the Stewards yet because she just desperately wanted to focus on Rafe.

Looking at the fish in the large saltwater tank in the waiting room, Eden was anxious to get started, so she could tell him about her weekend and about Rafe.

Dr. Cathcart opened his office door, looked out, and saw Eden was there for her appointment. "Eden?" he called, and when she turned, he waved her inside. "Come in," he said warmly. She entered, and he closed the door behind them. "How are your pain levels?" asked Dr. Cathcart as Eden entered the office.

Dr. Cathcart had seen Eden several years ago when she was going through issues with estrangement from her parents after coming out to them. He was familiar with Eden's ongoing problems with chronic anxiety and how it affected her—both emotionally and physically.

"Better," said Eden. She showed him her arms now clear of scratches and nail marks. "I haven't had hives or anything again, either."

Her last bad anxiety episode was the day she had received the photographs and the note Rafe had sent her. She ended up having to have a steroid shot for her hives and prescribed the Xanax soon after. Everything collided that day, and her anxiety took over her mind as well as her body. She had felt like Jake was still controlling her life with whatever he had told Rafe. Then there was her own inner turmoil about Rafe and her feelings. Seeing the photos and reading Rafe's note was just too much for her, and she had an anxiety attack.

"I'm feeling much better," she said, not wanting to relive the pain again in her mind.

"Very good," said Cathcart as they sat down across from each other and got comfortable. "Where would you like to start today?" he asked as he made a note.

"I finally saw Rafe this weekend," said Eden beside herself with frustration. "My god, she made me so..." she hissed, "angry."

"What did she do?" Cathcart asked calmly.

"She was swaggering around the beach," she said animatedly, "practically naked and kissing," she stammered angrily, "just anyone." She took a calming breath. "She told Abby she had promised to spend time with me. Why would she do those things while I was there?"

"You think she did those things on purpose to hurt you?" asked Cathcart.

"No, I don't know," she said confused. "I guess not. She didn't know I'd be there. So I guess Abby was right about the fact she didn't wear what she did to upset me."

"And the people she kissed?" asked Cathcart

"She..." Eden hesitated and backtracked, "she just kissed one girl, I guess. Maybe it didn't mean anything. We were in a competition, and she was messing with the minds of the people on the other team. But she didn't have to do it."

"So she didn't do anything to upset you purposely," Cathcart said, "but you're upset? Eden, what's really going on?"

"It's just a," she looked at the ceiling, "just the control thing she does."

"Control thing?" probed Cathcart.

"Like I told you," sighed Eden, "she tells Abby I have all the power and control. Then, over the weekend, I find out she promised she'd spend time with me but makes rules and statements like I have to 'remember she's not mine yet either' and I have to 'tell her what I want.' I don't know why she's doing those things."

Cathcart looked at Eden and put his hand on his chin. "Eden, it sounds like she is just trying to protect herself. Why do you think she says you're in control? What does she think you're in control of?"

"I don't know. I'm not in control of anything, and I feel totally powerless," cried Eden in frustration.

Cathcart waited until Eden gathered herself together and probed further. "Well, last week, you said Jake told her you were still in love with him, and he told her you and Bronte would be better off with him. Maybe she feels like she's losing you both. You *are* in control of what happens with Bronte. Have you told her you aren't in love with Jake?"

"No, I haven't," she threw up her arms in frustration. "I haven't seen her long enough to tell her anything." She looked up at Cathcart. "I'm not taking Bronte away from her."

"Does she know it for a fact?" asked Cathcart. "She did go to her lawyer and express doubt about what you wanted."

"I've always wanted Rafe to adopt her," Eden insisted. "Why does everyone always question me about this?"

"I can think of at least four things you have done that could be interpreted as you controlling Rafe's relationship with Bronte and, from her perspective, could look threatening to the adoption," Cathcart revealed. Eden looked up at him with disbelief, and he continued. "When you were with Jake, you said you kept Bronte from her and did things like failing to file the paperwork for the adoption. You didn't let her take Bronte to New York. Several times, when you were upset with Rafe, you admit you took Bronte out of Rafe's arms. You didn't tell her you were pregnant, so she had to find out by accident you were going to have Bronte. You really don't think you're in control of anything?"

"I didn't do those things to control her," insisted Eden.

"But you were in control," said Cathcart. "You were punishing Rafe with the power you have as the birth mother."

"I wasn't punishing her," Eden sobbed. "It's wasn't what I was doing. I..." she hesitated. "I had good reasons."

"Eden," Cathcart asserted. "There is never a good reason to use Bronte to hurt Rafe. Whether you can see it or not, it's exactly what you were doing." He let her think for a while before he asked another question. "Who decided you would be the birth mother?'

Eden looked up, not understanding why he was asking that question. "We decided together," she said nodding at the memory. "We decided I would do it. I wanted to do it."

"Rafe didn't want to be the birth mother?" pressed Cathcart.

"No, she would have." She hung her head slightly. "It was just, with her stressful career, her need to travel a lot for work, and the fact she made more money, it was better if I did it. I was ready, ready for a family, and so was she. I really wanted to have the baby."

"So she gave up the control and power of being the birth mother to you," Cathcart stated. "She trusted you, and now she is feeling betrayed because she believes you're in love with Jake. She believes you may go with him and take Bronte with you, which would be in your power as the birth mother since the adoption hasn't been finalized."

"It must be what she thinks," Eden said distressed. "Oh, my god," Eden whispered. "The letter she wrote in Canada to her mother and what Greer said makes sense. She thinks I'm taking her life away—she means Bronte. It's why she thinks I would want her to die," she choked, "to get her out of the way!" She burst into tears. "I don't want her to think that way! I'm not taking Bronte away!" Eden cried inconsolably. "I don't want her to die!"

Cathcart waited for Eden to calm herself again, and when she looked up at him, he knew she was ready. "I want you to think about how your actions might look to Rafe. Then you should talk to her and reassure her about Bronte. I think it will be important if you are to rebuild trust and be good co-parents."

"I've been trying to talk to her," Eden sniffed, "but it's not easy."

"Talk to her just like you've talked to me," he advised.

"I'll try, but it's not the same. At least, I know when I'll see her again." She looked up and tried to smile. "I'm supposed to see her Friday."

46

STEPPING OUT THE back door of his house, Flynn Ogden made his way over to Rafe Salvaggio's looking forward to spending time with her again. He went through the back gate and up to the patio door where he saw Rafe inside typing on her computer. He knocked on the glass door and saw her look up. She smiled at him and then made her way over to the door and slid it open.

"Hi," she said warmly. "Ready for another exciting night of furniture restoration and intrigue?" she teased. "I thought you'd be bored with all this by now."

"No, I really like it," Flynn assured her. "I like learning all about restoring stuff and thinking about what you told me about war and applying it to the scenarios you make up. So, what are we doing tonight?"

Rafe lead him toward the garage. "Do you want a beer?" she asked.

"Sure. I'll get them," Flynn said and went back to the kitchen, getting out two beers from the fridge, and then took them out to the garage.

Rafe took the bottle of beer Flynn brought her. "Thanks," she said and took a swig. She picked up one of the small wooden pieces of the chair and a piece of paper. "Take a look at this," she said and showed him her drawing. "Based on the rest of the pieces, and some research I did, I think this is very close to the original and should attach here," she said as held the drawing to the piece she held up.

"Wow," said Flynn impressed with the extremely detailed drawing with measurements for all the dimensions included. "So how do we get the piece? Do you have to send out for it?

Rafe laughed and shook her head. "No," she said and picked up a piece of mahogany, "I found this piece of antique mahogany. It matches very closely to what we have so we can carve the missing piece from it."

"Carve it?" asked Flynn nervously. "I don't think I can help with carving."

"It's okay." Rafe chuckled. "I have something else for you to do." She went to a shelf on the other side of her workbench and pulled out some small brushes, rags, gloves and a bottle of chemicals. "Okay, I tested the finish, and it was shellacked," she said as she ran her hand over the wood. "Since the whole thing is in such bad shape I think the best thing to do is strip off all of the finish and, later, put on a modern polyurethane finish to help keep the piece protected. This is a soy based stripper," she said as she handed him the bottle. "It is less caustic to the wood. So, if you use this on the main piece tonight, maybe I can get the rest later. Don't put too much on at a time because the shellac may strip off fast, and you need to get it off once it loosens so you don't harm the wood. Use the small brushes and cotton swabs to get into all the grooves of the filigree."

Flynn looked at the chaise and remembered all the hours he had spent just cleaning the piece up and cleaning the filigree with cotton swabs until Rafe was happy with everything. *At least I don't have to carve a piece,* he thought. "Okay, do you think this'll go faster than the cleaning did?"

"Absolutely." Rafe laughed. "I had you do it because I thought we might be able to save the finish, and I was worried about what would happen to the wood when we got all the dirt off. Mahogany is a solid wood, but it's susceptible to humidity, so I wanted to be careful of any cracks in the finish or severe damage since the piece is in such rough shape. We're lucky most of the damage is just small chips and can be repaired with mahogany filler. It's also why I kept making sure you used just a little water at a time."

Relieved it wouldn't take forever this time, Flynn nodded and put on the gloves. "Okay, great. So, what are we going to talk about while we work?"

"Tonight we're learning about infiltration, control, and manipulation," said Rafe as she got out her wood carving tools and put on her magnifying visor. She sat down and got out the other materials she needed to transfer the design to the wood.

Flynn smiled at the sight of Rafe in her visor and sat down on the floor in front of the chaise to start the stripping process. "So what's the scenario?"

"We're back on the island tonight," said Rafe as she clamped down her piece of wood and began to transfer her design to it. "It's you and one other person, the enemy, on the island. You must get close to the enemy without the enemy realizing what you're doing. He has to think he's in control. If he realizes you're controlling him, you're dead because he has a secret poison he'll use on you. You've found out about the poison and need to eliminate it to survive."

"Okay, what are my assets?" Flynn said and took a sip of his beer then decided to start with the filigree.

"You have yourself, of course, and some fish you caught with a homemade spear, and the spear too. The enemy has the poison and a knife."

"And it has to look like he is in charge?" Flynn mused and looked up to see Rafe nod. "I guess I could give him the fish and offer to catch more. Then maybe they will depend on me for the fish."

"You could..." Rafe paused to look at her drawing and then began to use her scribing tool across the wood making her basic outline. "But the key here is making it look like the enemy's in charge. Not dependent on you."

Flynn thought about the situation and couldn't come up with any ideas. "So what do I do?"

"Well," Rafe said as she considered the scenario, "you could tempt the enemy with the fish but tell him you don't know how to cook them. You let him take over the cooking. Then you act like you couldn't have survived without him and make him feel important and in charge. Let him tell you what to do, pretend to be weak. He may become over confident and then you can get close."

"So build his confidence?" said Flynn, liking the idea.

"Yes, but not too much, or it could backfire," mused Rafe as she tapped her chisel gently then sat it down and took a measurement. "Make him think he has an advantage he really doesn't have. For example, if he can lift a huge piece of driftwood and you can too, just tell him you can't, and he's stronger."

"Sounds like something I can do," Flynn said confidently as he began checking to see if the stripper was working.

"You can also do this technique where you refuse the first thing he offers no matter what it is, but always accept the second. It'll become a pattern he'll fall into with you, and when he finally sees the pattern, he'll start using it and begin offering you what he really wants for himself first, believing you'll refuse it. Then you can start to see the real intent of the enemy."

Flynn took another sip of his beer running the technique through his mind. "How does that control them?"

"It puts you in control because you can choose when to change your pattern to get what you want," explained Rafe.

"Cool, I can see it now," said Flynn impressed.

"Another way is to pretend you want something," Rafe paused to compare her work to her drawing again, "or don't want something, to mislead him into getting what you really want."

"How?" asked Flynn as he began cleaning off the stripper.

"Well, let's say you find some canned food washed up on the beach," Rafe pondered. "A can of beans and a can of peaches. Which do you want?"

"The peaches," said Flynn quickly.

"Really?" asked Rafe in surprise as she got out a wood carving knife for some finer detail. "Okay, but the beans will last longer in your system and provide strength while the peaches will taste good but only give you a quick sugar rush, and you'll be hungry again in a short amount of time."

"Oh, well, the beans then," Flynn changed his mind.

Rafe smiled, and her gray-blue eyes twinkled under her magnifying visor as she looked around at him. "Good, because I really wanted the peaches."

"But I thought..." Flynn frowned, "you said..." He shook his head.

"Flynn," Rafe laughed, "it's one can of food. It doesn't really matter what it is. I just want what tastes good."

"So I made the final decision you wanted me to make?" Flynn asked finally understanding what had happened.

"Exactly," Rafe smiled as she turned back to her work and took some measurements with a caliper, "and you thought it was your decision. It's manipulation. It can be a very powerful tool."

"I know," said Flynn thoughtfully. "I know someone who is very good at it."

"Well, if you know he's good at it, you can build a defense for it and possibly twist it back on him," said Rafe absently, concentrating on where she was putting her hook knife. "You just have to watch and see what lies he can't undo and the corners he's backed himself into."

"If I get the chance, I'll try," said Flynn. He watched Rafe looking through her magnifying visor and decided to try to get some information for Eden. "Abby said you're going out Friday night with Eden. Are you?"

Rafe looked at Flynn and frowned. "More like I'm going to The Kiki Bistro, and if Eden is there, we're in the same place."

"Oh, she made it sound like you two were..." Flynn let his words end, making certain he got the stripper out of the filigree with cotton swabs from the supply cabinet.

"Abby has a wonderful imagination," Rafe scoffed, "and she should keep it on her blog and out of my life."

Flynn wiped off more of the soy-based stripper and looked at Rafe hesitantly. "Weren't you guys really in love once?"

Rafe sat up and pushed her visor up then took a drink and looked at Flynn sadly. "Flynn, what do you know about love?"

Flynn kept his head down as he worked. "Not much really."

Rafe rubbed the back of her neck and sighed. "Eden knows I love her but she..." Rafe paused not wanting to say Eden loved Jake again because it hurt just thinking about it. "She isn't sure how she feels," she said instead, but it didn't feel right. "Or who she's in love with." She shook her head in weariness. "She wants something else—a man. So love can be very one sided sometimes. One-sided love really hurts," she said sadly.

"She seems nice," said Flynn wanting Rafe to see Eden as the good person she was. "I've been hanging out with her and Bronte sometimes."

Rafe frowned and worried he might get manipulated into something by Jake and Eden. "Be careful over there," she said as she took another measurement.

"I will," Flynn assured her thinking she was talking about the wood stripping. "She's worried a lot. Eden, I mean."

"Abby and Julia told me she was back on Xanax." Rafe frowned. "She was never very good in stressful situations." She wondered what exactly her stress was about but decided Eden's issues were Jake's problem now—if Eden was even really stressed. She could be lying to them too.

"I think she worries about you and her," Flynn said cautiously.

Rafe shook her head in doubt. "I'm sure she's worried about other things. There doesn't seem to me like there is much for her to worry about when it comes to her and me."

"What do you mean?" asked Flynn concerned.

"Flynn," Rafe sighed, "right now, there is no Rafe and Eden." *Because it's just the way Eden wants us*, thought Rafe as she looked at the broken chaise, *smashed into a million bits*.

"Oh," said Flynn as he shifted uneasily and wiped off more chemical.

Rafe turned back to her work and then dismissed the subject and moved on with the lesson. "Now let's talk about infiltration."

47

THE KIKI BISTRO was packed for the Friday night live music event with Corday. Everyone was excited to see the dynamic singer with her red glitter bikini top, her long locks, and sexy voice. Abby Van Falkov was already at a party table listening to the pre-show music. She was watching the people on the dance floor with Julia, Erica, Stacey, and Flynn. The mixed crowd was enjoying the pre-show DJ, and the waitresses and bartenders were making sure everyone had drinks and were having a good time.

Julia looked over the crowd hoping to spot Rafe. "Where's Rafe?" she asked with impatience. "I hope she wears something really sexy. I've thought of some great challenges for her."

"Julia, your dares aren't why she's coming," Abby said, annoyed at Julia for still making challenges for Rafe.

"I know I could make a fortune betting on her," said Julia with a smile. Her deep blue eyes sparkled knowing she was pushing Abby's buttons. "Why are you so against it?" she asked and looked curiously at Abby. "Do you want part of the winnings? You thought she looked hot too last weekend."

"I don't want any part of pimping her out," insisted Abby. "She'll be here to spend time with Eden."

"Speaking of Eden, there she is," announced Erica as she pointed across the bar.

"She's such a basket case," groaned Stacey. "Why is Rafe bothering?"

"Stacey, stop saying those kinds of things ," demanded Flynn not liking that she put down his friend.

"She needs to move on," Stacey pressed.

"Rafe loves her," said Flynn upset at Stacey.

"Hey, Eden!" Abby waved.

"Hi," replied Eden as she smiled and sat at the table. "Is Rafe here yet?"

"No, I was just looking for her." Julia smiled tolerantly then sipped her drink.

"She'll be here, she promised," said Abby

Stacey leaned forward, put her elbows on the table and her chin in her hands, and looked at Eden. "So why do you want to hang out with her? Do you just want to hurt her more?"

Abby shoved her so her arms came off the table. "Stacey, shut up!"

"Stacey, what's wrong with you?" Flynn demanded outraged.

"No, it's okay," said Eden as she looked anxiously at Stacey, knowing they all probably thought badly of her. "No, I don't want to hurt her."

"They have to talk, Stacey. They have to figure out everything," Abby said chidingly.

"You mean Eden has to figure out things at Rafe's expense." Stacey sneered.

Eden shifted uncomfortably, and she began to stand. "I think I should go."

Abby reached out for Eden making her stay. "Eden, she doesn't know what she's talking about. Stay."

"Look. There's Rafe. Just wait," said Julia as she frowned at Stacey.

Rafe walked up to the table with a disarming smile. "Hello, everyone." She looked at the troubled faces before her. "What's going on?"

Eden sat back down nervously. "Nothing. I'm glad you made it."

"I did promise." Rafe winked. "I think I'll go get a drink. Can I get one for you, Eden?"

"Thanks, I'll have a—"

"I know what you like," Rafe cut her off, smiled, and then walked to the bar.

Julia watched Rafe walk away. "How disappointing she's not showing all her skin tonight, but she does look good as her normal all put-together self." She grabbed Abby's arm suddenly. "Abby, look!" she said excitedly.

"It's starting out good," Abby was saying to Eden then looked up at Julia's outburst. "Oh, no." She groaned as she saw Rafe being approached by several women who gave her cards and others who had their phones out to hopefully get her number and take selfies with her. Apparently, her antics at the beach had gotten around even without being on her blog.

"Eden, do you want me to give her a challenge to keep things interesting?" asked Julia hopefully. "I think you might enjoy seeing her in action. I'm sure she can get a lot more numbers."

"Not tonight," said Eden weakly.

"How disappointing." Julia drooped with disappointment.

Rafe put a Long Island Tea in front of Eden and sat next to her. "Just like you like it. Cheers." She smiled and took a drink of her Whisky Sour then threw the numbers she had collected on the table. "Here you go, Julia. Have fun."

Julia picked up the cards and looked through them. "Rafe, did you forget my request about the clothes?"

"No, I didn't forget," Rafe said wryly. "Saturday was a one-time thing, to be repeated only on special occasions."

"Too bad." Julia sighed.

"Yeah, really, too bad," Abby agreed sarcastically and rolled her eyes at Julia.

Erica jumped up from her seat. "I'm going to dance. I like this song. Who's coming with me?"

"Let's all go. Rafe?" Abby looked at her encouragingly.

Eden smiled at Rafe. "Do you want to dance?"

Rafe looked at the dance floor. "No, not to this song," she said. "Maybe the next one."

Eden wasn't sure what to do. "Oh, okay," she said with uncertainty. "I'll stay here too."

"See you two later," Abby said as she walked away with the others.

"How are things at work?" Eden asked tentatively.

Rafe looked intently into Eden's eyes. "Let's not talk about work."

Rafe's eyes held Eden. She had not truly looked into them for a long time, and they still had the power to make her feel weak. "Okay," Eden said softly. "What do you want to talk about?"

"Anything else you want," Rafe said casually.

48

JUST OFF THE dance floor, Abby Van Falkov, Flynn Ogden, and Erica Sunley were standing together resting after dancing and watching Rafe and Eden. They were hoping the two women would start to get along and work things out one way or the other.

Abby was beside herself with anger at Stacey. "What the hell is wrong with Stacey?"

"I don't know," said Flynn upset at Stacey's antics too. "She's always doing those things lately and not thinking. I think she's been reading a lot of weird books for a new project, and I think they're affecting her brain."

"Are you sure she's not being affected by all the glue she uses?" Erica laughed.

"We have to keep her away from them," fumed Abby. "She's going to mess things up."

"I'll try to keep her away," Flynn promised.

"Look at how Rafe is looking at Eden," said Abby disturbed. "I don't know if I like the look she's giving her," she added with worry. "I hope she's not planning to do what Julia suggested."

"What?" Flynn asked.

"To seduce her," Abby said vexed.

"I don't think she would," Flynn reasoned. "Yesterday, she told me there was no Rafe and Eden."

"She what?" Abby screeched. "Why would she say that?"

"She said it was one-sided love, but I don't think it's true." Flynn sighed. "I think Eden wants her. She just has to accept it."

Abby looked back at Rafe and Eden. "Oh, no," she groaned. "What's going on now? Who are those people?"

49

WITH A HALF-SMILE, as she sipped her drink, Rafe Salvaggio was looking at Eden Kingsley intently and listening to her try to make small talk. Distracted during Eden's silence, Rafe looked across the room and saw a group of young women walking toward the table. She smiled bigger and leaned forward as she realized she knew one of them from the Conservatory. The brown-eyed girl and her friends invited themselves over and stood in front of the table.

"Dean Salvaggio?" she said as she reached out to shake Rafe's hand. "It is!" she exclaimed. "How are you? You remember me, right?"

Rafe smiled and pointed at her. "Of course, I remember you, Carolyn."

Carolyn gestured to her friends. "This is Emily and Janell."

Rafe shook their hands. "Nice to meet you," she said warmly.

Carolyn sat down, and the others joined her at the table. "I just wanted to thank you for letting me shadow you for two weeks for my assignment."

Eden looked warily at the girls who were clearly enthralled with Rafe. "Assignment?"

"I'm sorry," said Rafe. "Carolyn, this is Eden Kingsley," she introduced them. "Eden, this is Carolyn, a student at the Conservatory."

"Hi," beamed Carolyn. "I had to develop a web page for an instructor or staff member, and I was lucky enough to get Dean Salvaggio."

"Oh, it sounds like an interesting assignment." Eden smiled politely.

"Dean Salvaggio made it very interesting," Carolyn gushed. "Everyone loves it." She smiled thankfully at Rafe. "Mine gets the most hits, by the way."

"Fantastic," Rafe praised her. "I hope you got a good grade."

"She did," Emily interjected. "I wish I would have got someone as nice as you. No one else would let us take video.

The video where you're talking about how art enriches life and all is the most viewed clip."

"Really?" Rafe laughed flattered. She thought it was important to let the students use all the tools available so they could do their best possible work. She didn't understand why some teachers limited them all the time.

"The other vids you did are good too," added Janell. "But that one," she looked up searching for words, "it's like, almost hypnotizing."

"Hypnotizing?" asked Rafe as she looked at Eden, and then raised her eyebrows. "I guess it's a compliment."

"It really is," insisted Carolyn. "This is kind of embarrassing to tell a Dean, but I think you have as many guys as girls on campus in love with you right now. You're just amazing!"

Rafe smiled and took a sip of her drink. Then she thought, because of all the compliments, Eden might be feeling left out. "I don't know about amazing," Rafe said modestly. "If you want to meet someone amazing, you should talk to Ms. Kingsley. She works for *Ascesis Studios* now. She's been the catalyst for some really incredible things over the years."

Emily looked at Eden impressed. "Wow, really?"

"Yes, really," Rafe assured her. "She gets to choose what gets made into a film. You're all graphic designers?" she asked.

"Janell is," said Carolyn, "but Emily and I are in film and media arts."

"Even better," said Rafe approvingly. "Eden pretty much makes all the decisions for what gets made into film. Tell them what you do, Eden."

Eden looked at Rafe then at the students looking at her with anticipation. "Basically," she said hesitantly, "I'm just a script development executive."

Rafe looked at Eden, shook her head, and laughed. "Excuse me?" she said and looked at the girls. "She's their best script development executive. She works alongside producers and reads books and scripts and helps decide what will be perused for possible production. She has pitched a lot of great scripts and ideas. Once a project is chosen, she does everything from helping buy the rights to doing the budgeting. She knows a lot of writers, producers, directors, and others in the industry." She looked at Eden then back at the girls. "She also knows a graphic designer who works just outside of L. A."

"Really?" asked Emily excited. "So, Ms. Kingsley, can I have your card? Does your company do internships?"

"Yeah," Janell joined in, "and who's the graphic designer. Maybe her company does internships."

"I don't have any cards with me right now, sorry," Eden told them politely. "But we do have an internship program at the studio." She hesitated and looked at Rafe. "I don't really ever see that graphic designer anymore."

Rafe winked at Janell. "She broke up with him." She looked at Emily. "I'll get some of Ms. Kingsley's cards, and you can stop by my office and pick them up. She'll be a great contact for you when you're ready for an internship or after graduation."

"Oh, my god. You two are so cool!" Carolyn smiled. She looked around and grimaced with embarrassment. "Oh, I'm sorry. Are you guys on a date. We're so rude!"

Rafe laughed. "You're fine."

"It's okay." Eden smiled kindly.

Emily rolled her eyes at her friend. "Carolyn just gets so excited sometimes."

"Seeing you here just blew her mind," said Janell. "And we really wanted an excuse to meet you."

"Well, my office is always open," said Rafe.

"Ms. Kingsley, you're so lucky," said Carolyn enviously. "You have a cool job and get to go out with a really hot Dean."

"You can call me Eden," she said amused at their excitement.

"Dean Salvaggio's lucky too," added Janell. "Eden, you're beautiful. I haven't seen you around campus. Have you been to anything at the CCAD?"

Eden smiled at the compliment. "Not really." The only time she had been on campus was when Rafe was being held hostage, and it was not a pleasant day to remember.

"Maybe you can come and give a lecture on the film industry," suggested Emily.

"I'll think about it," said Eden congenially.

Rafe looked at Eden and smiled encouragingly. "You should do it."

"So, how long have you guys been dating?" asked Carolyn impetuously.

"Oh, we're not dating," answered Rafe. "Eden is my ex. We're just hanging out with some friends. They're all out on the dance floor right now."

"So, you're both single? Wow," blurted Emily. "Well, if you want to pick anyone up, you should sit at different tables. I mean it's totally intimidating to come up to a table with two hot women. It's too hard to decide which one to ask out."

"We're not really here to pick anyone up tonight," said Eden stiffly.

"So you're into men?" Janell inquired curiously. "The graphic designer was a guy? I can't believe some guy could steal you away from Dean Salvaggio."

"Oh, he didn't steal her away," confided Rafe with a tight smile. "She wanted to go." Eden looked nervously at Rafe, unsure why she was allowing this conversation to happen.

Emily looked at Rafe then at Eden. "Wow! Why?" she exclaimed.

"Well," Rafe explained pragmatically, "I made her very unhappy, and people just need a change sometimes when they're unhappy. And sometimes, what goes around comes around because I did steal her away from a man. What was his name, Eden?"

Eden looked into Rafe's inquiring eyes uneasily. "Jeffery," she said softly.

"Right," Rafe said as she snapped her fingers. "So there you have it."

Carolyn was enthralled. "You totally stole her from a man? I can see it."

Rafe smiled impishly. "Carolyn, stealing is wrong. But, then again, all is fair in love and war." She held up her drink in salute and took a drink.

Eden looked at Rafe feeling anxious and wanting to change the subject or leave. "The song changed. Do you want to dance now?"

Rafe looked at her with one raised eyebrow. "If you want to," she said. "Take my hand." Eden took her hand, and Rafe looked at the girls at the table. "You girls have fun. Maybe we'll see you later."

They walked onto the dance floor, and Rafe took Eden's hand in hers and wrapped her other around her waist while Eden put her other hand on Rafe's shoulder. They moved to the slow rhythm of the music. "They think you're beautiful," Rafe whispered into Eden's ear.

"But they're in love with you," Eden pointed out and nervously laughed as she leaned close and kissed Rafe's neck.

Rafe took a deep breath full of Eden's smell and closed her eyes to the pain in her heart. Eden's false kiss cut through her like a knife.

She whispered in her ear, "Who do you love?"

Eden stiffened in Rafe's arms at the unexpected question and looked up into Rafe's searching eyes. Her mind reeled in torment because of all the conflicting feelings she had, and she was unable to answer the question.

Rafe sensed no answer was coming, and she whispered again in her ear sadly. "Eden, I'm sorry. I shouldn't have asked." She held her for a moment longer, and pain shot through her head at the thought of what Eden was doing. "I thought I could do this, but I can't tonight." She lifted her head away from Eden's scent. "It hurts too much," she said under her breath without thinking. She broke away and turned from Eden as she pressed her hand to her temple. "I can't live like this much longer," she said hoarsely to herself and walked off the dance floor and out of the club.

Eden had heard what Rafe mumbled, and her confessions shook her. Tormented by her own inability to answer Rafe's question, she watched as Rafe walked away.

"Rafe," she called after her, too late.

50

FURIOUS WITH HERSELF, Rafe Salvaggio drove straight home. She had been doing so well, but then she let herself just get too close again. She thought she could go in and get Eden to slip up and say something, anything that might help expose the game she was playing. Instead, she failed to do anything remotely constructive and caused herself pain instead.

When she got home, she took something for her headache and changed into something more comfortable. She grabbed her stack of books and a six-pack of beer and took them onto the front porch to think and to study.

She finished her second beer, put the bottle back in the carton, and threw her book down as Jude passed by and saw her.

"Rafe?" said Jude as she walked up to her. "I thought you were going out tonight."

Rafe twisted off the cap of another beer. "I was out. I'm back in now."

"Early night?" asked Jude. "What happened with Eden?"

Rafe sighed and took a drink. "I guess I'm just not as good at intrigue as I thought I could be." She sighed and looked at

Jude sadly, as she pushed her carton of beers forward. "Want a beer?"

"Sure," said Jude as she let Rafe's words roll off her. Jude knew Rafe didn't mean for Jude to understand anyway. She pulled a beer out, sat down next to her, and twisted off the cap.

They sat in silence and drank.

51

RAFE SALVAGGIO'S HEAD throbbed. She felt like something heavy was pressing on her chest, and there was a constant banging in her ears. She fought her way up from the darkness of her dream. She opened her eyes and groaned as the banging got louder. She realized someone was banging on her front door.

Slowly, she got up to prevent more pain in her head. She put on her robe and stumbled to the door where she could hear Abby outside screaming.

"Rafe! Rafe! Wake up, Rafe! Open the door! Damn it, Rafe! Wake up!"

Rafe unlatched the door and pulled it open, thinking in her haze-filled mind, something might be wrong. "What's going on?"

"What's going on?" shrieked Abby. "Are you kidding me? What the hell are you doing?"

Rafe involuntarily put her hand to her head, and then her chest, and closed her eyes in pain. "What are you talking about, Abby?" she said groggily.

"Eden, what else?" she said agitated. "Why did you walk out last night? Eden freaked, and Flynn had to take her home! You promised you'd try!"

"I can't do it!" Rafe said in pain and turned her back on Abby. She went to the living room and flopped down on the couch. She saw Abby had followed her inside and sat next to her. "Abby, I can't give the rest of what is left of my heart to someone who doesn't even want it, someone who just wants to be close to me to hurt me. I did try, and I can't do it," she said firmly as she tried to breathe through her pain.

"Eden doesn't want to hurt you," Abby insisted. "She wants to try again with you."

"I think I know a little more about the subject than you do!" Rafe snapped, becoming angry at her pushing.

"I don't understand," said Abby softly. "You promised." She stood up and began pacing to calm herself. "Eden asked if I would get Bronte and bring her over today for her art lesson. What exactly did you say to her bad enough to make her want to stay away again?"

"I told her I couldn't do it," said Rafe remorsefully and looked away. "Maybe she would just be happier with someone else." She stood up shakily and took Abby by the shoulders. "Tell her she should keep Bronte at home today." She turned and walked into her room and closed the door.

"Shit!" said Abby bewildered by the pain she saw in Rafe's eyes. "What the hell is going on?"

52

AFTER GETTING BRONTE cleaned up from breakfast, and into her clothes for the day, Eden Kingsley released her daughter so she could play with her toys. She then walked back into the kitchen and sat down. She looked up gratefully at Flynn who was helping clean up the breakfast dishes. They had been in the middle of their conversation about what had happened last night when Bronte started doing her 'I want down, so I'll just go crazy to get my way' act and had to be settled and cleaned up. Eden had told Flynn everything Rafe said at the table with the students and out on the dance floor.

Flynn turned to Eden as she sat down. "She asked you who you loved, and you just stood there?" Flynn asked in disbelief. "Eden, you need to tell her Jake lied to her and everything. You need to figure out your feelings for her soon."

"I'm trying," Eden said sadly. "Every time we get together, something happens, and she leaves, or I leave." She hung her head in despair. "We never actually talk. And last night, we were ambushed by a bunch of her students. Flynn, she says she still hurts," she said as she looked at him sadly. "I wish I knew everything Jake said to her. I wish I could answer her and know for sure I'm telling her the truth." She turned at hearing a knock on the door. She took a deep breath and got up to answer it. "Hey, Abby. You're here early. I don't have Bronte packed up yet."

"I know," said Abby fretfully. "I talked to Rafe earlier this morning. She said you should keep Bronte home today."

"Did she say why?" Eden asked upset and held onto her arms in expectation of pain.

"She said some things," Abby stopped herself and shook her head. "But I think they'll just upset you more. I think she was just upset when she said them."

"Abby, tell me what she said. I have to know," Eden begged. "It's important. Please, tell me everything."

Abby watched as Eden took one of her pills and looked at Flynn with trepidation. She sat down at the table, looked up at Eden, and took a breath. "She said she can't give the rest of what's left of her heart to someone who doesn't even want it. Someone who just wants to be close to her to hurt her. I don't know what she means, Eden. Why does she think you want to hurt her?"

Eden looked at Flynn then back at Abby in confusion. "She thinks that? I—" she stopped and closed her eyes. "I don't know what she means."

"Well, she's not telling me why. I tried," Abby insisted. "Something is fucked up. She says you know everything already, and you're telling me you don't know. She says maybe you'd be happier with someone else." Abby could feel she was losing it and didn't know if she could go easy on Eden anymore. "Eden, I've helped you all I can. You told me you don't want to be Salvaggio's Paradise anymore—you want to be just Eden. Well, it looks like you got it. I guess Rafe has just done so many terrible things you can't decide one way or the other if you love her. Maybe Stacey was right about you. You really are trying to figure yourself out at Rafe's expense," she said with venom.

"Abby, I'm not—" Eden started her denial.

Abby cut her off angrily. "Do you even really know what it means when people call you Salvaggio's Paradise? You think it means you're no longer Eden or something? It doesn't. It means we could see your hearts were one, and you loved each other. It's not about ownership. It's about you loving her and her loving you."

Abby knew she was handling things badly, but she just couldn't stop herself from speaking her mind. "You once said you wanted Rafe to be your forever love. She can still be that. Don't you know you're just as responsible for creating the Salvaggio's Paradise title as Rafe was? You posed for that portrait! We all were there at the unveiling party when the whole paradise thing started, and we could see the connection between you two. The name of the painting is *Il Paradiso Terrestre, l'Eden*, for fuck sake! I looked it up. She's calling you paradise on earth!

Eden tried to speak, but Abby cut her off again and continued. "I know things are screwed up, but there's this thing called love and something called forgiveness you could both give to each other to start again. She really loved you. But now I guess she's right, and everything really is shattered! Why do you want to hurt her? I can't even look at you right now!" She bolted out of her chair and stormed out the door without looking back.

Eden looked over at Flynn, who was just as stunned into silence as she was, and she felt the anxiety building inside her.

"Flynn," she finally uttered miserably, "what am I going to do?"

53

FIRST THING MONDAY morning, Eden Kingsley called for an emergency meeting with Dr. Cathcart. She couldn't wait until after work, so she had arrived at his office in a high state of anxiety. Every time she thought about Rafe and Friday night, she lost her fight to control the panic inside over her inability to answer Rafe's question.

Cathcart sat Eden down and took her through some breathing exercises to calm her. When she was finally ready, he looked at her calmly and determined they could begin the session.

"Eden, now that you're calm, can you tell me what happened to upset you?" he asked softly.

Eden couldn't stop her tears and wiped them away with her tissue. "I've screwed everything up," she said speaking quickly to get the words out before she lost it again. "I should have told her everything, and now it's too late. She's done with me. I've lost any chance to figure things out."

"Eden, slow down," said Cathcart. "Start from the beginning."

"She promised to spend time with me." Eden took a breath. "We talked about it last session," she reminded him. "So we met at The Kiki Bistro. Everything was going fine. We were talking with some of her students who were there." She looked up at him with red-rimmed eyes. "She kept handing me opportunities to deny I still loved Jake, but I didn't do it. Then the song changed, and I asked her to dance. Then when we were dancing," she sobbed, "she asked me who I loved and… and I couldn't answer her! Then she said she couldn't do it. She said she hurt." She wiped her tears again. "Then she just left, and now I have no idea what to do."

Cathcart took a moment to take everything in Eden had spilled out so rapidly. "You've never told me why Rafe suddenly stopped talking to you," said Cathcart. "Did something happen between you?"

"No," said Eden as she shook her head. "I don't know why. She got sick, and she just stopped talking to me. Like I told you, she wouldn't let me touch her or anything. Then I thought she was going to die at the Conservatory, and suddenly, Greer was back. I thought Rafe was going to leave with her. It was Greer who told me Rafe and Jake had been talking with each other." She looked up at Cathcart debating on whether or not to tell him what happened with Greer and decided not to tell him. "I don't know why they were talking, but apparently, it was then when Jake told her Bronte and I would be better off with him."

Cathcart thought about the situation for a moment. "Eden, how did you feel after you found out Rafe was with Lauren?"

Eden was confused and didn't want to think about that painful day. "What does that have to do with anything?"

"Rafe is telling you she still hurts," Cathcart answered. "It's amazing she said it out loud to you since you say she has always bottled up her feelings. Your situations parallel each other. Don't you think it's possible she's feeling the same way you felt?"

Eden shook her head not seeing where he was going. "Our situations aren't the same."

"Not in your mind because you know the truth," said Cathcart. "You were spending time together, and in Rafe's mind, you were falling in love again. You said everything changed right after she got sick. I think Jake somehow convinced her you were in love with him, and it broke her heart. Whatever he said to her manifested itself into a physical illness, a kind of lovesickness."

"Lovesickness?" repeated Eden in dismay.

"I think so." He nodded thoughtfully. "Sometimes, people feel their emotions on such a high level," Cathcart explained, "the only way they can cope is through physical illness. Similar to how your anxiety causes you pain. The way you describe Rafe, it seems she always tries to keep her emotions in control, but this time, her body took over. Is it so hard for you to believe she can possibly feel the same deep emotions you feel?"

"No, I just..." Eden wiped another tear, "I just never thought." She closed her eyes to calm herself. "I guess our situations are the same for her."

"It's important you tell her the truth, Eden, and the sooner, the better," advised Cathcart.

"So, she may have been sick because of what Jake said to her?" Eden asked trying to clarify what he was saying.

"I believe she was," nodded Cathcart. "The way you described it, and her reactions to you, and now, knowing the time frame when she and Jake were talking, I'm fairly certain it's what made her sick. It's almost a classic case."

234

Eden dropped her head into her hands in anguish. "Oh, my god." She pushed her hair back from her face. "Abby said Rafe told her she thinks I'd be happier with someone else. I know she's talking about Jake. And she told her she didn't want to give me what was left of her heart because I didn't really want it, and I only wanted to hurt her. I don't want to hurt her," she cried as she tried to stop shaking.

"Would you be happier with Jake?"

Eden snapped her head up. "No!"

"Well, the reason I'm asking is because you're still struggling with your feelings for men, and if they include Jake, then Rafe is right to be cautious with her feelings toward you."

"I don't have feelings for Jake!" said Eden angrily.

"Then you need to be clear to both of them how you feel," said Cathcart. "It looks like Jake still has feelings for you, and if he can convince her you're still in love with him, then maybe we should look at why."

"But I don't love him!" Eden insisted angrily. "I don't love him, and I'm never going back to him. I've told him, he knows!"

"Good," said Cathcart softly and waited for Eden to calm. "But the person you keep saying you don't want to hurt still doesn't know. This is why you have to communicate with her," said Cathcart firmly. "Do anything. Write her a letter or email, leave her a message if you can't do it in person, anything," suggested Cathcart.

"I'm doing my best," said Eden softly as she got a new tissue and wiped her eyes and face. "You just don't understand. She locks herself away and doesn't make it easy. She's very strong willed, and right now, it feels like she's practically shut me out."

"How does it make you feel, to be shut out by Rafe?" asked Cathcart. "I don't remember you ever mentioning her doing it before."

"How does it make me feel?" Eden repeated avoiding the question. "She hasn't shut me out!" she said angrily. "I said it just feels like she has. We were working on things, Bill. She went to Greer. She didn't confront me about Jake, and that's not like her."

"Like I said, your situations parallel each other," said Cathcart, aware she hadn't answered his question. It was most likely because even just the feeling of being shut out made her angry. He also knew she was feeling guilty about her anger. "Rafe went to Greer for some comfort and to feel loved. You went to Jake. Were you working on things, Eden, or was it just Rafe who was supposed to be working on things?"

Eden looked at him shocked. "What do you mean was I working on things? I was going slowly so we could be sure."

"Yes, I know," replied Cathcart and nodded. "And Rafe gave up her so called power and control you're always complaining about, out of respect for your need to go slow. She didn't have to. I'll bet, if she pushed the right buttons, she could have done anything she wanted. You said yourself she's very strong willed. But she didn't. She was showing you there is more for her in this relationship than sex or being in control. But you weren't going slowly for her. You were going slowly for yourself." He paused as Eden shook her head in denial. "Do you think you can trust her again? During the time you were working on things, and you thought things were good, did she prove herself to you?"

"Prove herself?" Eden looked at Cathcart wondering if this was what she had been doing. Was she waiting for Rafe to prove herself somehow? She thought about what had been happening and tried to find the answer, but so many things rushed through her mind it was impossible for her to see anything clearly, and it made her so frustrated and angry with herself. "I don't know," she said shakily.

Cathcart redirected Eden because it looked like she was shutting down. "When you get to spend more time with Rafe now, how do you feel?"

"Now," she said with a short, anxious laugh, "I feel like I need to know where she is and what she's doing. After she got sick, I knew she didn't want me around, but I would go anyway. Sometimes, it terrified me to confront her, but I would find myself going over and doing it anyway. I thought I was going crazy because I just wanted to touch her," she said with a soft laugh more to hide her need to cry than anything. "I haven't done it lately though," she said and closed her eyes for a moment. "Even when I was with Jake, she was like, like this presence always in my mind. Sometimes, I would actually dream about her. She would just be smiling at me or saying things in Italian she used to say, and I knew she only said them for me. I wouldn't see her or hear from her for weeks or months, and I would find myself just... missing her," said Eden as the memories flooded her mind. "We hardly saw her, and it seemed like she was always the topic of conversation."

Cathcart frowned at what he was hearing. "Why was she always the topic of conversation?"

Eden bit her lip. "I think Jake was just always worried I would go back to her. He was worried she would hurt me again, and he was always concerned about the difficult position I was in with her and Bronte."

"Difficult position?" pressed Cathcart.

Yes." Eden nodded. "He knew people who were in situations like ours where the baby's parent was from another country, like Rafe's friend Gabri. He was our donor." She looked up at Cathcart and took a breath. "Jake said his friend's baby was taken away by her ex-husband to his country, and she never saw her baby again. He said the woman was devastated and she's still looking for her son. He was worried Rafe would take Bronte to Italy and thought I should demand she give us Bronte's passport." Eden shook her head sadly because those stories still affected her even though she was sure Jake was telling them to her to get her and Bronte to leave with him. "When we were in Canada, and I couldn't find them..." She stopped not wanting to bring those feelings of fear to the surface again.

"Has Rafe ever mentioned doing anything like taking Bronte away?" he asked with concern. "Did she ever threaten to take Bronte to Italy?"

"No," said Eden as she licked her dry lips. "Before Bronte was born, and I was living with her again, she talked about wanting to show her to Gabri."

"But she didn't talk about moving away?"

"No," she confessed.

"Was there anything else about Rafe you talked about with Jake?" asked Cathcart as he made a note on his notepad.

"We..." she cleared her throat, "we talked about the differences between Rafe and me."

"Which differences?"

"Oh, mostly he talked about how I wasn't the same as Rafe," she said and saw he wanted her to explain further. "We talked about how it was different for me because I had only been in a relationship with a woman for the four and a half years I was with Rafe. But Rafe had been with women practically exclusively all her life," said Eden not understanding why her conversations with Jake mattered. "He thought it meant maybe I wasn't supposed to be with women and was why I felt like I needed to be with a man."

Cathcart looked at Eden thoughtfully. "Why do you think he found it necessary to talk about those things with you?"

"I don't know." Eden sulked. "Maybe he was worried I would leave and go back to Rafe. When I broke it off, he accused me of going back to her. But it wasn't the reason—" She stopped herself realizing she was getting too close to revealing the information she was given about Jake.

"I think those conversations may have added to the already confused feelings you were having about Rafe and your fears," said Cathcart with concern. "Jake, while he may have been concerned for you, was not part of your relationship with Rafe, so he couldn't know your experience. I don't think those conversations with Jake were as helpful to you as you might have thought. It sounds like those conversations were more for his benefit than for yours. Making you doubt your relationship based on the amount of time you were with a woman, well, it belittles the emotions and the love you had for Rafe when you were together, and it suggests your relationship wasn't real," Cathcart explained. "Do you believe your relationship with Rafe and the love you had for each other was real?"

Eden looked at Cathcart in confusion. "Of course, it was real!" she blurted feeling affronted. "It was real."

"Good." Cathcart nodded. He was worried it was possible Eden thought her relationship with Rafe didn't have value and was relieved she felt it was a real relationship. He looked through his notes again. "A while back, we talked about when you told Rafe that Jake made you feel safe. Did you ever get to tell her she used to make you feel safe too?"

"No," she whispered miserably. "I had the chance, and instead, I put it off because I probably thought things were good and didn't want to bring up the past." Slowly she looked up at Cathcart anxiously. "Now I'm out here again without a safety net, and I'm trying to be one for myself, like Rafe. She can walk out the front door and find love," she gave a sad laugh, "but I can't get it right. I just don't know how. I try to find someone, and it turns out like Michael," she shook her head at the memory of that disaster. "Did I tell you, the first time we had sex, he was kissing me, and I was thinking about Rafe's eyes? I felt so guilty he thought he was the reason I was so ready. I couldn't even tell him I had to go home and finish what he couldn't satisfy. Who am I kidding? I wasn't satisfied then either," she said miserably. "Don't get me wrong—I'm sure it would have gotten better if we would have had more time," she assured him. "We only had one weekend before I found out…" She sighed because the doctor already knew Michael was married and had a family.

Cathcart could tell exactly what the tension was bothering Eden, but this was one he thought it would be best if Eden admitted it to herself. "It is important to be compatible in a relationship. If you feel you need to explore your feelings for men, we can discuss what it was that attracted you to Jake and what things made him a better sexual partner than Michael."

"Oh, god," Eden groaned and put her face in her hands. She didn't want to talk about Jake. Especially sex with Jake. She wanted to talk about Rafe. She looked up and saw Cathcart waiting for her to say something. She took a breath. "Sexually, Jake was just a guy who was willing to help me explore my feelings. I thought it turned into something more, but I was wrong."

"Okay," Cathcart nodded, "but there had to be some sort of compatibility for you to think there might be more."

"You mean did he turn me on?" asked Eden and sighed. "Of course, at first," she confessed and turned red. "I'm the one who wanted it, after all."

"So, did you leave the relationship with him because of sexual dissatisfaction?" asked Cathcart.

"No. I mean, not really. There were other things. It's more complicated." Eden stopped herself. She was really messing up this answer. "What I mean is, if not for some other things, I probably could have lived with the sex."

Cathcart looked at her for a moment with a frown and a furrowed brow. "Hmm."

"What?" Eden asked feeling judged. "He was responsive when I wanted it. After a while, he learned what I liked, and he let me go at my own pace when it came to doing things to him." Cathcart continued to look at her expectantly. "Okay," Eden sighed, "it wasn't long after I moved in with him before," she paused, "things stopped being, my body stopped being as responsive to him," she confessed. "I thought it was just because I was on the pill. We bought lube and other things, and it helped. He was very sweet about it. It wasn't all the time, either—it just wasn't like it was at first. Sometimes, odd things would lead to sex and not needing lube like after having a fight with each other or after one of us having a fight with Rafe. We put sex on a schedule because it was something his church counselor suggested we do to be sure we maintained a strong connection. But then, I started getting sick all the time, and it all went out the window."

Cathcart made a note on his pad. "As long as it was satisfying when you were actually having sex," said Cathcart as he wrote. He looked up. "Are you still on the pill?"

"Yes," said Eden.

"Yes, the sex was satisfying or yes, you're still on the pill?" asked Cathcart.

Eden's face flushed red as she looked at Cathcart, and she choked out her answer. "Yes, I'm still on the pill."

"Ah, good," he said and made a note. "So let me review. What I'm taking away is sex was new and exciting with Jake, but within months, you found it didn't satisfy you, yet you were willing to stay were it not for other factors." He looked up at Eden who was still a light shade of red. "My question to you is since you felt you had to leave Rafe to explore your feelings for men, did you also stay in your relationship with her for almost five years under the same conditions?"

Anger boiled up in Eden, and the heat of her anger replaced the heat she had felt for her embarrassment moments before. "No," she said through her teeth.

Cathcart could see Eden was angry but continued. "Good," he said calmly. "So, if you returned to a relationship with her, sexual satisfaction would not be an issue." He made a note in his notepad.

Eden's anger suddenly had nothing to hold it in place. "What?" she said surprised.

"Well, I assume the reason you want to spend time with her is to rekindle a relationship, and it would include sex. It's good to know a portion of the relationship if it becomes romantic, won't be a problem. Unless..." Cathcart trailed off.

"Unless what?" asked Eden apprehensively.

"Well, when you were spending time together, maybe you found you were not as responsive sexually to her anymore, similar to your situation with Jake or others you were with," suggested Cathcart.

Eden looked at him with a frown, angry at the comparison of Rafe with Jake or anyone else. "The sex was never like it was with Rafe, not with Jake or with anyone else," she said hotly. "I can still just look at her, and my body reacts, and I think she knows it. It makes me so mad sometimes I feel like I could scream." She sat back on the couch quietly calming herself for a while, and then she looked up at Cathcart who was writing in his dang notepad. "You're right about her," she said softly and crossed her arms. "When we were working on things, she could have done anything she wanted to me. She would come over and stay late. She would have my body and mind in such a state there were times when I found myself hoping she would just feel me saying yes because I wanted her to push every button she could find. By the time she left, I was ready to beg her to stay, and all she was doing was kissing me and holding me close."

She pushed her hair back and wiped the tears from her face. "Then she would leave, and my mind would start spinning out of control again while my body ached for her touch." She sat silently for a moment then looked up at the doctor. "When I thought about it the next day, it terrified me I had let myself get in that position. It's like I'm caught between two very different worlds, and I don't know which way to turn to find what or who I need or what I even want." She looked back down at her hands and began to cry. "I can barely sleep at night with all these thoughts constantly running through my mind. Even the pills don't seem to be helping like they used to anymore." She wept and felt hopeless.

Cathcart made a note then looked up again, waiting for Eden to regain control of herself so she could listen. "There's something else I want you to think about. Almost since you started coming into the office, you always start out with a list of complaints about Rafe. Most of your sessions are spent talking about her." He paused for a moment. "Why are you so angry with her?"

"I'm not angry. She's just..." Eden fought for words, "she just." She looked at Cathcart with uncertainty. "I don't know why."

"Why do you think you need to talk about her rather than work on your own feelings?" Cathcart asked hoping it would help her think her feelings through.

"I don't know," admitted Eden. "I just can't stop thinking about her and all the things she does."

"It sounds like you're hyper-focusing on small things and making them seem like bigger problems than they really are," said Cathcart as he looked at his notes. "You need to figure out why you're so angry with her."

Eden looked up at Cathcart and wiped her tears. She tried to think about why she was angry, but nothing came to mind. It was like white noise interrupted by replays of his question. Why was she so angry?

It was clear to Cathcart Eden couldn't answer, so he changed directions. "What did Rafe mean to you when you were together?"

Eden looked down at her hands searching for her words. "When I met her," she began, "I walked into a whole new world. I felt like," she paused, "like I was walking on a tightrope, and she was my safety net. She kept me safe and made me feel so loved. She wasn't like anyone else I knew. She just had this way about her, and it seemed to make everything okay." She wiped her face with her hand. "I guess she meant change for me too. So many things changed after I met her from my relationship with my parents to how I walked through life to how I dealt with stress. Look at me," she said and pointed to herself. "I'm a mess. I never had anything like this happen to me in the entire time I was with her, well," she said with a bitter laugh, "until I started having doubts."

"Why did you start having doubts," asked Cathcart gently.

"I don't know." Eden sobbed. "I thought I felt it slipping but figured it was just everything we were going through at the time, so I ignored it and tried to concentrate on other things." Eden sighed not wanting to admit to him what she had done online or to bring up those feelings that had surfaced then. "Then it was suddenly yanked out from under me when I found out about Lauren." She sat silently for a moment trying not to think about Rafe touching and kissing Lauren. "I thought I had it back," she sniffed, "but I was always in fear she would do it again. I guess my fear just kept growing, and I started thinking," she swallowed, "maybe I made a mistake in being with her."

Cathcart waited a moment for her to continue but she sat silently. "You left out you were dealing with the feelings you were having for men at the time too." He watched as Eden sighed and nodded her head. "So you used Rafe's affair as justification to go figure out your feelings for men. Your reasoning was because she had an affair, and you couldn't trust her, it was okay for you to leave her bed and go try to figure out your feelings for men. Can you see the problem there?"

"What?" Eden said shaking her head. "No, that's not what happened. I told you how, when I couldn't reach her, it made me feel like I didn't care and thought it meant we weren't meant to be together."

"Eden, it still sounds a little bit like you're blaming Rafe for the fact you left with Jake. Because she was unavailable one day, suddenly you found you felt nothing for her. Sounds like blame and denial."

"No, no, I'm not blaming her or denying anything," she insisted. "It was my decision to leave."

"Do you really think you didn't care or was her being unavailable just convenient because you were angry with her?" He watched Eden as she looked at him, unable to answer or figure out if she should be angry or insulted. "Let's think about what was happening. You said yourself she was being very good to you about everything, and you were already feeling guilty about the feelings you were having about men, feelings you were having before you became pregnant." He watched her look down at her hands then nod at hearing her own words repeated. "Being angry with her would have only added to your guilt. So the best thing for you would be to feel nothing. Then all you would have to deal with were the feelings you were having about how you should be in a relationship with a man." He paused for a moment. "If you didn't feel anything for her, why did you tell her about your feelings for men?"

Eden looked up at him with a confused frown. "Well, because," she started, "because she deserved to know why I was so distant and..." she trailed off, "I had to tell her."

"Okay," said Cathcart, "but you could have told her you were distant because of the affair, and you were still angry with her. You could have separated and handled Bronte's adoption together. Then you could have handled your feelings about men after you moved out without her ever knowing about them. Why did you have to tell her?" he asked again.

Eden looked up at him, and her face bloomed red with anger. "You think I told her to hurt her," she said softly. "You think I was mad and wanted to hurt her the way she hurt me, so I threw the feelings I thought I was having for men in her face, don't you?" she asked angrily.

"I don't know, Eden," said Cathcart calmly. "Is that what you did?"

Eden looked at Cathcart shaking and angry. "That's not what happened! She told me to go figure out my feelings!"

"Yes, you told me she said she gave you a trust. Should she have trusted you?"

"I—" Eden choked out, "she—"

Cathcart knew what he was going to say next would be hard for Eden to hear but thought there might be some truth in it somewhere. "You were so angry with her you wanted to hurt her, and having an affair with a man, in her home, and then leaving without a word with Bronte did hurt her. And now, you're still angry." He paused to let his words sink in as Eden cried. "I know this is hard," he said calmly. "I'm not judging you or saying you're a terrible person because you're not. I know you didn't make a conscious plan to hurt her. I doubt at the time everything was happening you even realized why you were doing the things you were doing. But whether we like it or not, there are real reasons for why we do things, and sometimes they don't paint us in the best light. Even good people lash out when they get hurt, and in doing so, sometimes we make mistakes and hurt others."

248

"I didn't want to hurt her. I don't want to hurt her." Eden sobbed as she wiped her tears with a tissue. "I don't want to be angry."

"Eden, you say you're over Rafe's infidelity," Cathcart asserted, "but I think you're suppressing your most painful feelings about it."

Eden shook her head in denial. "But I am over it. I told Rafe I was over it."

"You're not over it, Eden. It's why you're so angry," said Cathcart and paused for his words to sink in. "It may also be why you believe you're having such a difficult time figuring out your feelings. It seems like your saying you want to stay in Rafe's world but don't feel safe in it without her, so you're looking back to a time when you were a completely different person and trying to make it work for you again. It may even be why you left, and you thought you found a kind of similar safety again in a relationship you thought would be easier, or you were familiar with, a relationship with a man, specifically Jake, and it just didn't work for you. No relationship is going to be easy or familiar all the time, no matter if it is with a man or a woman. The entire equation for your feelings shouldn't be based on how easy or familiar a relationship is with a certain gender. You were willing to stay in an unsatisfying relationship out of guilt because you got into it as a result of anger."

Eden's eyes filled with tears again as she struggled to speak. So many thoughts and emotions were running through her mind it made it hard for her to think at the moment. "I really just don't know who I am anymore. I just can't sort through all of these feelings," she choked, "and I don't know why."

"Eden," Cathcart said with sympathy, "you're hiding your true feelings and pain in all of your complaints about Rafe." He looked at his notepad. "Complaints about her emotional abandonment, her controlling, her power, the fact she's so wrapped up in herself and her career, her making you feel lost or being unable to hold on to your identity. The list goes on and on. I think most of those complaints are just excuses you use so you can keep yourself from loving her or trusting her and telling her how you really feel. Do you trust her?"

"Trust her?" Eden repeated not knowing what else to say.

"The only way to truly be close to her again is to trust her," said Cathcart. "Do you trust her," he asked again.

"I don't know," cried Eden. "I'm just so afraid. What if she loses control again? I was so," she paused shaking, "so humiliated and felt so betrayed. I just couldn't take it if she did it again." She looked up with fear in her eyes. "She is supposed to be strong," she cried out. "She doesn't lose control! I can't." She breathed unsteadily. "I can't go through something like that again. I just can't!"

Cathcart shook his head with concern. "Eden, Rafe can't always be the strong one. Everyone loses control sometimes in many different ways. No one is perfect. What she did was painful, and I'm not excusing what she did, but from what you've told me, she was working very hard to earn your forgiveness and trust. What does she need to do to earn it?"

"I don't know," said Eden at a loss. "I want to trust her; I want to love her." She closed her eyes tight trying not to cry anymore. "I'm just so... afraid."

Cathcart smiled because, for the first time, Eden had almost admitted in session what he suspected. The fact she still loved Rafe. "Eden, it's okay to want those things. I think you may be angrier with yourself for still having feelings for her than you are at Rafe. It's okay to want to love her even though you're still hurting."

"I do want to love her," said Eden softly. "I don't want to be angry," she sighed, "at her or at myself."

"You just have to stop making up all these excuses to be angry then, and really look at your feelings for Rafe," said Cathcart gently. "You do know how you feel about her. You said you want to love her. Why do you want to love her?"

"Why do I?" Eden started and looked at him mystified. "Because," she paused, "she—" Eden fought the words wanting to come out of her. "I can't help myself," she whispered. She looked up at Dr. Cathcart in torment. "I hear her voice in my head. I keep seeing things that remind me of her," she said manically. "I dream about her," she took a breath, "and when I actually see her, I just. I just..." she swallowed, and her face flushed red, "I can't help how my body reacts, and I just want to be close to her."

"It's okay for you to have those feelings for her and not anyone else," Cathcart assured her. "Don't be angry you have them anymore. Think about it, and you'll see it's true."

Eden looked up at him and took a breath. "It's not just sex," she blurted and blushed again. "I mean, yes, my body does react sexually to her, but it's more than sexual. I don't know if I can explain it." She hesitated as Cathcart waited patiently. "There's always been something there since the first time I really saw her as more than just someone I spent time with sometimes. Rafe called it *zingari magic*." She gave a small laugh at the memory. "Even when we were with other people, I could feel it with her. It's like something that makes a hard thump in my heart sometimes, or it fills my heart, so it swells and then pours warmth through my body, or sometimes it rushes through me and makes me dizzy like I'm drunk. It just happens, and a lot of times, she really isn't doing anything. I just look up and see her. I thought after I left her, I wouldn't feel it anymore, but it never went away. I tried pushing it away, believe me," she said softly, "but I don't think I ever really had control over it."

"They're your feelings," said Cathcart. "Why don't you think you have control over them?"

"I just don't'." Eden sighed. "I don't know if those things kept happening because of my feelings or if they kept happening because of Rafe and what she was doing."

"What was she doing?"

"She was being Rafe." Eden breathed a short laugh through her nose. "She should have been angry. People said she should have done a lot of things she didn't do. A few weeks after I moved out, she agreed to meet with me. I was nervous because, well, I left her. She came into the restaurant and greeted me as if we were old friends. She kissed my cheek, and then it was like all she wanted was to make sure I was okay, and I was happy. She saw the folder I had on the table, took it, and began looking through it. Before I could say a word, she took out her checkbook and wrote me a huge check to help with Bronte. Then she said she would take the folder and would go over things, and I should let her know if I needed anything more. I remember sitting there after she left just looking at the check wondering if she was glad I'd left her.

"I found out later she ended up paying almost all the bills in the folder directly because I got the paid statements in the mail. The unpaid bills were returned to Jake and me." She looked at Cathcart and gave him a wry smile. "Mostly, they were bills Jake had slipped in for things like tithes to his church for what he considered my share, or my credit card bill for the closet organizer and some other things I bought when I moved into his place. I don't know why he thought she would pay for those things. I sent her a note apologizing for those bills being in the folder, and Jake was mad about that too." She sighed and shook her head wishing for the thousandth time she had never met Jake.

"Rafe never asked for the keys to the house back either," she continued, "but I gave them to her anyway. She started paying child support and lost almost every argument over visitation with Bronte for eight months. She kept paying for things even after I accused her of throwing her checkbook at problems. She never sued me or sent Katheryn, her lawyer, after me to argue for her. She paid the medical bills, even ones I didn't ask her to pay. She remembered my birthday. She invited us to every big party and event, but we never went and never sent Bronte. I stopped telling Jake about them after a while because it seemed to make him jealous Rafe was still contacting me." She closed her eyes and shook her head at the memory of all those arguments.

"I invited the girls to some of our parties," Eden continued, "but Jake didn't want me to invite Rafe, so I didn't. None of the girls ever came, and I think not inviting Rafe was the reason. I had lunch with Abby sometimes. She would say things in passing like, 'Rafe says you're welcome at her house anytime if you want to swim,' or 'Rafe said you would want to know this information or something was happening,' or 'Rafe said your lilac is in bloom.' Sometimes, Rafe would send things to me through Abby like herbs from my herb garden. She had the landscaper start taking care of it after I left. She'd send things for Bronte with Abby too, like a toy or clothes. I would go home and cry. Jake thought it was because Abby was being horrible to me and didn't want me to see her anymore, but he couldn't have been more wrong. He never figured out the things I brought home were from Rafe." She pushed the hair from her face and leaned her head back.

"Then I'd see Rafe somewhere, and it would happen," she said softly, "that thump in my chest." She looked at Cathcart. "She was supposed to hurt me and make my life hard. She was supposed to make me jump through hoops and worry about what she would do next. She was supposed to make it easy to stay away. Jake told me she must have been up to something, and he had me really scared about what might happen. He said most people would have gone to court for visitation and would have made me litigate and force them to pay for anything. But she didn't do any of it. Why do you think she handled things the way she did?"

"Maybe that's something you should ask her," said Cathcart softly amazed she still couldn't see the answer.

"I want to," said Eden softly, "but it's just so hard to talk to her sometimes," she complained.

"I think the first thing you need to do is talk to her and end her suffering," suggested Cathcart. "You need to tell her Jake lied to her. If she could end your suffering, wouldn't you want her to?"

"Yes, I would," Eden whispered.

"You also have to tell her your fears and anger are still there about the affair, and they are very real," said Cathcart. "She needs to know what you've been going through and the reason for some of the things that have happened. It won't be an easy conversation."

Eden looked at Cathcart thinking about what he said about how she left with Jake and using Rafe's affair to justify herself even though she told Rafe she was over it. "I know now it was a bad decision to leave like I did, and I should have talked to her more. I should have talked to you too maybe, before I..." She sighed and couldn't finish her thought. "I've just really messed up my life and Rafe's life too."

Cathcart looked at Eden then made a note on his pad. "I want you to stop taking the Xanax since they aren't helping you. I don't think a higher dose is really what you need right now. I'm going to give you some relaxation techniques, and if you can't sleep, take a mild over the counter sleep aide. I want you to talk to Rafe as soon as possible. I think talking will help you more than anything else will because holding in your guilt and anger seems to be causing you both problems. You need to talk to her right away. The more you delay, the harder it will be to resolve things and close the gap growing between you."

"I will," promised Eden, "as soon as I can." She looked up at him sadly. "Bill, I may never get the chance." She burst into tears again, and they streamed down her face. "I may have already lost the only chance I had," she sobbed, "and she just walked away."

54

RAFE SALVAGGIO WALKED back into her office from her Monday afternoon lunch and found a couriered package on her desk. She sat down, opened it, and took out its contents. She leaned back in her chair, smiled as she read the cover letter, and looked through the rest of the package. She leaned forward again and pressed her phone intercom.

"Brandy, confirm President Biggalow is in her office, and pull out the budget files for the new video media lab, the new digital equipment, and for the expansion of the computer graphics and design department. Let me know when you have them on your desk."

Rafe's eyes twinkled as she took out her phone, and typed in a text message. A few minutes later, her phone buzzed, and she pushed the intercom button. "Yes, Brandy?"

"Dean Salvaggio," Brandy said through the intercom, "she's in her office, and the budgets you requested are on my desk and ready for you."

"Thank you," she said and made her way out of her office. She had the package in her hand and picked up the budget folders as she walked past Brandy's desk. "I'll be back soon," she told the teaching assistant happily.

She made her way through the corridors with a smile on her face for everyone she passed. She turned toward the administration section of the campus and made it to Clarice Biggalow's office. "Is she in?" she asked, and she walked past the nodding secretary into Clarice's office. "Clarice, how are you this afternoon?"

"Dean Salvaggio," Clarice took off her readers, "what brings you here?"

Rafe gave her a big grin and placed the budget files on her desk. "I just wanted you to look at these budgets and to make sure they were the first ones funded when money comes available. I was hoping to get your signature on them today."

Clarice chuckled and shook her head. "I don't usually approve budgets until the funds are in, Dean Salvaggio. You know the rules."

"What if I told you my department will be getting a half a million dollars within the month?" Rafe smiled and raised one eyebrow.

Clarice looked at her with surprise and stood up. "You mean?"

"We got the Jackson-Goyer," said Rafe beaming with pride. "Here's the confirmation letter," she said and handed her the package. "They'll make the finalist list public Wednesday. I just have to fly to New York for the presentation of the award and to finalize the fund transfer paperwork. The first meeting with the board and the press is Wednesday afternoon, so I'll leave tomorrow night." She tapped the budgets on the desk. "So, how about those signatures?"

"For you, I'll break my own rule." Clarice laughed as she opened the files and signed the budgets.

Rafe picked up the signed budget folders. "Thank you." Rafe flashed another smile. "I'll get started making travel arrangements today. I'll leave Tuesday night, stay through the weekend, and be back in the office on Monday. I'll expect a big homecoming."

"You'll get it," promised Clarice. "I'll make all of the arrangements, and we'll have a big party to celebrate."

"Make it really big." Rafe winked at her and made her way back to her office.

55

TUESDAY MORNING AT nine a.m., Rafe Salvaggio sat in Katheryn Hardam's Law Office waiting for Eden to show up. Katheryn had called the meeting to update them on the injunction proceedings. While they waited for Eden, Katheryn was looking over some additional changes Rafe had indicated for her will, and Rafe was texting on her phone.

Eden arrived and stopped just inside the doorway of Katheryn's office when she saw Rafe sitting in the leather chair looking at her phone. She knew Rafe would be there, but after talking to Cathcart, and dealing with some hard realities she was still working through, it was hard to face her at the moment.

Katheryn looked up and saw Eden. She stood up and walked around her desk. "Eden, come in and sit down please," she said. After she shook her hand, Katheryn leaned back against her desk. "I'm assuming at the moment your feelings about the adoption are the same and neither of you has changed your mind. After our little chat a while back, I thought it was important we all get together and make sure we're on the same page." She looked at Eden. "Eden, you said you still want to fight the injunction, and you want the adoption process to continue. Do you still feel the same?"

Eden looked at Rafe then Katheryn. "I absolutely still feel the same."

"Rafe, what about you?" asked Katheryn.

Rafe looked at Eden and hesitated. She looked at Katheryn. "Yes, I still want it if Eden is okay with it."

Eden looked at Rafe anxiously trying not to get upset. "Rafe, I've always been okay with it, more than okay with it. I've always wanted it this way. Please believe me." She looked at Rafe, but Rafe just sat silently and looked at Katheryn or her phone.

"Well, good," said Katheryn and went back around to sit behind her desk. "Since we know everything is going ahead let me give you an update. The court date will be coming up soon unless something goes wrong, but right now, things look good. The group filing the injunction, the *Stewards to the Protection of the Innocence and Morals of Youths*, has been filing amendments. They've been frivolous up to this point, and I've managed to have them thrown out. But yesterday, an amendment was filed that has proven to be harder to show as frivolous."

"What is it, Katheryn?" Rafe asked concerned and took a quick look at Eden. "I've been so careful. I can't believe I've done something wrong with Bronte."

"She's barely been alone with her since the abuse charges," Eden said looking at Katheryn.

"You have done a good job, Rafe," agreed Katheryn. "But this has nothing to do with your time with Bronte," she paused, "this has to do with the immoral environment issue."

"What immoral environment?" Rafe asked confused.

"They're really stretching this, Rafe." Katheryn hesitated then began to explain. "Apparently, a presentation you gave at the CCAD on the 'human form in art' has been webcast on a pay per view site through the CCAD. They're using it to prove not only will you subject the child to an immoral lifestyle according to them, but also you condone putting the child's picture in with other, again this is their words, other 'pornographic' art. This, coupled with your own deviant sexual behavior they apparently have well documented, they claim makes you unfit to be an adoptive parent."

"What are they talking about?" asked Eden as she looked at Rafe. "What presentation? What pornographic art is Bronte's picture with?"

Outraged, Rafe stood up and paced the office. "I did not put Bronte's picture with pornographic art!" She turned to Eden. "Eden, I did a presentation at the CCAD on the human form in all mediums. I told you I was doing one. I used many art pieces to prove points about the power and nature of the human form. All of the art pieces I used are considered masterpieces. They are not pornographic! I used the photos I took of Bronte in one section of the lecture about emotion. I swear there was nothing pornographic about the lecture." She turned to Katheryn. "How can they take my lecture and twist it like this?"

"Rafe, I need a copy of your lecture," Katheryn said firmly. "I'm sure they've edited it to look like they want it to. Can you get me a copy today?"

Rafe was reeling and furious, but she managed to control herself and looked at Eden. "You believe me, don't you?"

"Why would you use her pictures?" asked Eden aghast. "What were you thinking?"

Rafe noted Eden didn't answer her question, but she attempted to explain. "I used them to show innocence. They're beautiful pictures. How could I know this would happen? I'll show you the presentation. There's nothing immoral or pornographic about it."

"Rafe, can you get me a copy today?" Katheryn asked again attempting to refocus her client.

Rafe paced the room again struggling to control herself. "Yes, I'll get you a copy today," she confirmed and looked at Katheryn. "I have a gallery show at the school my photographs will be in. Some of the pictures are of Bronte" She looked at Eden then back at Katheryn. "Should I take them out?"

"Sit down," suggested Katheryn, and she waited for Rafe to comply. "My advice is, don't change anything yet, unless you feel strongly you should. Let me look at the presentation, and then I'll know more."

"Eden, you know I would never do anything to hurt her or put her in jeopardy," said Rafe distressed.

"I know you wouldn't hurt her," said Eden troubled. She looked at Rafe accusingly. "You let them put her picture on the internet?" she asked in disbelief. "It's putting her in jeopardy, Rafe." A chill ran through her at the possibilities of what could happen and what the Stewards were doing to her and other people.

Rafe looked at Eden with horror on her face and started pacing the room again. "I'm sorry. The art club just. I can't believe this!" she said in a fury. "I'll tell them to take it down today," she promised fervently. "I didn't mean to do anything like this."

"I know you didn't mean to, and I'm not accusing you of doing it on purpose," Eden tried to assure her.

Rafe turned heatedly to Katheryn. "What else do I need to do?"

"Sit down and calm down," Katheryn said firmly, and she waited for her to sit again. "Rafe, I don't want you to stop living your life, but it seems like every time I turn around, these people come up with something to add to this injunction." She walked around her desk and opened the file. "Every time they file something, the court date has a chance of changing, and the adoption gets pushed further back. It's already changed twice. I've gotten statements about your sexual activity and, believe it or not, a picture of you kissing and groping a girl on the beach and arguing with her girlfriend. I've managed to get it all thrown out, but you need to be more discrete." She closed the file. "It's like they're following you everywhere just looking for anything to use against you." She looked at Eden thinking about the information she gave her and then back at Rafe.

Aggravated but trying to calm herself, Rafe looked up at Katheryn. "I didn't do anything wrong, Katheryn. It was a competition. We were playing a game. Did they also tell you I was out having drinks with those people afterward celebrating?"

Katheryn dismissed her excuses because they were mute at this point. She looked at her and spoke calmly. "It would be useless for me to tell you to watch your every move because it seems like they can make something out of nothing. Don't stop doing what you normally do. Just be aware of what's going on around you, and be more careful."

Rafe leaned back and crossed her arms as the vein on her head throbbed. "I can't really win this, can I? Everything I do is going to be wrong no matter what."

"Oh, we'll win," declared Katheryn. "I'm going to eat these people alive. Just try to be more careful, and not just with Bronte, but with everything. And please, try to be more discrete with any personal interactions you may have."

"Katheryn, I haven't even been with anyone since..." Rafe looked at Eden and frowned. "Since—"

"Since Greer?" asked Eden softly.

Rafe rubbed her temples as her head throbbed with pain and felt her chest tighten. "Yes, Greer," she spoke softly in pain, "since Greer," she repeated, "Greer," she whispered again. "I can't do this," she moaned. She looked at Eden with eyes full of pain and accusation. "They'll get what they want no matter what I do, won't they? I've got to go," she said in a fury and stormed out of the office as Eden watched in distress.

Katheryn stood up and walked around to stand in front of Eden. She looked at her sternly. "Eden, you need to rethink keeping this from Rafe. I don't know how these people are getting information on her. It's like they're watching her every move. I just don't know what these Steward people are capable of, and if anything, and I mean *anything,* happens even slightly worse than what I've been dealing with," she paused, "I'll have no choice. I will tell her. I'm seriously considering telling her anyway."

"You promised you wouldn't reveal your source," Eden reminded her nervously. "Are you going to keep your promise?"

"I'll keep it," Katheryn confirmed. "But Eden, I think you're making a terrible mistake."

56

IN NO MOOD to go back to work, Rafe Salvaggio took the rest of the day off and got home early. She made calls to the school, took care of the video, and had her assistant send a copy to Katheryn. After she had taken care of everything, she called Lydia to let her know she could bring Bronte home early and then double-checked her travel arrangements and her suitcase while she waited. As soon as Lydia dropped off Bronte,

Rafe called and asked Jude to come over so she wouldn't be alone with her.

The three of them were in the backyard sitting in the grass now saturated with bubble residue. Rafe was blowing bubbles while Jude and Bronte were trying to catch them without breaking them. They had already spent a lot of time popping them as they floated down. After blowing a long stream of bubbles, Rafe took up her camera and snapped pictures of Bronte and Jude. They were laughing, and Bronte was squealing in delight at the sight of the bubbles as she clapped them between her hands like Rafe had shown her.

"She's so amazed by them," said Jude laughingly.

"The advantages of being one." Rafe laughed with her and blew more bubbles.

"Here's a big one. Bronte, get it before it gets away," said Jude to the little girl. She helped Bronte get the bubble as Rafe took their picture.

"Bronte, come here," called Rafe. She sat down on the ground and put Bronte in her lap, holding the bubble wand in front of her. "Can you blow? Blow, and you'll make some bubbles." She showed Bronte what to do, and Bronte tried, but nothing happened. "It's okay. Let me dip it again." She dipped the wand again and held it in front of Bronte, and she blew and made some bubbles. Bronte laughed and tried to grab them. Rafe and Jude laughed with her. "You're great at this, B Girl!"

Jude looked up and saw Eden had been watching them. "Hey, Eden."

"Hi. It looks like you guys are having fun. Can I play too?" Eden asked tentatively.

Rafe gave her a troubled smile. "Of course. Here. You can be the bubble maker for a while."

Eden took the bubbles and the wand and began making bubbles for Bronte. She looked up at Rafe. "What made you think to get her bubbles?"

"I loved them when I was growing up," Rafe answered with a shrug. "My momma brought them whenever we went to the park and had a picnic. I loved watching them float and the colors the sun could make them turn."

Eden watched Bronte and Jude chase down bubbles to pop them. "It looks like she really loves them too."

Jude sat down next to Eden panting and holding Bronte who was ready for more bubbles. "You should have seen her eyes when Rafe blew the first one." Jude chuckled as she wiped Bronte's hands with a towel. "They were huge! She almost cried when it popped until Rafe made a bunch of little ones. Then I showed her how to pop them with her finger, and Rafe showed her how to clap them between her hands and step on them."

Rafe looked at Bronte's sticky hands and clothes. "Sorry about the mess," she said to Eden. "I'll take her in and clean her up."

"It's okay," Eden assured her. "Let her play some more." She looked at Bronte then at Rafe. "You're really great with her. I'm so glad you're her mom." She smiled and hoped Rafe believed her. "I don't know when I would have thought of this." She blew more bubbles for Bronte to chase.

Rafe looked away from Eden. Their visit with Katheryn was still fresh in her mind. "I gave a copy of the presentation to Katheryn, and I have a copy for you too. I had them take it down." She sighed and shook her head. "I'm not her mom yet. Eden, I hope you understand how important being there for Bronte is to me. I love her, and I want to be part of her life. If you'll let me," she said softly remembering the conditions Jake had mentioned. "No matter what it costs. I just want to be there for her to share things with her my mother shared with me."

"I know how important it is," Eden assured her, "and it's why I'm doing the things I've been doing."

Rafe looked at her and was unsure how to take her statement. "I know I'll never be her real mom—" she started.

"You will, you are her mom," insisted Eden interrupting her. "I say you are, and Katheryn says the law is with you too. You'll always be her mama, no matter what."

Still upset about the new charges against her, and not really believing Eden, Rafe gave a small nod just to keep this time with Bronte. "You better start blowing more bubbles. Jude, get ready to lift Bronte up high, and I'll take her picture. It'll look like she's flying through them."

57

RAFE SALVAGGIO AND Jude Atwood were sitting together on the porch relaxing and drinking beer. About an hour earlier, Eden had taken Bronte home. Rafe was glad Jude had been home to help her with both Bronte and Eden. She felt like everything she did now was playing out exactly as Jake said it would. There seemed to be no way to win except to give Eden whatever she wanted. If she lost the injunction, she would have to make some hard life changes.

Rafe looked over at Jude and passed her another beer in silence. She waited to speak until she had opened the bottle and took her first swig. "I'm leaving for New York. My car should be here soon," she said quietly.

"New York?" said Jude, surprised. "What are you going to be doing there?"

Rafe grinned, happy at least one thing in her life was going right. "I have to go pick up a lot of money for the CCAD." Her cellular phone buzzed. "Excuse me." She tapped it and read a text message. She shook her head as she gave a small laugh and then put the phone down. She took a sip of her beer then looked at Jude. "I have my first meeting over lunch tomorrow."

After a while, Jude spoke again. "How long will you be gone?"

"I'll be back on Sunday," answered Rafe. "I'm staying over the weekend." She sat silently for a while.

"So you won't be back for the art class," said Jude.

"No."

Jude took a swig of her beer. "What are you going to do?"

"I'd like to visit some projects I helped with before I sold my company that should be finished," said Rafe. "Maybe visit some museums and other places." She picked at the label on her beer bottle for a while. "I'll probably try to see some friends I haven't seen to for a while too." She took a long drink. "Yesterday, I took care of all the arrangements for while I'll be away. Eden has Bronte the rest of the week and the weekend, so she's taken care of while I'm gone too." They looked out at the night sky, and Rafe could smell the lilac bush Eden had planted when she moved in years ago. Another reminder of what she had lost.

"I still have the key to your house," Jude reminded her.

"Good. Keep it," said Rafe and took the last sip of her beer. "I'll leave my flight, hotel, and other information on the dining room table in case you need it." She looked at Jude with a smile. "No parties inside my house while I'm gone."

"No problem," agreed Jude with a grin and took another swig of her beer.

Rafe looked at the time on her phone. "Well, I'm going to go put my things to the door," she said as she stood and stretched before going inside.

There was a feeling almost like relief building inside Rafe as the reality she was getting away from everyone and everything for a while got closer. Once she was in New York, she would see how the feeling developed.

Maybe being away from my life for a while is exactly what I need.

58

WEDNESDAY MORNING AT The Kiki Bistro, Abby Van Falkov was having what had become her ritual mid-week morning breakfast with coffee before work with Julia, Erica, Jude, and Stacey. The group caught up about the events of the week and made plans for the weekend as they ate. They were enjoying their final cups of coffee, and the topic at the table had finally turned to Rafe and Eden since Abby couldn't stop talking about them.

"I told you she was just figuring out things at Rafe's expense," said Stacey knowingly.

"This whole thing is fucked up." Abby sighed hating the fact Stacey might be right about anything.

"Maybe it's better they aren't together," suggested Erica as she added more sugar and some flavored creamers to her coffee.

"Rafe should just go back to Greer or find someone else." Julia sighed, tired of talking in circles about the whole thing. Rafe was stubborn beyond reason, and Eden, well, who knew what was going on with her. The more she thought about it, the more Julia thought maybe Rafe needed to be with an older woman who had the patience to deal with her. At the moment, her hopes of ever dating Rafe were waning.

Jude put down her coffee cup. "She might just be going back to Greer," she revealed.

Abby snapped her head up in surprise. "What do you mean?" she demanded.

"She left for New York last night," she said and took another sip of her coffee.

"New York? Why?" asked Abby, agitated she didn't know the latest piece of gossip.

"Something about the CCAD and visiting galleries and people she hasn't seen for a while," said Jude then toyed with her coffee cup.

"So, you really think she's meeting Greer there," asked Stacey curiously.

"She was there the last time Rafe went," said Abby, troubled. "Eden *so* fucked this up."

"Do you think she knows Rafe went to New York?" Erica pondered.

"I don't know," said Jude. "Rafe didn't say anything to Eden when she picked up Bronte last night."

"Who gets to tell her if she doesn't know?" asked Julia wondering if Rafe really did change her mind about Eden after all.

"Not me," said Jude as she put her hands up in front of herself.

Stacey raised her hand like a schoolgirl. "I'll do it!" she said giggling with anticipation.

"No, we can't let you do it, Stacey. You'll just make it worse." Abby sneered.

"Worse? I don't think it's possible," exclaimed Stacey.

"I can't do it." Abby shook her head not wanting to be the bearer of the news. "I can't look at her right now."

"I'm out," said Erica as she waved off the task. "I don't know her like that."

"I guess it leaves me," Julia said in dread at dealing with Eden. "I feel like I'm betraying Rafe, but I guess Eden has to find out sooner or later."

"Maybe we should just keep our mouths shut," suggested Jude. "We really don't know if it's why she went." She took a drink of her coffee. "She told me another amendment to the injunction was filed against her."

"What for?" asked Erica shocked.

"They're accusing her of putting Bronte's picture with pornographic art because of her lecture, and they're bringing up things like they think she is immoral and a sexual deviant again," Jude said quietly.

"What the hell?" Abby shrieked.

"Rafe would never do anything to hurt Bronte," asserted Julia.

"Well, the lecture was sexy and so was Rafe when she gave it. I know a lot of people who are downloading it just to watch her," said Stacey as she arched her brow.

"Does that include you, Stacey?" retorted Abby irritably.

"Of course," Stacey answered Abby with a smile, "but I did it for the art."

Abby rolled her eyes "Right. You should go find a boyfriend."

"Whatever," Jude yelled to stop their arguing. "Guys, it's fucked, and Rafe was really upset about it. With the injunction, and the thing with Eden, who knows what she'll do in New York. She may just stay in her hotel room so no more amendments can be filed."

"Jude," Stacey said sharply, "a sexual deviant in a hotel room? They can make anything out of that!"

"Shut up, Stacey," Abby said disgusted with Stacey. "Go do your funeral make-up and put yourself into a six-foot hole."

Stacey laughed and grinned at Abby. "I'd just come back as a zombie and eat your brains."

Julia stood up ready to leave the table and the drama behind. "Well, I agree with Jude. Rafe is going to do whatever she wants, and if Eden does nothing, then," she said dismissively, "it's on her. At least Rafe said she'd be back." Julia looked at Abby. "Remember when she disappeared for four months? It ended up she had decided to take some girl to Amsterdam for Pride, and they stayed."

Abby rolled her eyes at the memory. "That was so fucked up," whined Abby. She looked at everyone's curious faces. "I thought she had been kidnapped or something," she complained. "But they were shacked up and partying."

"Not the whole time," Julia reminded her with a laugh. "She did end up getting some restoration contracts while she was there."

"Whatever." Abby scoffed.

"Yeah, she probably just got those to make sure her father didn't go ballistic about her being gone so long," Julia added. "Well, I'm off. I've got morning meetings to attend."

Abby watched Julia walk out the door and looked at the others who were getting ready to leave and start their days. "It's not who Rafe is anymore," she said sullenly, worried she might be wrong and Rafe might really be going back to her wildling ways.

"Speaking of Pride," said Jude wanting to change the subject, "are we still meeting?"

"Let's all meet here after the parade," suggested Abby, glad to talk about something that would turn her mood around. "I have the best outfit picked out." She looked around at everyone. "We should probably ask Eden."

"I'll ask her," said Jude. "I'll see her on Saturday."

59

I have had not one word from her.
Frankly I wish I were dead.
When she left, she wept a great deal;
she said to me, "This parting must be
endured, Sappho. I go unwillingly."
I said, "Go, and be happy but remember
(you know well) whom you leave
shackled by love.
~Sappho

EDEN KINGSLEY HAD taken Bronte for her Saturday art class and was disappointed Rafe hadn't shown up for it again. Eden was sure Rafe was still upset about the new amendment added to the injunction. She also knew her inability to answer the question Rafe had asked on the dance floor made the situation even worse.

Today, she wanted to take Dr. Cathcart's advice and tell Rafe that Jake lied about everything. She couldn't let her hurt anymore. She would tell her about the fears she had and about how she was trying to work through them. Maybe they could help each other. She wanted to tell her everything she had talked about with the doctor, and she wanted to love her and to be sure of herself, and not be angry or afraid anymore. She just hoped Rafe would give her the time she needed to continue to work with Cathcart so she could resolve all the things she was dealing with inside.

Carrying Bronte on her hip, Eden knocked on the door. No answer. She knew Rafe had to be there because she could see her car was in the garage. She walked to Jude's house to see if Rafe had talked to anyone there. Jude had talked about going to Pride later, but after, she would be busy, so they hadn't talked about anything else. She knocked.

No answer again, but the main door was open, so she called inside. "Hello?" She opened the screen door. "Flynn? Jude? Stacey? Is anyone here?"

Eden looked around and saw the key to Rafe's house on the hook by the door. She hesitated but then took the key down. She found a pen and paper and wrote a quick note letting them know she borrowed the key to check on Rafe. She also wrote to say they should come over if they found the note so they could carpool to Pride. She walked out quickly with Bronte on her hip and headed to Rafe's house.

Standing in front of Rafe's door, Eden wasn't sure if she should go inside. She knew Rafe probably didn't want to see her, but she was worried she might be sick again. Plus, she had promised herself she would talk to her today. She finally built up her nerve and put the key in the lock. She opened the door and walked in quietly.

The house was silent.

She went to the guest room and put Bronte in her playpen to play. She walked to Rafe's room to check on her and knocked on her door. No answer. She opened the door and looked inside. She saw immediately it was empty and closed the door. She walked to the patio and looked out at the pool.

No Rafe.

Eden turned around and started toward the kitchen. As she passed the dining room table, she saw some of Rafe's photographs. She stood at the table and looked at them. The photographs varied in size and shape, and they were ready for matting and framing. There were several photos of Bronte with titles like 'Flowers are for Picking After All,' 'Bronte and her Beach Castle,' and 'Angel Dreaming.' Eden smiled as she looked at their beautiful daughter.

She looked at all the other photos of different people, some she knew and some she didn't, and others who must be students. Eden shifted through the small piles and suddenly stopped. She held up a large photo and read the title again. 'Greer's Claim Over Rafe.' She looked closer and realized the person in the photo was Rafe.

Her Rafe.

Rafe's face was hidden in shadow and was turned in profile. She was wearing only her matching black bra and underwear. On her tawny flat stomach, there was a drawing enhanced somehow so it almost glowed. Eden looked at the photo puzzled. She turned it over and saw there was writing and she began to read Rafe's clear, neat handwriting.

~Greer's Claim Over Rafe~
> The hand is making the sign for *I love you*, because, Greer loves Rafe.
> The middle knuckles are pyramids to represent time, longevity, something they wish they had.
> The R filling the index finger is for Rafe.
> The G filling the little finger is for Greer.

The Egyptian eye of Horus between them represents healing, something they both need.

The large ornate G in the middle of the hand is Greer's mark. Greer's claim over Rafe.

The paisleys and organic forms filling up the thumb and the rest of the hand represent the nature of love as a living thing that grows and dies but is always born again.

Something we need to always remember.

Original Artwork by Greer Noble

Photography by Rafe Salvaggio

Shaking as her mind reeled in torment, Eden turned the photo over again. She looked at Greer's artwork on Rafe's skin and sat down as her body weakened unable to take her eyes off Greer's claim on Rafe's body.

Greer loves Rafe.

Eden's anxiety built inside her and caused a shortening of her breath. Eden put the picture back on the table and put another photo on top of it so she wouldn't have to look at it again. As she moved another picture over it to help hide *Greer's Claim,* she uncovered a sensual picture of Greer with a secret and seductive smile. The warning Greer gave her was ringing in her ears. If Rafe went to her, Greer would never give her back.

She picked the photo up to turn it over, and a sheet of paper clinging to the picture slipped free and fell to the floor. Eden picked it up and looked at it. As she read what it said, tears began falling from her eyes and her throat closed up so she could hardly swallow as the dread built inside her.

The paper showed Rafe's travel information for her trip to New York.

Eden looked at Greer's picture. She looked at the dates on the travel information again. Eden's heart crashed into her chest. Rafe had been gone since Tuesday night. She realized it was the night they had spent time making bubbles with Bronte. She had been gone since—Eden lost her breath again.

Rafe was gone.

Greer loves Rafe, she saw in her mind.

Through her tears and panicking breaths, Eden looked around the house she had once called her home with Rafe. The place where she felt the most loved with Rafe. The place where she once always felt safe with Rafe. The place where she had kept her heart and dreams for so long. The place where Rafe loved her.

Rafe was not here.

Rafe's love for her was not here.

Eden then realized Rafe's love for her had died and it was born again for Greer.

Greer loves Rafe.

Rafe had gone to Greer, and she would never get her back. The pain from this cut of knowledge washed over her.

In the nightmarish empty silence, a wave of bleakness washed over Eden and stripped away all of her chaotic feelings and emotions, leaving her heart desolated and barren. The house was so quiet and empty—like her life had become. No sound, no feeling, no sensation could make it from her mind to her body. She slowly stood up and walked in a trance-like state into Rafe's bedroom, a place she had barely seen for over a year, and she sat down on the bed.

Rafe's bed.

Lying down on the bed, she suddenly felt tormented by a familiar scent. The scent had haunted her no matter how hard she fought to exorcise it and caused her senses to betray her with their eagerness to recognize it, desiring it.

Rafe.

More tears fell, and she cried silently with loss echoing through her empty chest. She pulled her phone from her pocket, and with a shaking hand, she dialed.

Eden struggled to talk between her cries of anguish. "Flynn? Where are you? Rafe. Rafe, she's gone. She really is gone. I'm at her house. She just left without a word. She's gone. Flynn," she whispered. "She loves her. She loves her. She went to her." She sobbed as she hung up the phone. "I'm sorry," she called out in anguish. "I love you," she finally said with a sob, but it was to an empty room.

She kept pouring her words out to the empty room in a broken voice as she wept in misery. She begged through her tears for Rafe to come back. She regretted her lack of strength over her fears. When she only had tears left, she buried her tear-stained face in the blankets, raining tears of sorrow, regret, heartache into them.

60

SHUFFLING OUT OF the bathroom after her shower, with a towel covering her wet hair, Jude Atwood headed for the kitchen to make a snack. She was always hungry after helping with the art classes and watching the kids eat paint. Her plans for the day were on her mind because she wanted to go out and enjoy the Pride events. She already told the gang she would be there so was trying to hurry. She looked down at the kitchen table and found Eden's note. "Shit," she whispered. Eden was supposed to be on her way to Pride. She tossed the towel onto a chair, threw her shoes on, and walked next door knowing Eden would find an empty house.

When she entered, she could hear Eden crying and followed the sound to Rafe's bedroom. She found Eden weeping in Rafe's bed. "Oh, no." She groaned. "No." She pulled out her phone and dialed. "Abby, you have to come over to Rafe's house. No, I didn't break any of her artwork. I know you're in the middle of the parade. It's Eden. She's here. She got the key from the key rack. Just come over. She's in Rafe's room crying."

She hung up then walked over and sat down next to Eden. "Eden, it's okay. Please don't cry. I just can't take it when girls cry." She reached out tentatively to pat her shoulder. "Abby will be here soon. I'm... I'm going to check on Bronte." She got up, went into the guest room, and found Bronte playing happily in her playpen. "Hey, Bronte. Are you hungry? I am," she said as she picked up the baby. "Let's go raid Mama's kitchen."

It only took Abby thirty minutes to make it to Rafe's house wearing her skimpy Pride outfit, and Flynn arrived at the same time. When the two walked inside, they found Jude playing with Bronte in the living room.

Jude looked up and pointed to Rafe's room. "She's still in there crying on and off," Jude said with worry. She looked down at the doll she was holding and quickly gave it to Bronte.

"Okay." Abby sighed as she ignored Jude's attempt to hide she had been playing dolls with the baby. She went into Rafe's room and kneeled by the bed. She put her hand on Eden's back as Flynn stood in the doorway. "Eden," she said quietly, "Eden, it'll be okay. Rafe will be back tomorrow."

Eden looked up at Abby with red-rimmed eyes filled with sadness. "I think she's gone to be with Greer. It's where they met before. You were right." She sobbed, and her body shook.

"Shhh, Eden, you don't know for sure," Abby consoled her softly. "She just had to go for the CCAD for the grant thingy."

Eden shook her head in despair. "I saw the picture," she said through a sob. "She loves her. She, she—" A wave of tears and sobs wracked through her.

"I'm sorry about what I said," Abby told her as she started to help Eden up. "I was just upset. Come on. Let's get you home. You shouldn't be here right now. Rafe will be back tomorrow."

Flynn went over to help Abby get Eden up. "Come on, Eden. Don't worry. She'll be back. You can talk to her tomorrow."

As Abby straightened the bed, Eden spoke mournfully and shook with sobs as Flynn helped her out of the room. "Abby,

Flynn, she's gone," she whispered. "I'm too late. She's really gone. She's gone. I've lost her. I lost her," she whispered in despair.

61

SUNDAY AFTERNOON, THE private car service carrying Rafe Salvaggio home pulled into her driveway, and the driver helped her unload her luggage and packages. She took everything inside and deposited her items in different areas of the house. A new toy and some books for Bronte in the living room, the press package for work on the kitchen counter, and a small painting she found in the Village in the dining room with the photo's she was getting ready to have framed, and her suitcase into the bedroom. She stripped out of her clothes, took a long hot shower to relax, and got dressed in some comfortable lounge pants and a soft bamboo shirt.

She went back into the dining room and saw her pictures had been moved out of order. She fixed them assuming Jude had looked through them. She looked at the photos and smiled. She was excited about putting them in the gallery. It would be the first time she displayed her photography work.

She couldn't stop her yawn and could feel the jet lag coming on. She decided to go lie down for a while and try to read herself to sleep. She took her book into bed with her and tried to concentrate on what she was reading, but it wasn't happening for some reason.

She suddenly found herself thinking about Eden again. Eden. She thought about her all weekend. Rafe wondered if Eden was playing a game with her by saying she was doing these things because Eden knew it was important to Rafe to be part of Bronte's life. She knew she had to try again to be close to Eden, but it hurt so much, and she was sure Eden must have figured out what she was doing.

She should never have made all of those remarks about graphic designers and men. She should never have asked her who she loved, but she couldn't help it. Her patience just ran out. All her strategy research shot out the window. She just couldn't use it on Eden.

At least it gave her an excuse to take the time to build the walls around her heart—a wall she would need. She was sure Eden understood Jake had revealed their secret to her. It probably was no coincidence right afterward, another amendment to the injunction was filed. They were just waiting for her to slip up. Why was it so hard to stop loving her?

How much more pain can I put myself through?

Rafe took a deep breath. "My god, I must be going crazy," she complained to herself. "I want her with me so much I can actually smell her." She shook her head and got out of bed even though her body needed the rest. She knew rest would not come for her mind at the moment.

She walked to the kitchen, put some water in the electric tea kettle, and turned it on. When the water was ready, she poured it into her teapot and let the chamomile tea begin to steep. There was a knock on the door. She sighed and went to answer it.

"Abby," she said with a groan when she saw who was there.

"So, you're back," Abby said smugly.

"I am," said Rafe and smiled halfheartedly, assuming Jude had told Abby about her travel plans. "What brings you over here?" she asked and opened the door so Abby could come inside.

Abby walked in and sat on the couch in the living room. "Rafe, you really are thoughtless. Why didn't you tell anyone you were leaving town, and why didn't you return any of my calls yesterday?"

Rafe went back to the kitchen to get her tea, and Abby got up and followed her. "What are you talking about? I told Jude. And you obviously knew. And you know what? I can leave town anytime I want to without checking in with anyone." She made her cup of tea and handed another cup of tea to Abby. She walked back into the living room and sat in the chair as Abby sat down across from her. "I didn't return your calls because I didn't want to talk to anyone. I needed some time away from everything and everyone."

Abby blew on her tea to cool it off and looked at Rafe over the cup. "So how was it?"

"If you're referring to my trip to New York," she said exhausted, "it was blessedly uneventful."

"Uneventful?" Abby said suspiciously.

"Yes," Rafe answered and took a sip of her tea. She looked up at Abby who clearly expected more information. "I did my duty for the school and attended the Jackson-Goyer Foundation presentation ceremony, and then I got to make nice at the obligatory dinner and after party, which I left as early as possible without seeming rude."

"Is that all?" Abby pressed.

"No," Rafe said then took another a sip of tea and leaned back in her chair.

"Well?" said Abby exasperated. "What else did you do?"

Rafe looked at her and yawned. "Abby, I spent the entire work week keeping my appointments with the Jackson-Goyer Foundation to get all of the fund transfer information for the school into their system and signed off on all of the paperwork, going on tours and making nice in interviews. The rest of the time in the evenings and on the weekend, I spent wandering around the city. Why are you so interested?" she asked perturbed.

"So," she said slowly, "you didn't meet anyone?"

"I met a lot of people," Rafe said confused and exhausted.

"I meant anyone specific," Abby said meaningfully.

Rafe leaned her head back on the chair. "Abby, just spit it out. What exactly do you want to know? I'm too tired to play games with you."

"Did you meet Greer?" asked Abby happy to get to the point.

Rafe looked at Abby and frowned. "No," she said with a yawn. "Why?"

"No reason," Abby lied. "It's just she was there the last time you went."

"I see," said Rafe and sipped her warm tea.

"You see?" asked Abby, wondering what Rafe saw.

"Yes, I do," said Rafe leaning forward. "You think I'm breaking my promise to spend time with Eden, and I went running to Greer."

"Well," she said slowly, "it looked like you did."

"I admit I was glad to go to get away from everything for a while," said Rafe candidly. "Going to see projects my company had worked on was a lot of fun, but it was also heartbreaking to me." She looked at Abby and knew she couldn't understand how much she missed the work she used to do at her old restoration company and how frustrating it was she felt like she had sold it for no reason. Now it seemed Eden was taking everything else away. If she had any clue all of this would have happened, she would have never sold the company. She rubbed her temple and tried to push the frustration away. "Visiting places I used to go and seeing people I hadn't seen for a while I think was good for me. Walking through the streets of New York," she hesitated, "it just seemed to revitalize me. Between Eden and the injunction, I felt like I was being dragged down into hell."

"So you didn't see Greer?" Abby repeated wanting to be very clear.

Rafe looked at Abby irritably. "Greer is still my friend. I still talk to her sometimes, but I didn't meet her in New York. Greer knows I'm trying to figure out things where Eden is concerned. So drop it."

"Why didn't you tell Eden you were leaving?" asked Abby ignoring Rafe's irritation.

"I really didn't think she would care," Rafe answered as she leaned her head back and closed her eyes.

"Well, just so you know," Abby paused, "she did care." Abby sipped her tea and went on with her questioning. "So, when do you want to spend more time with her again? Are you still going to keep your promise?"

"Yes, I'll keep my promise." Rafe yawned. "I don't know when I want to spend time with her again. I'm too tired to think about it right now. You figure it out for me."

"Rafe," Abby said cautiously, "did you mean all the stuff you said about her just wanting to be near you to hurt you? Do you really think she wants to hurt you?"

Rafe sat up and put her tea on a coaster. "She is hurting me," she said frustrated Eden had them all fooled, and they were never on her side. She stood up and yawned again. "I've got to get some sleep. You know the way out. Lock the door." She left Abby sitting in the living room as she went to her room, closed the door behind her, and fell exhausted into bed tormented she couldn't rid her mind of Eden's scent.

62

LATE SUNDAY AFTERNOON, Eden Kingsley was lying in bed, her eyes just opening from her drug induced sleep. She sat up suddenly, and her heart skipped a beat. Then she remembered Bronte was with Letty and Ephraim, and Abby had taken her there last night. She put her hands to her head and closed her eyes as she remembered yesterday. Abby and Flynn brought her home from Rafe's house and stayed with her for a while and then she took her sleeping pills and went to bed crying.

Bringing her hands down, she opened her eyes and looked up at her quiet room and the all the things Rafe had filled it with. The sleeping pills had left a bad taste in her mouth, and as she swallowed, she felt the emptiness inside her swell up.

She was alone, alone in her apartment, alone in the world.

She had never felt such an empty feeling in her life. She laughed and sobbed at the same time because, until yesterday, she was so full of conflicting feelings, she thought she was going mad. Now there was just an empty place inside her. The reason for her living and feeling at all was gone.

Rafe was gone.

New tears made trails down her cheeks. She leaned forward and put her hand to her aching heart. She never realized how full it was when just the possibility Rafe could be hers was in it. How could she not know all this time there was so much of Rafe in her heart? How could she go on now knowing what she had lost? She was the cause of her own pain now, as well as Rafe's.

Greer loves Rafe.

Rafe's pain was being soothed right now by Greer.

A wave of pins and needles made its way over her body, her soul's way of conveying her inner torment would never end now that she had lost something irreplaceable. Eden sighed heavily against the weight of her sorrow and forced herself out of bed. She went into her bathroom to shower and to try to wash away some of the sorrow as well as try to get the bad taste from the pills out of her mouth.

She turned on the shower and stepped in. Then her thoughts crashed into her heartache and tears began to fall again. The hot water rushed over her hair and face, taking her tears with it down her body, but the sorrow just would not wash away.

As she was drying off, feeling clean but not refreshed, she realized she felt nothing but the emptiness and sorrow because she had cried everything else out again.

She put on some clean pajamas and shuffled her way to the kitchen. "Jeez, Abby!" she screamed out in fright. "What the hell are you doing here? You scared me!"

"I've been waiting for you to wake up," Abby stated in a serious tone. "I still have your key from last night." She laid the key on the table and pointed to a cup of coffee. "I heard you get in the shower. Sit down and have some coffee."

"Thanks," said Eden as she sat down and looked into the coffee cup emotionless. "How long have you been here?"

"Not long," admitted Abby, "an hour or so." She hesitated as she looked at Eden and the blank expression on her face. "Rafe's back."

"She is?" Eden said softly, preparing herself inside for the worst.

"Yes," Abby confirmed. She watched Eden toy with her cup without expression. "Eden, she didn't tell you she was going because she didn't think you would care."

"Oh," was all Eden could force herself to say.

Abby looked at Eden's expressionless face and got angry. "You know," she snapped, "you really do need to figure out your feelings for her."

"Abby, I—,"

"Just hear me out, Eden!" Abby cut her off angrily. "You need to figure things out because you're causing a lot of people a lot of pain. We all love you, but we can't stand by and watch you destroy Rafe's chances for love with Greer if you really don't care for her. We love her too, and it seems like she's the one being hurt the most in all of this."

Eden leaned on the table and put her hands to her head. "I know," she sniffed in misery.

"She went to New York for work," Abby said firmly. "That's all. She didn't meet Greer there. You still have time to figure things out."

Eden looked up, feeling a sudden shift in her heart, and could barely speak. "She..." she choked, "she didn't?"

Relieved at finally seeing some kind of expression on Eden's face, Abby took a calming breath. "She's still keeping her promise to spend time with you." She looked at Eden as she trembled across from her. She hoped she and her other friends were doing the right thing. "I've talked to everyone, and we're all going to have a casual dinner party and drinks at Rafe's house on Wednesday night. Rafe said it would be okay. Maybe we'll play cards or something. Anyway, you should plan to come. Okay?"

Eden nodded her head slowly as a tear of relief broke away. "Okay."

Abby got up and went around the table to hug Eden. "Well, I've got to go," she said releasing Eden from her hug. "I'll see you and Bronte Wednesday night for sure."

Eden watched Abby walk out of the apartment through her tears. She turned and laid her head on the table and whispered to herself. "Thank you, thank you. I haven't lost my chance. Thank you."

63

THE NIGHT WAS warm and quiet as Eden Kingsley paced below the porch light of Rafe's house. She had been debating with herself for hours and finally decided she had to tell Rafe the truth about Jake and his lies. She had to do it tonight. She couldn't wait until morning—or even another hour. She had to tell her how she felt and declare she wanted her, needed her, and loved her. She wanted to tell her about her fears and wanted to hold her and feel her arms around her again and feel her lips on hers. She had her chance back, by some miracle, and she didn't want to waste it.

She nervously rang the doorbell and waited, her anxiety increasing with every passing second. She broke out into a sweat across her brow and the back of her neck as the minutes passed, which seemed like forever, with no answer. She wished she had her Xanax, but she knew talking with Rafe would be the best medicine. It always had been. Even the doctor agreed. She rang the bell again and knocked on the door.

The door suddenly swung open, and Rafe appeared wiping her hand across her eyes trying to wake up. "Abby, I wish you would," Rafe looked up sleepily and confused as recognition filled her hazy head. "Eden? What's wrong? Where's Bronte?"

"She's with Letty," said Eden anxiously. "Can I come in? I..." she swallowed nervously, "I need to talk to you."

Rafe frowned not understanding why Eden would come over in the middle of the night. She had finally been able to get some reasonably restful sleep, and now it had been taken away.

"Sure," she said in a haze and feeling more exhausted than when she had gone to bed. "Okay. Is something wrong?" she asked as she led her inside to the living room.

"No," Eden said shaking her head as she followed. She sat on the edge of the couch nervously. "I-I'm glad you're back."

Rafe sat sleepily on the other end of the couch and tried to focus on Eden. "Eden, I'm sorry. I'm still half asleep," she said as she yawned. "Jet lag, I guess." She blinked to clear her eyes. "What is it you want?" she asked more gruffly than she had intended. She was still unhappy about everything happening with the injunction and seeing Eden was just a reminder of the problem—and of Jake's words.

Eden hesitated for a moment under Rafe's harsh words but forced herself to move closer to her. She took Rafe's hand and kissed it. "Rafe," she said and looked into her face. Rafe's frown made her nervous, but she forced herself to speak. "I know you talked with Jake, and he said some things to you." She felt Rafe tense. "I talked to him," she said softly. "He said he... he told you I love him." She kissed Rafe's hand again then looked up into her wide gray-blue eyes full of liquid pain. "Rafe, I don't love him," she said solemnly.

Rafe's mind was reeling, and she tried not to react. "I see."

"Do you?" whispered Eden as she moved closer and caressed Rafe's hair and face. "Rafe, he lied to you. You have to believe me."

Rafe remained silent.

"You asked me what I wanted." Eden leaned in and kissed Rafe's lips. "I want you, Rafe. I need you." She kissed Rafe again. She kept her lips against Rafe's and pulled her close, wanting to kiss her more deeply, as she ran her hands over her.

Rafe's heart was beating fast as the woman she loved kissed her and touched her. But in her mind, alarm bells were ringing—she knew Jake had revealed their secret conversation. She pushed Eden away and looked into her eyes then whispered painfully, "Eden. Eden, you don't have to make this sacrifice. I'll give you whatever you want. I'll do whatever you want," she promised. "Please, don't do this."

"Sacrifice? Rafe, I lov—,"

"Stop!" Rafe cut her off and put her hand over Eden's mouth. "Don't say those words to me. Don't!" Rafe stood up and backed away.

Eden held her hands out to Rafe. "Rafe, I—" She tried to say she loved her again but was cut off.

"I think you should go now," said Rafe and moved toward the front door.

"Please," Eden begged desperately, "please, don't make me leave."

Rafe could not stop thinking about the things Jake had said to her. She couldn't handle the thought of Eden doing this, and she couldn't fathom her reasons. Since Jake had told Eden they had talked, Rafe knew Eden had to be trying to do damage control and convince her Jake had lied about everything.

"I can't do this," Rafe said softly then turned and walked into her room and locked the door. She sat on the floor with her back to the door holding her head in her hands as tears loosened from her eyes. She shook with pain as she felt the pressure against her chest again and knew her only defense now was distance so she could think. She had to figure out what to do now. She couldn't imagine why Eden thought doing this would get her anywhere. The only rational explanation was Jake hadn't told her everything they had said in their conversation—if it could be called a conversation. It was more of a warning that felt like a threat.

Eden leaned against Rafe's door and begged through the crack. "Rafe, let me in," she cried. "Please. Rafe?"

Rafe lifted her head up and leaned it against the door. "Please, just go away. I need time to think," she said shakily.

"You have to believe me," pleaded Eden. "I love you."

"Don't say that to me!" yelled Rafe as she covered her ears with her hands. She didn't understand how Eden could use those words with her so easily, so heartlessly.

Eden pressed her body against the door and cried. "Rafe. Rafe, please, I need you."

Rafe clutched her hair in her hands and rocked forward. "Go away. Go away, please, just go away," she said softly as she put her hand to her head and to her chest in pain.

"Rafe," Eden said knocking on the door, "don't make me go. I want to stay with you. Please."

"I can't do this anymore," Rafe whispered and shook her head trying to control the emotions rolling inside her.

"Rafe, please. Let me in," Eden cried out. "I want you, I do."

"Eden!" Rafe screamed out in fury. "I need to think! Please, just go away!"

Leaning against the door, Eden's face was wet with her tears. "Don't make me leave," she cried out, "please!"

Rafe was shaking with pain and anger. She could feel the heat of rage building in her at what Eden was doing to her. She had to get away from her. Further away. "I just," she choked, "I just need time." She breathed hotly. "I told you, I need to think!" she yelled. "Please, go away!" she cried out in torment her voice breaking with the strain.

Rafe crawled in agony to the other side of the room and pulled her pillows and blanket off the bed, laying down as far away from the door as she could, and then buried her head under a pillow, so Eden's cries for her sounded muffled and far away.

Outside Rafe's bedroom door, Eden slid down the door in misery still twisting the locked door handle. "Rafe, please let me in," she pleaded. "Please believe me. I've... I've just been so afraid all this time." She tried to tell her everything hoping she could understand. "Rafe? Rafe," she whispered. "Rafe," she sobbed.

There were no more responses from inside the room.

Eden cried and stayed by the door hoping Rafe would let her in, but the door remained closed. After a while, she knew Rafe had cut her out again. Eden pulled herself up slowly, walked out the front door, pulling it closed behind her, feeling lost and crying.

64

LOOKING DEFEATED AND tired, Eden Kingsley arrived after work for her regular six o'clock Monday appointment with Dr. Cathcart. She sat down in the chair across from the doctor. Her eyes were ringed with dark circles. She couldn't stop the tears that had been waiting all day to fall.

Cathcart handed Eden a box of tissues and waited for her to calm herself. When she looked like she had gained some control, he began to try to find out what was troubling her.

"Are you ready to talk about it?" he asked softly.

Eden wiped her eyes. "I just," she stammered, "I just keep doing everything wrong."

"What did you do wrong? What happened?" asked Cathcart calmly.

"I told her," Eden said as she looked up at him in misery. "I told her Jake lied to her."

"Very good," Cathcart commended her.

"I love her," she said as tears ran down her face again.

Cathcart smiled, glad she had finally broken through her barrier. "So you stopped making excuses. What happened to make you realize you loved her?"

"I thought I lost my last chance with her," she said despondently. "I thought I lost her." She shook at the memory. "She left and went to New York. I thought she went to... to her.

When I thought she was gone," she sniffed, "everything inside me just—stopped." She looked up at him in misery. "How could I have not been sure?" she asked desperately. "I feel so guilty it took the reality of losing her forever to make me admit I'm still in love with her."

"Eden, emotions and feelings are hard to cut through sometimes, especially painful ones," Cathcart assured her. "You shouldn't feel guilty about your feelings and what it took to break through them. I think you were sure about your love for Rafe. You just felt confused and conflicted because of the fears and the anger at yourself, and at Rafe, you were holding inside. The fear of truly and completely losing her outweighed all of the other fears at that moment."

"But it really could have been too late," Eden said as she wiped her eyes. "She really could have been gone forever. I just felt," she stopped to wipe her eyes, "so empty when I thought she took her love to someone else and wouldn't be in my life anymore. But now," she agonized and looked up sadly, "I think maybe I've still lost her."

"She's still there for you, Eden. She didn't leave," Cathcart pointed out. "Why do you think you've lost her?"

New tears broke away from Eden's eyes. "I went to her last night. I told her the truth about Jake. I told her I wanted her and I needed her. I... I kissed her, and she pulled away." She looked up at Cathcart with reddened eyes. "Sh-she wouldn't let me tell her I loved her. She locked herself in her room and told me to go away."

"Did she say why?" asked Cathcart with a frown of concern.

"She said," Eden sobbed, "she said she needed to think."

"What did you think would happen?" Cathcart pressed.

More tears spilled out if Eden. "I don't know."

"You told her a lot at once." Cathcart pondered the situation. "Maybe she does need time to think. Did you think telling her the truth about Jake would make everything right?" He watched Eden shrug. "Eden, the truth isn't a magic pill that will solve everything. It is a big step in the right direction, but is hardly ever an instant cure."

"I just don't understand why she needs time to think," Eden stressed through her tears. "Everyone keeps telling me she loves me. I told her I wanted her. She told me to tell her what I wanted. It seems like she'll be with everyone else. Why doesn't she want me?" she asked in anguish.

"So you expected her to have sex with you?" Cathcart asked troubled. "Eden, you just dropped a bombshell on her. She has been living with a lie for," he paused to think. "What was it, over a month? And you expect her to believe you suddenly and sleep with you?"

"She sleeps with everyone else!" said Eden angrily. "Did I tell you she had three girls coming out of her room one time?"

"Did she love them?" asked Cathcart calmly.

"I don't know. I think she loved," she looked away, "loves Greer."

"Eden, when she was with those women—who were you with?" pressed Cathcart.

"Jake," she said quietly. "But she was with Greer after," she sobbed, "after I wasn't with him anymore."

"But she's not with her now," Cathcart stated, and Eden shook her head no. "You can't hold the things she does while you're apart against her. She has a right to a life too, even if you weren't with anyone."

"I know." Eden nodded. "I'm sorry." She looked up desperately. "I just don't know what to do now."

"You need to give her time," advised Cathcart. "She was willing to give you time when you needed it. Do you think you can give her the time she needs?"

"I guess," Eden agreed sadly. "Yes."

"I don't know what's really going on in Rafe's mind, but I think your friends are right," Cathcart said supportively. "I think she does love you."

Eden looked up with tear-filled eyes. "You do?"

"I do," nodded Cathcart. "She's so good at hiding her emotions, but some of her actions, when looked at from a distance, expose her."

"What do you mean?" asked Eden with uncertainty.

"Well, one example is she let Julia move in with her," Cathcart stated.

'So," Eden said with confusion.

"So, according to what you've told me, Julia is one of Rafe's oldest friends. She's known her since they both were taken from a home they knew and dropped off in an unfamiliar place an ocean away. They've been friends and at times rivals for a very long time. You told me your friend Abby was complaining about how they were teaming up again like they used to when Rafe was single. I think, in order to find a familiar comfort, she let Julia move in with her as her way of taking herself out of the present painful situation and hiding in who she was before she met you."

"I don't understand how living with Julia proves Rafe loves me." Eden sighed and wiped her eyes.

"You don't?" Cathcart said and collected his thoughts. "I think Rafe justified going back to spending time with Julia because she allowed, and even encouraged, her to go back to being who she was before she met you. It made it seem like she was fine without you. She didn't start trying to live a life and look for someone to love until after Julia got her to go out and start meeting people again. You being happy with Jake, and Julia's encouragement to regress back into a different yet familiar routine, must have been, for Rafe, like giving herself permission to start over."

"Why would she do that, need permission for that?" asked Eden confused.

Cathcart decided to try a different direction. "Eden, I think Rafe does love you. From what you have told me, Rafe is a very strong person to the world and to the people around her. She doesn't wear every emotion on her sleeve, but inside, she has just as fragile of a heart you or anyone else has," he said and watched Eden nod at his assessment. "She, like everyone, wants someone to love. When she thought it wasn't going to be you, she found Greer. But she had to really work at blocking you from her heart. Because she went to Greer a second time, I think you're right—they did love each other. But now, Rafe has promised to spend time with you. She's been telling you she's in pain, but she keeps coming back to try with you. She wouldn't be doing those things if she didn't love you."

"I really hope you're right." Eden sniffed. "It seems like she doesn't want me near her now."

"You've accomplished a lot," Cathcart said encouragingly. "You've done something very hard. You've been through a difficult emotional event. You've told her the truth, and now you have to work on trust. Both of you have to work on it. When you get through this issue, then you can talk to her about your fears and the anger you've been dealing with about the affair, and talk about the other things that have happened since you've been apart. I think you should wait until she comes to terms with what you told her last night first, though. You say you love her. Now you just need to trust she feels the same way and give her the time she needs."

Eden looked up at the doctor and took a shaky breath. "I do love her." She wiped the tears from her eyes and hoped again she wasn't too late. She also hoped she could find the strength to take the doctor's advice and tell Rafe everything. *Well, almost everything,* she thought. She knew she still couldn't tell her about Jake and the Stewards until she could find a way to fix the mistakes that had led to them infiltrating their lives.

To be continued in Book Four — Wildling's Claim...

Salvaggio's Light

Book Four
WILDLING'S CLAIM

C.L. Cattano

NOTES

Translations: For translations of Italian, French and Spanish use: www.Babblefish.com

The chapters in this book were arranged with the intent of saving paper. This chapter style saved 23 pages. Original Total Book Pages 336 — Final Pages 313.

Music mentioned in this book.

No financial incentive was given for the mention of the following artists in this work. The author is a fan and felt mentioning them worked in the story. For the use of their name, credit is given, and links to their work are below.

Enjoy!

Jennifer Corday

Website: https://www.corday.net/
Facebook: https://www.facebook.com/JenniferCorday
Twitter: https://twitter.com/jennifercorday
iTunes: http://itunes.com/jennifercorday
YouTube: http://www.youtube.com/jennifercorday

ABOUT THE AUTHOR

C.L. CATTANO LIVES in the Midwestern U.S. with her partner and their dog somewhere between the city and the forest. With a joy for traveling, she and her partner have visited many countries and have a love for meeting people and learning about the places they visit. When possible, she likes to include references in her work about the things she has learned, the places she has been and people she has met while on her travels and in her everyday life.

Cattano has a variety of creative interests including, but not limited to, creating fine art, writing, photography, and supporting women in the arts. She considers herself a 'Jack of All Trades' dabbling in what she terms the 'whimsies of her soul' pulling her toward happiness and fulfillment.

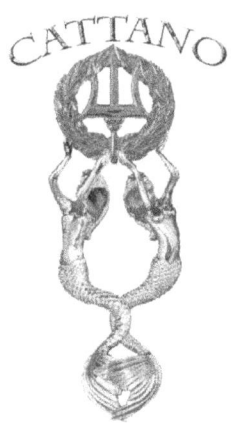

OTHER BOOKS

By C. L. Cattano

Cursed Hearts is a love story that transcends time and gender. Separated from by a gift from a bored demon on All Hallows Eve two souls connected

by the power of love have been searching through time for each other and incarnated as both men and women.

Over time, the gift became a curse and a game for the demons.

Now the souls have finally met again, and they must fight for a life together.

Will love prevail? Will they finally be able to live together again for a lifetime? They have one night to figure out the riddle and get it right to break the curse.

NOTE: 18+ Lesbian Romance. Some light erotic moments.

Available on Amazon <u>Cursed Hearts</u>

Salvaggio's Light Series

Available on Amazon
<u>Shattered Paradise</u> — Book One
<u>Blue Inferno</u> — Book Two
<u>Secrets & Rivalry</u> — Book Three

REQUEST FOR REVIEW

Thank you for reading **Salvaggio's Light** — *An Epic Contemporary Romance Serial.*

I hope you enjoyed book three, **Secrets & Rivalry**, and will consider leaving an honest review. It only takes a few minutes, so I encourage you to go now and leave a review!

Check out the Salvaggio's Light Facebook page to join in the discussions and fun!
www.facebook.com/pg/SalvaggiosLight

Join the CL Cattano Mailing List www.clcattano.com

I love getting fan mail, and you can contact me at
clc@clcattano.com